SAVAGE BEAUTY

ARROW TACTICAL SERIES

ISABEL JOLIE

ISABEL JOLIE

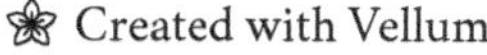 Created with Vellum

"Until we stop harming all other living beings, we are still savages."

— THOMAS EDISON

PROLOGUE

Sloane

What am I missing?

The hard edge of my nail clicks lightly, tapping out a beat on the plastic key, the keyboard as my instrument.

Tap tap da tap tap tap da tap tap tap

Am I clear in my discourse and presentation of data?

The sharks will rip it apart. As they should. That's the point of a peer review.

But is this ready to be shredded?

There's no one to ask. Of course, there's no one to ask. It's Sunday afternoon on island time.

I'm the only one who works on Sunday in this sun-soaked town.

Even the cleaning service only works Monday through Saturday. On Sunday, the offices are divine solitude. But today, isolation is an unfortunate reality. It would be beneficial to have someone to read through my premise, the evidence I've collected, and my conclusions. Someone to challenge me before I publicly share what I've found.

If I'm correct—and I *am* correct—there's no way they'll stop funding my research.

A shadow darkens the sun's rays over the white tile squares on the lab floor. *Why didn't I hear footsteps?*

Light rays stream around the tall, muscular man wearing a black button-down dress shirt with sleeves folded up his sinewy forearm. The top two—no, three buttons of his shirt are undone. A heavy gold necklace glints above a nest of curly chest hair. Two gold rings glimmer, obscuring the black ink on his fingers. The thick black hair atop his head matches his full, trimmed beard. This man is not a scientist.

With his back to the sun, the shadows conceal the contours of his face, but I can see enough to know he's handsome in a rugged, bad boy way. He could be a model on one of the mafia romance books my sister Sage likes to read. Or the ones I read when my brain is too tired to absorb material with sustenance.

"Why are you here?"

Those worn black boots and jeans don't match the tourists' outfits. Hawaiian shirts, shorts, and flip-flops, or possibly a t-shirt with an idiotic saying on the front are what tourists wear. And I've never met a bad boy scientist. I've read about them. Characters in a Penny Reid book, maybe? But those men aren't hairy.

"Saw a gorgeous woman through the window. Sitting all alone on a beautiful day."

I haven't showered since Friday, and I'm in a hooded sweatshirt, running shorts and sneakers. I didn't apply the eyeliner like Sage showed me, didn't curl my eyelashes, and the roots of my hair are slightly greasy. Maybe he's horny. Or drunk. Studies have shown drunk men find women more attractive than sober men.

He pulls out a cigarette.

"You can't light that here." There are rules, and even growly, book-cover-worthy men need to obey them.

"Who says?"

Click. A yellow flame shoots up near his thumb.

"This is a non-smoking building." I'm up, off my stool, report forgotten. "Sir, you cannot smoke in here. Exposure to second-hand smoke causes an estimated forty-one thousand deaths annually in the United States. Data isn't publicly available for the Cayman Islands or the Caribbean region, but it's reasonable to assume the results translate to all regions."

He holds the cigarette between two fingers, lifting it higher, as if out of my reach. But I'm five-foot-nine.

"Sir." My fingers are inches from the tip. "This is a non-smoking building."

"Why don't you come outside with me?" He grins.

I snatch his unlit cigarette out of his fingers, break it in two, and drop it into a black plastic trash can. I brush my hands to clean them of the offending item, but I need a sink. Who knows where that thing has been?

"Don't like smoking, huh?"

I twist the knob on the stainless-steel sink. Sinks are in all the labs here at Origins. The soap at this sink needs to be refilled, but there's enough for two pumps of milky white antibacterial soap to fill one palm.

"What's your name?" His deep voice bears a distinct accent, but it's not Caymanian. European?

"Where are you from?" His smile widens, exposing crooked teeth and a missing incisor. When he doesn't smile, he resembles a book cover model. When he smiles, the urge to back up stirs. His shadow darkens the tile all the way to the toes of my running shoes.

"Belarus." Caymanian, Jamaican, Filipino and British are the four most common nationalities in the Grand Cayman Islands. Belarus is an outlier. "What's a beautiful woman like you doing inside on a gorgeous day like this? You belong in a bikini."

A vacuous comment from an aesthetically pleasing male. Predictable. "Do you have business with Origins?"

"More or less."

My gaze traverses his halfway unbuttoned shirt, worn jeans, the thick black leather belt, and the holster with the grip of a pistol. A firearm can be legally owned on Grand Cayman only with the express consent of the Commissioner of Police, and on Cayman Brac and Little Cayman with the express consent of the District Commissioner, after a thorough application and vetting process.

He does not look like one of the investors from last week. Those men wore business suits. They didn't wear ties, but on the islands, ties are often set aside. Their suit jackets were pressed. And they wore polished leather business shoes. This man's shoes are not polished.

"Are you a police officer?"

"Do I look like a police officer?" He grins, but it's a closed-lipped grin. It's a better look.

"What will it take for me to get you out of the office? To enjoy the sunshine. I'll take you for a ride on my sailboat."

"I don't go on boats."

"Are you afraid of boats?"

"No." I need space, so I take a step back. "An estimated one hundred million people go on boats for recreational purposes in the United States. It's estimated there are over four thousand boating accidents each year, but only approximately five hundred deaths worldwide. The chance of death is statistically insignificant. I suffer from motion sickness."

"Have you been to the marina?"

"No. I moved here for work."

He grins, but I look away quickly to avoid those teeth.

"The weekend has almost passed you by. Let me whisk you

away for a glass of wine overlooking the marina. We can watch the ships pass from the safety of the dock."

"I'm supposed to call my sister soon. Sunday is the day we do our video call. I need to be back at my apartment."

"I promise you, I'll have you back."

"Why?"

He chuckles, and his hands rest on his waist. There's a noticeable bulge in his crotch. *Intriguing.*

"Like I said, I was passing by and saw a beautiful woman, and I thought to myself, 'she needs fresh air.'"

The outline running along the side of his zipper means he might have an erection. Horny or drunk? I don't smell alcohol.

It's been months since I had sex. William returned to Switzerland after getting a better-paying job with one of our investors. Sex with William was fulfilling. Since William, I've been relegated to my vibrators. My gaze flicks over to a supply closet where William and I used to regularly have sexual intercourse.

I don't have relationships, but I enjoy sex. It's been a long time since I've had an orgasm with something other than my fingers or a vibrator. I have spare condoms in my backpack.

My screensaver plays across my screen in twisty, vibrant hues. After my call with Sage, I'll re-read the report. Dr. Kallio won't read it until the morning.

"Okay."

"Yes, you'll go with me?"

"Yes." I nod, save my report on the server, disconnect my laptop, and place it in my backpack. "To the marina."

"Is that everything you need?"

"Yes, it should be."

He lifts the shoulder of my backpack, and I snatch it back.

"Easy, there, tiger. I was going to be a gentleman. Carry it for you."

"There's no need for that." His gentleman reference clashes with his bad boy vibe.

Outside the offices, there is one lone car in the parking lot, and the front windows are rolled down. My bike is in the shade, locked in the bike rack. Sometimes I walk, but today I rode. Walking works a different set of muscles than riding a bicycle does.

He opens the passenger door for me. Inside, on the console, are two water bottles.

"Thirsty?"

I am thirsty, but I don't like the idea of getting in a car with a stranger.

He gestures for me to get in.

"I have my bike."

He ducks into the car, grabs a bottle, and hands it to me. It's already been opened, but the water is full. Reusing water bottles is a wise choice for the environment. The water is slightly cooler than room temperature. Maybe the bottles were recently in the refrigerator.

He leans against the car, arms crossed below his chest while I take a swallow from the water bottle.

"You're going to the marina across the way?"

"Yes."

"I'll meet you there."

Sage always tells me I'll never meet anyone if I spend all my time in the lab. But I met William. He moved, but still, we had sexual relations for over a year. And now, I've met another man while working in the lab. Two instances of meeting someone in my lab. Sage will be floored today on our video call.

"Can I take your picture?"

"Mine? Why?"

"My sister would get a kick out of seeing you."

"And why is that?"

"You look like one of the men on her book covers."

"You talk to your sister a lot?"

I unzip my backpack, searching for my phone. "Yes."

"Where does she live?"

"In the States."

Locating my phone, I pull it out.

"Don't take a picture of me out here in a parking lot. Wait until we're at the marina. Better background."

Consideration should be given to the background when taking a photograph. The most memorable photographs feature an off-centered object with a background of interest.

"Get in the car."

I shake my head and go to my bike. The marina is close. I'm not going to leave my bike here. Then I'd have to come back to get it, and I might be late for my call with Sage.

He slips behind the wheel and starts the ignition as I turn onto the street. He catches up to me with his window down.

"What's your name?"

"You're just now thinking of asking my name?" He chuckles, like it's funny.

"You don't know my name either."

I lift the bottle from the holder on my bike and chug a swallow of the tepid water. The sun is bright, and after putting the bottle back into the holder, I shield my eyes from the sun.

Why did I agree to go to the marina? It's not like we're going to bonk in public. And I won't invite a stranger to my place. William and I had been together for at least two months before I brought him back to my place.

Of course, if he tries anything, I'm not defenseless. No, if he behaves badly, I will make him regret it. Thanks to my brother's training, I do not fear men.

"Oh, but I do know your name."

The tips of my sneakers graze the sidewalk as I slow to a stop.

He's driving slowly to keep pace with me, and a hotel van honks before speeding past him.

"You're Sloane Watson."

Maybe he was with the investors on Friday. Facial recognition is a weakness of mine. My mouth feels parched. I chug more water and use the back of my hand to dry my lips. The tap water he used to refill this plastic bottle is unexpectedly crisp, with a slight citrus zest. I drink more.

I hop off the bike and walk it in the direction of the marina. A sailing mast protrudes above the low, curly trees.

He's beside me, watching me, matching my slow speed.

"How do you know my name?"

"I'm Anton. What do you like to do in your spare time?"

Spare time. I assess the deeply tanned man driving beside me. He's not dressed for beach activities, but he possesses spare time. You don't get a tan like that unless you have spare time or you work outside. "What do you do?"

We're getting closer to the marina. There's a small parking lot without a bike rack, but I can always find a place to park my bike. He said we'd get a drink here, but I don't remember there being a bar. I'm not sure I want to drink alcohol. I haven't eaten today. A veil of exhaustion falls over me.

"I'm getting tired."

"No wonder. You work all the time."

He's right. I do. I slept little this weekend. The sun warms my skin, and the breeze cools it.

"Are you sure you don't want to get in the car?"

My feet are heavy, as if my sneakers are weighted. We're so close to the parking lot. There are people milling around.

He stops the car, gets out, and guides me to the passenger side of the vehicle. I lean against him.

"You're being nice." It's true. He is. But I suspect he may not be trustworthy. Why is he being nice? He's not drunk, and I haven't showered.

"So are you."

"I'm not sure I want that drink. I'm sorry. I think I need to go home." Why am I so tired? The seat in his car is warm, heated from the sun.

"Close your eyes. Rest. We'll be there in a little while."

"We're right here." I point into the parking lot. There is an abundance of empty parking spots.

"But you said you want to go home. Right?"

Right. That's right. I do. I want to wash my face. Brush my teeth. Crawl between the cool sheets on my bed and sleep.

CHAPTER 1

One Month Later

Max

Doctors and nurses pass in the manila hallway with stern expressions and swift steps.

"Have you been to the Petronas Twin Towers?" Mom asks.

I'm speaking to my mom through my earpieces, and she doesn't hear me as well when I do that, so I've got the phone held up to my mouth like it's a microphone. None of the physicians or nurses spare me and my mumbling a second glance.

"Riva, he's not there for a joyride," Dad pipes in. He's on the line, too, because yes, my folks still have a landline and one phone in the den and one in the bedroom, specifically so when I call they can each easily join in on the call.

"But surely he has some free time. You have some free time, don't you? There's also the Batu cave, and you liked Chinatown in New York City when we took you. You might like it there too."

Mom continues reading through a list she must've prepared

specifically for this call when a dark-haired, middle-aged man about six-foot-one and wearing a money suit, slows near Sloane Watson's hospital room. My buddy Knox approaches him.

The guy's hands aren't near his waist, but from this angle, I can't tell if he's packing.

"Mom, Dad, I'm gonna need to go. I'll call you in a couple of days."

"When's your flight—"

"Riva, you know he can't share that."

"Love you guys."

I end the call but remain on the bench, wary of the suit. I increase the volume on the earpieces, using the devices like a hearing aid.

"Can we go outside? My car's in the parking lot." The suit's question to my friend has me wondering who the hell he is. We're in Kuala Lumpur, for fuck's sake. Lawyer? Unlikely. High-end hired assassin? Conceivable.

"Why would I go outside with you?" Knox asks nicer than I would've.

Knox and I served on the teams together. Not the same team, but we know each other, and when we left the military for the private sector, we joined the same outfit.

"So we can speak. Without being overheard." Who does money-bags think, besides me, is listening?

"And you are?" Knox asks.

"Tristan Viognier. We met once on a business call. You might remember me as Nomad."

Ah, that makes sense. He's Interpol. They provided us with the intel that led us to Sloane Watson, the woman we extracted from a hostage situation. We're still piecing together all the whys.

Sloane is the sister of Knox's girlfriend, Sage. She's also the sister of Sam Watson, a former SEAL who died in combat two years ago. That's probably a big reason Arrow, the black ops security firm we work for, took Sloane's case pro bono. The interest from the CIA in the eleventh hour was an unanticipated bonus for our private security firm. The CIA is just one of the government agencies on Arrow Tactical's client roster.

Knox and Sage haven't left the hospital since Sage arrived fifty-two hours ago. Each night, I've gone back to the hotel alone, and their room has remained unused.

"She's groggy. She's been in and out of sleep all day. We haven't questioned her yet. I don't have anything to share with you."

Knox speaks the truth. The escape plan the CIA concocted for us to rescue Sloane from a Cambodian compound entailed unanticipated complications. Therefore, here we sit in a hospital on foreign soil.

"Let's go see if she's ready to talk," Knox says. Together, Knox and the Interpol officer enter Sloane's hospital suite.

I remove my earpieces. This guy isn't here to hurt anyone. Knox must've come to the same conclusion, or he would've never led him into the suite with the Watson sisters.

I edge my way into the doorway behind them.

Sloane rests on a stack of pillows in her inclined hospital bed.

The family resemblance between Sloane and her sister, Sage, is undeniable. But there are distinct differences too. Sloane's tall and lean, for one, whereas Sage is petite and curvy. Sloane's a darker brunette, and her straight hair, in the right light, has a lustrous black sheen. Sage's hair is wavy, full of body, a lighter, semi-chocolate brown, and she almost always wears it pulled back.

Knox fell hard for Sage, claiming she possesses that mythical heart of gold. I'll admit, when I first met her, I was slow to warm to her. She had one wild story, and Knox fell too fast. Way too trusting. My man put his heart on the line within days of her showing up on his front stoop. But with time, I've come around. Knox called it right. She's a sweetheart. And she loves my buddy. She'll be good for him. I hope.

Sloane, however, is her sister's opposite. By all accounts, she's sharp like a knife. Cutthroat. We're still gathering information, but we all suspect she's not entirely innocent and her poor choices played into her abduction. We fully expect she willingly broke the law. But they've got her hopped up on meds that keep her floating in and out of consciousness, so we have yet to press her.

They lowered the dosage of whatever's been keeping her sedated. We should get answers soon.

We aren't law officers. If she broke any laws, she did so outside of US territory. If anyone will investigate the matter, it will be Interpol or the Cayman Islands police. And the Cayman Islands aren't going to send investigators to Kuala Lumpur.

"Sloane, this is Tristan Viognier. He's part of the team that helped us find you. If you feel up for it, he'd like to ask you some questions." Knox steps away after making the introduction.

"The nurse said they may discharge me in the morning," Sloane says to the room with no noticeable acknowledgement of the stranger.

Mr. Interpol drags a chair up beside Sloane's hospital bed. He removes his sportscoat, revealing a close-fitting, lavender dress shirt with gold cufflinks. He's positioned himself at a lower height than Sloane, presumably to set her at ease. The effort seems lost on Sloane, who maintains a listless stare out the window.

"Do you feel up to answering some questions?"

Knox fumbles with his phone, and I'd bet he's setting it to record. Smart. Our team back home has questions. One of our own died protecting Sage. Our best guess is whoever abducted Sloane came after Sage to use her as a tool for coercion.

"What do you want to know?" Sloane jabs her temple with her index and middle fingers. "My head hurts."

"I shall strive for expediency." Tristan leans back in the seat and crosses an ankle over his knee, exposing purple paisley dress socks. The guy has a British lilt to his words that matches his odd fashion sense.

Sloane closes her eyes. She's clearly not too concerned about the Brit. I'm not sure she's even looked at him.

"Fine. Let's get it over with," she snaps.

"Very well. I'll be as brief as possible." The officer's posture strikes a classically friendly interrogation position. "Can you tell us what happened?"

Sage's head dips, then jerks. She's struggling to remain awake. I tried to send her and Knox home countless times, only to be rebuffed.

Sloane had a bad allergic reaction to the pill we slipped her in Cambodia, and her dehydrated state intensified the reaction. The pill was supposed to make her lose consciousness so no one would question her being taken to the hospital in an ambulance. Unfortunately, the reaction was so severe we had to fly her to Kuala Lumpur to save her life. Sloane didn't wake up from her medically-induced coma until early this morning, so I can't blame Sage for insisting on remaining by her only living relative's side.

"It's my understanding you were taken against your will," he prompts. He reminds me of a lawyer. Or maybe a politician. This is my first interaction with Interpol, but this guy isn't what I expected. "Do you know why they took you? There was no ransom, which is typical in an international incident. We're quite curious, as I'm sure you can understand."

"He took me on a boat. I told him I get seasick."

"Does this man have a name?"

"Anton. That's how he introduced himself. I overheard others address him as Solonov. I assume his name was Anton Solonov."

Tristan turns slightly in the chair, meeting Knox's gaze. I don't recognize the name. But maybe I should. "How did you know Mr. Solonov?"

"I didn't know him," she snaps. Tristan appears unfazed by her attitude. Sage comes to stand beside her sister, physically blocking her view of the window. She brushes her sister's hair behind one ear and leans closer, setting her face near Sloane's.

"Sloane. Do you think you could tell us what happened? Just start from the beginning." From this angle, it's difficult to read the exchange between the sisters. "Where did you meet this…Anton?"

"The man is a psychopath. Possibly a sociopath."

Sage picks up her sister's hand and rubs her thumb back and forth over the back of it. "Let's start from the beginning. Where did you meet him?"

"The lab. It was a Sunday. An hour and thirty-three minutes before our Sunday video chat. He asked me to go for a ride."

"Had you seen him before?" Sage asks.

"No."

Sage looks distraught. "You got in a car with a man you don't know?"

Sloane says something to Sage I can't hear. Knox smirks. Intriguing. Sloane's voice grows louder. "I'm not stupid. I agreed to meet him. I had my bike. He showed up after I finished a report. I needed a break before I double-checked the numbers in my analysis."

"You met him in your lab?" Tristan asks for clarification.

"I thought he was an investor. They were there earlier in the week, and I overheard them. They were referencing incorrect financial projections. I didn't want them to cut funding, so I dug deeper into the data."

"What data?" Tristan asks.

Sloane's lips purse as she presses her temple.

Sage leans closer. "Sloane?"

"Transplant survival rates. I overheard people talking in the Bodden building. And the numbers cited were significantly off. Yet familiar. It bothered me. I went back and checked peer reviewed research. I was right."

"About what?" Sage combs her fingers through Sloane's hair, the movement as soft and comforting as her tone of voice.

"It doesn't matter." Sloane's gaze settles on the top right corner of the room. "You won't understand."

Sage smiles and continues combing her sister's hair with her fingers. "You're right. I probably won't. Can you still tell me? Simplify it. Tell me like I'm a third grader."

The Interpol suit leans forward, losing his patience with the sister talk, and asks, "Sloane, the Bodden building. Is that part of Origins Laboratories?"

"Yes. We don't do research in that building, but they hold meetings there. Investor meetings."

Sage brings her sister back around to the questions we all have. "So, I'm a third grader. What were they wrong about?"

"The survival rates they were referencing were wrong. Five to ten percent off. More. The complications. Hepatitis C. Cancer. And they weren't comparing live versus dead donors. They were just…wrong. I needed to show them they were wrong, because if they believed those numbers were right, they might not continue funding my research."

"And exactly what research do you do?" Tristan interrupts.

"Organoid research. I'm working on growing organs from stem cells."

"Past fourteen days?" Tristan asks. This is where we'd known she was breaking international law, but I don't get the sense anyone really cares about that law.

"Yes, past fourteen days. We're making progress, too. Growing organs in a lab is an ethical solution to the world organ shortage. But the survival rates the investors touted were off. And I figured it out."

"What was wrong with their numbers?" Tristan prompts.

"They were quoting numbers from studies coming out of India and Taiwan. Both studies attempted to discern variations in results on black market organs. Gathering black market data is quite difficult. For obvious reasons. Anyway, I spent a week compiling a report on all black-market transplant surgeries versus both live and dead organ transplant surgeries in the United States and the United Kingdom and prepared a discourse on the variations and how lab-grown organs would not suffer the same results as those in alternative countries. I also located more recent data on our server from non-specified locations. The location field had been deleted, but I located the source file. The results were noteworthy and worth peer review. It appears survival rates on black market organs are trending downward in specific source regions. The cancer rates for three years post-surgery for recipients with organs sourced from specific regions in Asia were extraordinarily high. Twenty to thirty percent higher than standard norms. Obviously, it needs to be shared broadly. Peer review. I might have missed something. Tabulated something incorrectly."

"Did you share this report with anyone?" Tristan asks.

"No. The psychopath arrived before I double-checked my analysis. I'd been working on it for days. I saved it to the network, but I wanted to review it again before sharing it with my boss."

"Did you talk to Anton Solonov about your work?"

"No."

"Did he inquire about your research?"

"No."

"So, what happened? After you left the lab?" Sage asks. I'm not sold on the heart of gold, but she's got the patience of Job.

"I woke up vomiting in the bottom of a boat. I thought I would die. When we made it to land, I told him I would do anything as long as he didn't make me ride in a boat again."

"I thought you said you didn't get in the car—"

"I didn't. He gave me a water bottle. The last thing I remember is him driving alongside me while I walked my bike on the sidewalk. I could see the marina, but I was so tired. He must have drugged the water."

"How did you end up in Cambodia?"

"We docked somewhere and boarded a small plane."

"Did you…did he touch you? Hurt you?"

Sloane shakes her head slightly. "I couldn't stop vomiting. Dry heaving."

"What about the people in Cambodia?"

"Anton told them he'd be back to get me. He told a guard no one was to hurt me. Before you ask, I don't know why. Whoever his boss is, they gave specific instructions I wasn't to be hurt. I heard him instruct more than one person."

"Were you ever held against your will in the Caymans?"

We're all interested in hearing the answer to this question of Tristan's. We'd originally suspected she was being held in the Caymans. But by the time Arrow got involved, she'd been missing a while. We didn't have much to go on.

"No." Sloane is curt. Dismissive, even. "How quickly can we arrange flights home? I need to get back to work."

Sage places her sister's hand, the one without an IV, on her thigh. She's leaning on the bed, and she seems to be working to get her sister's attention. "They believe you resigned."

"I didn't resign. I need to get back."

"Not so fast, love," Tristan says with quiet calm. "Anton Solonov is a known assassin. There's what's called a Red Notice placed on him. Which means he's considered to be highly danger-ous. We've been quite aware of him for years. Someone hired him. Someone with extensive means because he doesn't work for just anyone. Can you think of any reason someone would hire him to abduct you?"

Sloane's brow furrows, and it's clear there's a discussion going on in that head of hers. "I figured out why they had me doing blood tests."

"Why?"

"Organ matches." She licks her lips, and Sage gets up to get her water. "The people in the compound will be harvested for organs. Or at least, that's my assumption based on the records they were keeping on them. But anyone could do those tests. Once I figured out what they were doing, which was on the first day when I saw the data they were collecting, I refused to be a part of it. But then they told me they'd hurt Sage."

"And you don't have any idea why they picked you?"

Sloane shakes her head, lips firm and tight, gaze downward.

"Could it be this report you created? Is there someone who wouldn't want it shared? Data, perhaps, that someone might not want uncovered?"

Sloane pushes the glass away when Sage approaches, refusing the water. She closes her eyes and rests her head against the pillow. "It wasn't our research. I accessed a database we pay to access. Multiple parties contribute data. I was making the case to the investors that organ development will be profitable because I overheard one of them questioning the financial return. If anything, the risks inherent in trafficked organs will be absent from lab grown organs. And based on the data I was putting together, the risks of black-market organs are increasing. Significantly higher cancer rates. Like I said."

"How closely does Origins Laboratories work with Lumina International?"

"They're an investor."

"So, you don't work closely with them?"

"I never work with them. My old supervisor took a job with them in Geneva. The headquarters." Her gaze drops to Sage's hand over hers. "I was close to him."

Reading between the lines, my guess is this old supervisor is an ex. But if the Interpol suit picks up on that, he doesn't care.

"Has he remained in contact with your project?"

"No."

Tristan fumbles with his coat like he's done. That's a shit interrogation.

"And your supervisor's name?" He reaches in his coat pocket for his phone.

"William Salo." He taps the name into his phone.

If he's wrapping up, there's no need for me to stand in the doorway like an outcast.

I rap my fist against the doorframe, and Knox waves me inside. "Tristan, this is Max Hawkins. He's a colleague of mine."

I assess Sloane as I approach. "How's the sleeping beauty?"

"Grumpy," Knox mumbles low enough the women can't hear. I clap him on the shoulder. If we weren't in the company of ladies, I'd give him some shit about the family he's considering marrying into. Of course, I doubt my buddy's thinking marriage quite yet. He fell hard, but he didn't hit his head when he nosedived.

"Well, I think I've had the most pressing questions answered," Tristan announces to the room. "Lovely to meet you all. My department would appreciate inclusion on any reports or summaries."

Knox leaves the hospital suite with the Interpol goon, and I hang back, observing the two sisters.

Sloane's objectively a beautiful woman. I'd describe her as elegant and refined. Porcelain skin, a straight nose, curved, perfectly shaped eyebrows that frame intelligent oval eyes, and rose-colored lips. Knox says she's over-the-top brilliant. All she needs is a pair of black-framed glasses and a skintight, rear hugging pencil skirt and she'd make one helluva sexy librarian on Halloween. The kind who doles out punishments for speaking. Yeah, I can almost see the flush undertones on those high cheekbones in response to a little dirty talk. Those thick eyebrows would knit together, her dark eyes would narrow, and those pink lips would pucker.

And yeah, I need to blink that away.

"You hanging in there?" I've had minimal interaction with Sloane since giving her CPR in the back of an ambulance, so the question is directed at Sage.

It's hard to believe it was only a couple of weeks ago that she showed up at our apartment building back in Santa Barbara, scared to death. Sloane was missing and someone broke into Sage's home, trying to kill her.

Sage stretches her arms out before her. "I'm good."

"Why don't you go back to the hotel? I'll stay here. I got this."

We don't expect anyone else to come for Sloane. But if they do, I'll be here.

"Thanks, but you can go back. I'm fine staying here."

"Come on. You've got to be jonesing for an actual bed. You guys have been camping out here for days. That sofa out there is comfortable, but it's not all that."

Sloane's sharp tone cuts through the air, a quick reminder she's no longer medicated. "Sage Watson. You need rest. You, of all people, need your sleep."

"I'm fine," Sage argues, but the sunlight streaming in through the window highlights her bloodshot eyes, undermining her state-ment. From what I understand from Knox, Sage had a heart trans-plant as a teen. He said she's healthy now, but it's a fair assumption that her sister hasn't forgotten the past.

"Sage. You need to rest. Go." Sloane barks the words out. She could stand to be a touch softer.

"You and Knox get out of here. I've got things covered," I say, modeling appropriate behavior for the bedridden grump.

"What's everyone up to in here?" Knox asks as he re-enters the room. "Ready for some dinner?"

"Max and Sloane are ganging up on me to get me to leave."

Sloane closes her eyelids and rests her head against the stacked pillows. "Max says she hasn't left the hospital room. Take her back to the hotel. Make her shower and rest."

Sage stands tall, not having it. "You don't get to tell me—"

"Have you been taking your medication?"

Oh, boy. A sister war. I take a step back.

"Yes," Sage insists. "You can't kick me—"

"Talk to the hand," Sloane says, palm up, eyes still closed, chin thrust in a regal position. "You're not getting sick or worn down on my watch. You need to be rested before boarding a transcontinental flight. Sagey bean, go. Get out of here."

CHAPTER 2

Sloane

The hospital door clicks closed, and the sound strikes like an axe against marble. The constant throbbing on the back of my skull aches with the pain of a thousand knives pricking skin. I brush a hand over my forehead, and a pull on the back of my hand sends a painful tearing sensation up my arm. I squint to see the source of pain, and light intrudes with another blade to my temple. Thick, semi-transparent tape covers a needle dug into the back of my hand.

"It's the IV," a masculine voice rumbles. "Remember? It's for fluids. You were chronically dehydrated."

The doctors and nurses have told me this. My bad for forgetting about the IV in my hand. Dried blood colors the underside of the milky white medical tape.

"You tried to rip it out earlier. Does it hurt?"

"Everything hurts."

"Let me get a nurse for some pain medicine. They cut you off this morning."

"No." I inhale deeply and rest my hand on my thigh, eyes sealed shut. "I don't want pain meds."

"I get that. I'm not a huge fan of them either. At least, I don't like it when they put me off my game. What was the dehydration about? Did they withhold water?"

Bile rises in the back of my throat as I visualize the water bottle I drank from. Thin, crinkly plastic with a green label. Not again. "Anton poisoned the water. I couldn't trust them."

"Was he there with you in Cambodia?"

"Not for long. The water out of the pipes was tinged brown. It needed to be boiled."

"That sucks."

If I wasn't in so much pain, I'd laugh at the Jolly Green Giant's succinct way of summarizing the situation.

My eyelids are closed but damn this pain. And what's worse, a tanned, hairy beast occupies the space behind my eyelids. I can't believe I thought that monster was handsome. From here on out, I'm sticking with nerdy scientists. Maybe someone has done a study on that. How would you structure it? Group men by physical attributes, IQ, and career, then rank prowess in the bedroom, and what…likelihood to kidnap someone and stick them on a sailboat?

Heavy footfalls pace the room.

Bep. Bep. Bep.

Stir. Stir.

Is he dragging his feet?

Nausea swirls, and the discomfort extends from my throat to my abdomen. Peeking through eyelid slivers, I make out his dark, bulky form. I could ask him to leave, but I don't want to be taken again.

"Can you not move?"

"Sure. Sure. Sorry." He plops down in the armchair by my bed with a round of loud squeaks. The squeaks stop, replaced by an air noise. I crack an eye. He's breathing. Too loudly.

As if that's not enough noise, he sighs and stretches. His back cracks with his stretch.

"You don't have to stay here. Go back to the hotel." I've spent much of my life in hospital chairs. They suck. At one point, I considered medical school, but my hatred of hospitals diverted me onto another path.

"Nah. I'm happy hanging out here."

"I don't want you to stay here." The most direct approach is the most effective approach, and while I do like the safety of him, the man is far too loud. He is a noise creator.

"I get that," he says. "But Knox and Sage won't rest easy if you're alone."

"But you're loud. And it hurts." The tips of my fingers knead my temples so he shouldn't require further explanation.

"Tell you what. Let me get you some pain meds. I get not wanting to feel groggy, but you're already groggy, right? You're not going anywhere for the rest of the day. You might as well sleep. I'll stay here. I'll be on lookout. And if you're sleeping, you won't hear me."

The chair squeaks because he probably can't be quiet. But he's made some good points. The pain is awful. With the nausea, it must be a migraine. My skin hurts.

"What do you say?"

He's waiting for me to consent. I suppose pain meds in a supervised setting are acceptable. "Yes. Okay." His shadow remains. "Please."

Minutes later, a second pair of footsteps, lighter and without as much sliding noise, accompany his heavy footfalls.

"You're in pain?" a feminine voice with an unfamiliar accent asks.

"Yes."

She talks me through what she's doing, and a coldness creeps up my arm as the medicine infiltrates my body.

Within minutes of her leaving the room, the throbbing in my head eases, as does the nausea.

I twist my head into the pillow, angling it so I can better observe the odd, burly, Nordic man who has posted himself as a lookout. His shoulders are broader than Knox's, and he has lighter hair. He's the opposite of Anton Solonov, the hairy man I mistakenly fancied to be a mafia cover model.

"Do you have any tattoos?"

He snorts. Or maybe it's a half laugh. It's not a full laugh. "Yes, I do."

Hmm. Not the exact opposite of Anton Solonov.

"Anything I can do for you?" he asks.

"Can you stop breathing?"

"Ah…"

"You can leave now. I'll be fine." I hope. I close my eyelids, letting him think I'm falling asleep.

When Sage was in the hospital, once she fell asleep, my parents said we could leave. I'm pretty sure there were evenings when Sage feigned sleep so we would leave.

"No can do. But I'll be as quiet as a church mouse."

"That's an ignorant saying. Mice are unaware of the building they occupy. They would make the same level of noise whether in a church or a bowling alley." The chair squeaks. Because of course it does. The man probably weighs close to three hundred pounds. "How much do you weigh?"

"Two-fifty. Why?"

"I was close."

"You were wondering how much I weigh?"

"You said Knox and Sage won't rest easy unless you're here. Why?"

"Well, based on what I heard of your conversation with Interpol, you are aware of what happened. You were abducted. And you had to be rescued. We'd prefer to not have to rescue you a second time."

"You think Anton will come to find me again?" I won't go with him. I won't go anywhere near that man.

"Why do you think he took you? It's just me and you here. I don't care if you broke the law. But if we know the truth, we can better protect you. We can provide a better assessment of what level of danger, if any, you might be in."

For whatever reason, I visualize Anton in his dingy white tank top on the boat, and my stomach churns. I force my eyes open to erase that unappetizing image. "The man from Interpol seemed to think it was something I was working on."

"The organoid stuff?"

"You wouldn't get it. It's complicated."

Cool air flows through my nostrils. Tension has replaced the unbearable pounding in my cranium. I listen, and maybe the pain medication dulled my hearing, but I don't think I hear him breathing.

"Try me. I'll disregard anything that's outside my IQ range."

I narrow my eyes. Is that sarcasm? If so, it's uncalled for. I was simply being direct. I don't want to close my eyes because my stomach can't handle any more nauseating images, so I focus in Max's general direction.

"I oversee two studies. In one, we use stem cells to create artificially grown miniature organs."

"Whoa. Impressive."

"Exactly." He does get it.

"Fully functioning organs?"

"Well, no. Not yet." The cells can only be viewed and studied with a microscope. "We're going to get there, though. We're also experimenting with using adult skin cells to regenerate functional human heart tissue."

"And what part of that is illegal?" His seat squeaks, and the soles of his shoes tap the floor.

"Are you against using stem cells?" My temples pulse, and I grimace. I don't wish to debate ethics with this noisy man.

"Nah. I'm only asking 'cause you're based in the Cayman Islands. That was kind of our assumption."

Oh. Right. "There are fewer restrictions and oversight. What we're doing with stem cells and with our organoids is… It doesn't matter. It's not illegal, per se."

"All right. It's not illegal. Any guesses as to why someone would hire an international assassin to abduct you? I mean, they kept you alive, and this guy's skillset is in killing, so—"

"Red Notice. That's what the Interpol man said. My fantasy of him being a mafia guy wasn't far off."

"Your what, now?"

"Forget I said that." I scowl at his grin. It was a first impression and a prime example of why first impressions should not be trusted. The guy was a monster. But I don't need to worry myself with that guy. This Max guy is correct. What I need to figure out is who did this to me. Who do I know that would know how to hire an assassin? "How hard is it to hire an assassin?"

"Why?"

"Because I want to figure this out. Who would do this to me?"

"And Sage."

"Why do you say, 'and Sage'?" He's got my full attention. "They were lying about having her."

"They were lying to you, but someone hired guns to come after her. Twice. Not Anton, but other men with the same skill set. Killed one of my buddies who was defending her. Which is another reason I'm sticking by your side. We want to find these bastards."

Dizziness sets in. The room spins ever so slightly. "You're sure about this?" I think back to Mr. Viognier and Knox. "They didn't tell me any of this."

"You didn't ask them any questions, did you?"

"Why wouldn't they tell me?" I push up off the pillows. "Is Sage safe now?"

"Yes." He's at my side, hand on my shoulder. The man's hand is enormous. It spans from the nape of my neck to my arm. His skin is warm—no, hot. It's as if he's radiating heat. "You don't need to worry. We've got you. And Sage. Knox isn't going to let anything happen to Sage. He loves her."

"No, he's a family friend. We're not that close."

The mattress sinks with his weight. I shift my legs away from him, giving him more room. He wears an odd expression. Amusement, perhaps? But I didn't tell a joke.

"You missed a bit. Knox and Sage…they're an item now."

I study him for any hint he's joking. "Seriously?"

"Yep."

"She had a crush on him when she was younger." I think back to the way she would act around him. I'd teased her.

"Well, then, I guess she'd say you getting abducted was a good thing." He's grinning.

"No. She wouldn't."

"I'm joshing with you, Watson."

I don't like jokesters. "Mr. Hawkins, can we try to stay focused? If someone might come after Sage, then we need to figure this out."

"Alrighty. I agree with you there. How valuable is this research you're doing? Sounds pretty valuable to me. Are there competitors who might try to nab you?"

"Competitors? No. It's not… Everyone considers what I'm working on to be a long way from earning out. So much so I had to beg to continue. They gave me another project to oversee. Comparatively, the other project is boring. I'm testing to determine the most effective dosage of rapamycin for anti-aging purposes. There's a lot of money to be made if you can get the dosage right, but we're hardly the only ones working on it. Once they discovered that patients taking it to prevent organ rejection were aging slower, it became a field day to every skin care line out there."

"You don't sound impressed."

"Organs or wrinkles? Which is more important to humanity?" One of his thighs presses down on the hospital bed, and the metal grinds under his weight. His muscular thigh is probably the width of both of mine. "Did you play football?"

"Talk about left field. I thought you wanted to focus."

"I do. But you're huge."

"You're an interesting one, Watson. I never know what you're going to say."

"I say what I think. Keep me on track." I snap my fingers. It's a technique I learned that helps to sharpen my mind. Bring my brain to heel. "Mr. Viognier. I told him I'd been working on a report when I was abducted. He seemed to think that's why I was taken."

"The report you were preparing for peer review?"

I rub the point of my finger between my eyebrows and visualize the report. "When they put me on that other project, it was only natural I'd fear they'd pull funding on the long-term project. It won't earn out, whereas this other one will be an ATM machine." It's a phrase I overheard an investor use once. "I had to do everything I could to preserve funding."

"For the organ research?"

"I wouldn't fight for wrinkles."

"Of course not."

He gets it.

It all clicks. "That report. The data I found from accessing the databases we subscribe to. Someone must've been alerted when I was accessing those external databases."

"Okay. But if someone feared you would share data, why not just kill you?"

I bite at my thumbnail and pull my finger back, surprised at the length of the nail, but happy it's clean. Grime had been building up beneath my nails in that filthy compound.

"I don't know why they wanted me alive. But someone did. I heard the guards warn people more than once they couldn't hurt me."

"And in Cambodia, you said you were testing the people?"

"For organ compatibility." It had to have been. But my research really isn't related at all to what they had me doing in Cambodia.

"Can you perform transplants?"

"I'm not a surgeon. But, if anyone saw what I was working on, they'd know I was preparing it for peer review." I clap my hands. "That's what I need to do. I need to look at that report again and see if this theory has merit. If it does, I'll spread it far and wide. Then there'd be no need to come after me. Or Sage." My throat is dry. Parched. "Can you get me some orange juice?"

There's a pitcher of water by the side of the bed, but I don't want water. It's too heavy or…I don't think I like the taste. I used to, but not now.

"Sure."

He picks up a phone and places an order for orange juice. This place is nicer than the hospitals back home. There's even a view of an expansive lawn. When Sage was in the hospital, her view was usually of a parking lot or the side of another building.

"Are you up for food? Want dinner?"

"Tomato soup." The advice I administered to Sage holds true for me, too. I need my strength to travel. If my immune system is lowered, I might get sick after the flight. Around twenty percent of passengers develop cold symptoms after a commercial flight. I once read that up to eighty percent of travelers have some negative symptoms, ranging from digestive tract issues to flu-like symptoms after vacation travel, but they did not cite the details of the study. This is not vacation. Most definitely not vacation.

If they were after me for that report, wouldn't they go after others that I worked with too?

"Am I the only one they came after? What about Dr. Kallio? Is she okay?"

"No one else from the laboratory has been reported missing. When your sister called your place of work, they informed her you resigned."

"I would never resign. This research is important to me. I need to talk to Dr. Kallio."

"That's probably not the best idea." He's seated in the chair. The side of my hospital bed must have been uncomfortable. "Remember what the Interpol suit told you? Red Notice? Not a good idea to go barging back."

"I need to let her know I didn't resign. My research projects." I push up off the bed and ignore my scratchy sore throat. "Mr. Hawkins, I need to get back to them." The light in the room feels brighter. I need to go.

"Call me Max."

"Max—"

"Sloane." He says my name slowly, imbuing it with care and an unstated request to listen. "We need to take this slowly. Someone burned down your sister's home in Asheville. These theories are good, but we need to proceed with caution." An uneasy feeling washes over me. "Whoever hired Anton Solonov, and the other two tangos, Omar Cardenas and Alexis Flores, is still out there."

"They killed someone?"

"Felix Hernandez. A good man. One of the best."

"They told me they had Sage and that they wouldn't hurt her." None of this makes any sense. But they killed someone. And burned down Sage's home?

"Who told you they wouldn't hurt Sage?"

"The man in Cambodia. Not Anton. Another man. I don't know his name. He said he'd hurt Sage if I tried to escape. But I was skeptical of the photograph he showed me. But I still did what he wanted. He could've hired anyone to do what I was doing." The pulsing in my head intensifies, and I place my forehead in my palm.

"Sloane, none of what happened is your fault. But it's important you accept that you can't go waltzing back to your office. Someone hired these men. For all we know, it could be this Dr. Kallio you're mentioning."

"No. She's my friend. But there are others." We're always looking for investors. Maybe someone else…maybe someone felt the report I put together would curtail investment? I compiled the data to prove our lab is a solid investment and my research will earn out, but maybe they looked at the cancer rates and interpreted the data differently?

"Sloane…whoever is behind this is powerful. You're still coming off the meds. Let's take it slowly. Maybe you'll remember more. But waltzing back into your office before we have some answers is not an advisable game plan."

"Mister…Max… Is that your full name?"

"People call me Max. It's short for Maxwell."

"Fine." I blink. Focus. I need to figure this out. The puzzle pieces need to fit together. "That Interpol guy…he asked your team to share any reports. Is there an incident log? I need to know everything."

CHAPTER 3

Max

Sage didn't want to barrage her sister with questions or bring on traumatic memories too quickly, so we've been pussyfooting around her all day. Bringing her orange juice. Letting her sleep. Answering questions about why she's in the hospital. Until the Interpol guy appeared, no one asked a single goddamn question of importance. But of course, now that she's completely lucid, they're gone, and I'm the one here to lay it all out there for her.

She's no longer squeezing her eyes shut in pain, and she sounds sincere.

"I'm not sure we have much more knowledge than you do. There's no report to share. Not yet."

"Why not?" For someone who took a job abroad so they could skirt international laws, she's got a lot of self-righteousness jammed up her ass.

I sit up a little straighter. She's not my commanding officer, and our company has taken tremendous expense to save the prickly PITA. "On this case, we don't actually have any paying clients—"

"Who is 'we'?"

"Arrow Tactical Security. It's the company Knox and I work for. Missing persons is just one example of the work we do. After the man broke into Sage's home—"

"When was that?"

Damn if I can remember. I pull out my phone. It's a Blackberry. Got used to the thing and have refused to change. I log onto a VPN to pull up our Slack channel.

"What are you doing? Are you—" She leans forward, squinting those eyes as if it's possible for her to see my screen.

"Patience, woman. Close your eyes and breathe."

"Saying 'woman' in a derogatory manner is unacceptable."

I probably should have expected a woman like Sloane would take offense at that offhand comment. "Didn't mean anything by it. Don't be sensitive."

"I am not sensitive."

I blow out my disagreement with that statement in one loud huff. "Just give me a minute. I don't have the date memorized."

"Do you keep a diary?"

"Sure do." Her glare has me grinning. "No, Watson. I don't keep a diary." Me and a diary. That's a good one. "Checking our project log." It takes a second for me to synch through the VPN. Since I'm outside the US, I need to enter a code that changes every five seconds.

"There. I'm in." I go back through the notations. Bingo. "Someone broke into her house at approximately two a.m. on July eleventh."

"That's two weeks after Anton Solonov took me." She chews on a fingernail. Her eyes are open, but there's a glazed effect over her dark brown eyes and minuscule pupils, as if she's not seeing anything at all. "I was still trapped in a boat at that point. They wouldn't let me out of the hold. I thought I would die. Why go after Sage?"

"We have a couple of working theories. But we could never

interrogate anyone to confirm anything." Her steady gaze through the window has me pushing up out of the chair and checking the view to see exactly what she's staring at. My knees pop, and the familiar ache flares. I dig out an Advil pack from my pants pocket. "One theory is that they thought she knew something about what you were working on."

"She knows nothing."

"We're aware. But whoever took you might not be." Her lips purse as if she's giving this idea consideration. "We also considered that she's the only person who would search for you."

"That's not true. Dr. Kallio would search for me. Or William. For that matter, any number of my colleagues would search for me."

"Who's William?"

"William Salo. He was my boss. He took a new job in Switzerland, and they hired Dr. Kallio."

"According to your employee file, you resigned."

"But that's ridiculous. I didn't resign. I already told Sage. And you. Why aren't you listening?"

"There's an email file on your employee server."

"I didn't send an email."

"Someone did. From your account."

"I haven't had access to my email since that psychopath drugged me and locked me on a boat."

"So, you didn't do it, but someone did. They probably did it so your colleagues wouldn't wonder what happened to you. You know, your boss, Dr. Kallio, she's the one Sage talked to first when you didn't return her calls. She's the one who told her you emailed your resignation and said you'd fallen in love and were going to leave to go sailing around the world."

She removes her finger from her mouth and studies it. I suspect she just chewed a piece of her nail off.

"Admittedly, many companies keep a limited amount of information on employees, but there was no notation of concern from your supervisor."

"Dr. Kallio wouldn't make a negative notation in my employee file. I do twice the work of any other researcher." She still has that faraway look in her eye, looking in the general direction of the window, and it feels like she's talking to herself, not to me. "I need to get my laptop. I can access the server. See what's going on."

"That sounds like a remarkably stupid idea." Yeah, now she sees me.

"I'm not stupid. I am highly intelligent."

That's not the response I was expecting, but I'll give it to her. She's refreshingly straightforward. "You realize that if it wasn't for Arrow taking on this project, you'd be trapped in Cambodia taking blood samples indefinitely. You get that, right?" A little thank you might be nice.

"They were getting ready to move me."

"To where? How do you know?"

"I heard a man speaking. He spoke in Russian, but I understood some words. I think that's what he was saying. That I was to finish with the blood samples, and I'd be moved. He assured whoever he was talking to that I was okay. I thought they might put me on another boat. That's why I took the pill without knowing what it was. Even though Knox said he'd be back, I couldn't wait."

"When did you hear them say they were going to move you?"

"The day before Knox showed up. I assumed the man was speaking to Anton, but that was a fear-based assumption. I have no fact-based evidence. He was speaking Russian, but that's circumstantial."

Fear-based and fact-based. Sage's sister disseminates information like a pro.

"It's a good hunch," I admit. "We're looking to see if there's a connection between Omar Cardenas and Alexis Flores to Anton

Solonov. We suspect either he hired them, or the same person who hired Anton hired them."

"You said you had theories. Plural. What are your other theories?"

"That they wanted Sage to force you to do something."

"They lied to me. They told me they had her. But they wouldn't let me speak to her."

"Did they harm you?"

Those dark eyes seem to double. "They drugged me and locked me in the bottom of a boat. I'd say that's harmful."

"Yes. I agree. But did they do anything more? Hit you?"

"No. But I watched them beat a young man. They told me that would be me if I didn't do as they wanted."

That counts as a form of torture. "And what did you do?"

"I told them to go ahead and kill me. I think he would've liked to, but his boss told him not to hurt me."

"He told you that?"

"No. I already told you. I overheard them." That actually matches with what Knox had been told when he entered the compound. When a guard entered, he acted like he was coming on to her, and the guard told Knox there were other women he could have sex with, but not her. Of course, she heard all that. She was standing with Knox when it happened.

"Whoever orchestrated this didn't want you hurt. Otherwise, they would've beaten you into submission. And they wouldn't have differentiated you between the other women in the compound."

"They do hurt those people. The ones working on the computers."

"I didn't actually enter the compound, but that's our understanding, yes."

"If people know about that place, why hasn't anyone stopped them?"

"It's connected to a powerful man. A Cambodian senator. He

claims the people are there of their own volition and they keep no one against their will."

"That's not true." The faraway off look returns. "I need to get my computer. After I distribute my report, I need to publish an account of what I observed in the compound. I have a contact at *The New York Times*. She's in sciences, but—"

"Sloane, I don't know you from Adam. I'm here on the job and for my friend Knox. But I strongly advise letting this go. You're playing with dangerous people. And from what I can tell, connected people. Someone was protecting you. If you go after them publicly, whoever is doing this might not be so willing to let you live."

"They didn't let me do anything. You and Knox got me out of there."

"True." Can't really argue with that. "So, tell me something. How do people make money from the research you're doing?"

"Usually, people ask me to tell them about the research I'm doing."

"I've got the general gist. You're a cellular biologist. You were working on the effects of rapamycin on cells, and you had another study growing organs in test tubes."

"That's not—"

"It's close enough, right?"

"Yes."

"How do people make money off it? I'm asking because right now we have a lot of questions. And generally, when people go around criming, they do it for money. How do people make money from what you do?"

"Our investors and the laboratory will make money if either of my projects prove successful. The rapamycin is simply trying to ascertain the best level of the drug to reap the antiaging benefits without the negative side effect of lowering the immune system. If we can determine the optimal dosage level, it stands to be in greater demand than multivitamins. No one wants to age."

"Yeah, I'd imagine that's a pretty big market."

"Projections set it as a thirty-eight-billion-dollar worldwide market by 2028."

I whistle because, yeah, people have killed for a shit ton less.

"But I'm not the only one conducting research of that kind. There are multiple companies doing research right now."

"I'd imagine so."

"But what I'm doing with organ cellular growth? Imagine a future where someone you loved needed an organ. I could take their stem cells and grow them an organ. There would be no wait list. We could grow organs and have them ready for patients as needed. No one would have to become weak or close to death's door to receive an organ. Transplants would occur on healthy individuals. Recovery rates would rise exponentially." Those intelligent eyes sparkle like she's describing nirvana.

"That's what you were working on?"

"No." She waves a hand dismissively. "Well, yes, that's the long-term vision. Right now, we can legally grow organs up to fourteen days. There's this ridiculous international law. That's why we're working out of the Cayman Islands. Because I have cells that have continued to live substantially past the fourteen-day mark. They don't become functional organs. But we're making progress. And that's why I have to go back. Everything I was working on is in the labs. I don't think the investors believe in my project. I overheard one of them sharing survival rates, and he was wrong. He was quoting black market data. I don't know where he got it, but that's what I was trying to show."

"Show what?"

"Black market organs have issues." She says it like I'm a simpleton for not understanding. If she'd been my lab partner in high school, I would've wanted to strangle her.

"I'd say black market organs have a pretty big ethical issue."

"No." She waves her hand dismissively, once again acting like I'm naïve or ignorant. "Not that. It's that many of the donors have alternate health problems. The testing for compatibility isn't necessarily as strong. Hospitals and surgeons who complete the surgeries aren't as equipped and trained as more reputable hospitals that would never step outside of international guidelines. The long-term results are inferior to ethical transplants in the US. I was trying to extrapolate the long-term results in an environment without donor health risks. From a financial perspective, if I can grow organs, it would be a financial windfall. Based on my preliminary analysis." She lets out a sigh. "I need to review the data sources I found on our network. I need to get back there to figure out what is going on."

There's not a single person she can trust back there. Any one of them could be complicit in her abduction. "You can come back with us to California. We've got a tech team. They can break into anything. We'll get you on your network."

"No. I need to go back to Grand Cayman. Everything is in my apartment."

"Pretty sure they cleared out your apartment."

"Who?" Another wave, but this time she dismisses herself. "It doesn't matter. I have to go back."

"Sloane, you're dealing with dangerous people. I can't emphasize that enough. People who stand to gain a lot of money with either your silence or your knowledge. The people holding you in Cambodia? All hired guns. The Wagner Group. Some of the best hired guns money can buy. Anton Solonov? He's not a cheap hire. You don't get to hire someone like that without connections. You can't go back. It's too risky."

"The work I'm doing could change the world. Isn't that worth taking some risks?" We stare each other down, locked in a battle of wills. I don't blink, but deep in my bones, I know I'm going to end up helping this mad scientist. "What do you do?"

"Me?" I really do not care for how she looks at me like I'm a simpleton. "Well, I told you. I work for a—"

"Were you in the military? Like my brother?"

"Yes."

"So, you're like my brother, Sam Watson?"

"I'm a lot like your brother was. Determined to make this world a better place."

"And you're one of the best, right? That's what he loved. Being among the best."

Hearing it phrased like that, coming from her mouth, leaves me speechless. I nod as I let the pride filter. Yeah, we are among the best. We're among the most highly skilled in the world, trained by one of the world's most advanced militaries.

"Well, Sam believed in taking risks. To better the world. And that's what I'm going to do."

CHAPTER 4

Sloane

"What about your sister?"

The question is an accusation that I'm not concerned enough about my sister, and that I don't have my priorities in line correctly. But she's the reason I need to figure this out.

"She's a teacher. She's going home. Jimmy will take care of her." I'd like to believe my research will help Sage, but unfortunately, the timeline probably won't allow my work to save her if she finds herself in need of a second transplant. Research and development is a slow, onerous process. But my work can save another family. Future children.

"Pretty sure Knox will have something to say about that."

Knox Williams. Sam told me if I were ever in trouble, I should go to Knox. Sam suffered from paranoia.

A battery of images floats by. Knox touching Sage's shoulder. Bringing her coffee. Watching Sage intently. Max said they are together.

"Did Sage have sex with Knox?"

"I'd say that's a safe bet." The lines around Max's face quiver, as if he's trying not to laugh. But I didn't make a joke. Sage once told me she didn't have any interest in sex, but she's physically healthy. Logically, her libido and sexual desire would increase. I don't know if she's on birth control. I'll need to speak to her to ensure she's being safe.

"You don't look happy."

Max's deep voice disturbs the quiet, reminding me of his presence. As Knox's friend, he possesses information I can't ask Sage. "Will Knox be careful with her?" He lives far away. "Does he want her to move?"

"Hey." He presses his back against the wall and does things with his arms to stretch his muscles. Those things cause his shoulder and pec muscles to flex. The broad-shouldered man is exceptionally fit. A unique male specimen. "Those are all questions you're going to need to ask your sister."

"But I asked you. Sage is inexperienced. She's never dated before."

"Well, like I said, my boy has fallen in love with your sister." He said that? "He'll die before he lets anything happen to her. It's my understanding he's considering moving to be with her, but you'll need to talk to your sister."

"The world order has shifted."

"What was that?" Now he's stretching his right arm over his head, and his torso bends. "You always say the most unexpected shit, you know that?" He stretches his left arm, and the bicep bulges. "Sloane?"

Oh, right. He's talking to me. "You should stop doing that." I wiggle a finger in his direction in case he doesn't understand me, keeping my gaze on the cumulus clouds out the window.

"Stretch?"

"You're distracting." My mind shouldn't be reacting to him like this. I have an IV line digging into the back of my hand and the remnants of a vicious headache. But I bet he has this effect on all women, and he knows exactly what he's doing. Who stretches on a wall?

"Sloane?"

"Yes?"

"I asked you a question."

"No, you didn't."

"Yes, I did. I asked you if you find me attractive."

I twist, lift a pillow from under my head, and throw it as hard as I can. He laughs. He literally laughs as a sharp pain shoots up the back of my hand and through my lower arm.

"You're physically attractive, and you know it." I'm sure they put the IV in my hand because of my small veins, but it hurts. I let out a long exhale, stretch my fingers, rest the hand on my thigh, and close my eyes. I need to focus on what needs to be done. Not a Thor doppelgänger and his calisthenic stretches. "We're planning to leave tomorrow, right?"

I keep my eyelids squeezed closed. Doing so blocks out the light and the distracting man. Scientists will be the only men in my future.

"I believe so."

"Do you have my passport? Or my credit cards?"

"Last I heard, Jack was pulling strings with the embassy to get you a replacement passport. Do you know where yours is?"

"In my apartment, in my home file."

"Solonov never showed your passport at any country's entry point?"

"No. They smuggled me around like contraband."

"I suppose to them you are. The big question is who was calling the shots. The fact they went after Sage…it's almost like they had a plan to force you to do something. Why else keep you alive? Who did your former boss go to work for? I think you said his name is William?"

"William would never do this. And he went to work for a

multinational conglomerate. They'd never take on the legal risk of violating international law."

"You may be right."

"I am. I need to gain access to my credit cards so I can schedule my flight."

"Arrow's taking care of your return trip."

"And where is Arrow flying me?"

"To Asheville. With your sister."

"Sage needs to go to Asheville. I need to go back to Grand Cayman. If necessary, I'll connect in North Carolina, but it would save time if I didn't have to do that."

"You're not going to listen, are you? Hold on a second." His deep voice sounds farther away. "Yep. All's good. Knox is back at the hotel. I'm here for the night shift." I squeeze open one eyelid and take in Max's profile, one beefy arm holding a cell phone to his ear. "Copy that."

"Who was that?"

"Office."

"Rather quick call."

"They wanted to be sure they got a message to me. Two men passed through Kuala Lumpur's customs ninety minutes ago. Could be nothing, but they're on Interpol's watch list and known associates of Anton Solonov."

"You think they're here for me? How would they know where you took me? You flew me here, right? There's nothing on me for them to track. I don't have my phone. The way we left, I left every-thing behind. Again."

"What do you mean, again?"

"They put me on that boat without any of my stuff. I mean, I had my phone but haven't seen it since he drugged me. My wallet and a pocketbook. Gone. And my clothes."

"Where'd you get the clothes you were wearing before they admitted you to the hospital?"

"When I got off the boat, they kept me in a house for a couple of days. They had some clothes. A small satchel. Some used books. Not a great selection. I left behind all of that." Yet another reason I want to go home to my apartment.

The phone is back to Max's ear. This time he's facing me.

"Do you know what happened to Sloane's clothes after we arrived at the hospital?" With swift steps, he approaches a paneled door, taps it, and the spring lock opens, exposing a closet. The ugly gray dress hangs clean and pressed. I do not want to put that back on. It itched. Max bends, giving me a fine view of his muscled derriere. He pushes back up off the floor, and I'm pretty sure I hear his knees crack. He holds up a shoe.

The cloth shoe has a woven textured base. He tucks the phone between his ear and shoulder and pulls out a small knife from somewhere on his waist. The silver blade shines beneath the fluorescent lights. With a twist, he digs into the bottom of the shoe.

He can destroy the shoe for all I care. I do not wish to wear that outfit ever again. It's what all the women in the compound wore. Drab, poorly fitting clothes. Although, I was one of the few women given a dress. Some wore the same loose pants and shirt the men did.

Max holds up a small silver dome. "Yep. They had a tracking device in the sole of her shoe. Fuck." He drops the shoe back into the closet and closes the door. Holds the device up and dumps it in a cylindrical metal trash can. "Copy that," he says and ends the call.

"Okay. I'm going to see about getting you out of here early."

"Why would they want me? They can't be here for me." None of this makes sense. If it's about the report, I don't have my laptop. I don't have access to the report.

"I'm not sure what they want, but we're getting you and Sage back Stateside."

"No." He can't force me. I have choices. "You don't have any answers. And I'm the only one who can get those answers. If I'm in danger, I'll rely on Knox. That's what Sam told me to do."

"No."

I narrow my gaze at him and all his hotness. Fine. He's attractive, but he doesn't get to call the shots, as Sam would say. Nope. Those are mine to call.

"Knox is with your sister. He's been a wreck since your brother died. And the guy is finally happy. I'm not letting you take that away from him. Your sister has to get back to her job, right?"

"Yes."

"Well, she'll go back. Knox will go with Sage to ensure she's safe. She'll be safer in Asheville with Knox. I'll go with you. If you think answers are back in your apartment, I'll go with you."

"I can go on my own."

"No. You can't."

"I'm not leaving my research."

"There's a very good chance your lab, or someone at that lab, is behind your abduction."

"We can agree to disagree." That's what I say, but there's a chance he's right. Doubtful, but an annoying nagging insists it's conceivable. It's hard to say. "But whether they are or are not involved isn't the point. I'm going to figure out what's going on, turn the responsible parties in to the authorities, and get back to my work." Because my work is important.

"Fine." The tone of his voice and the meaning of the word conflict. "But you're not doing it alone."

CHAPTER 5

Max

"Hey. Sorry to wake you, but we've got to move. Sloane and I are headed to the airport."

"Wait. What happened?" Knox sounds groggy. "Hold on a minute."

I wait, sitting back in the den section of the hospital suite. There's a nurse beside Sloane, preparing to remove the IV line. The doc cleared us to leave, but I've got a whole page of symptoms to watch out for. The flight we're about to board is a long one, and Stella couldn't get business class seats, but she managed to get us two first-class seats at the last minute. I can't even imagine how much those puppies cost.

Click.

"Hey, I'm out in the hall. Sage is sleeping."

"Figured. Sorry about that, man. We got an alert that two men connected to Solonov went through customs in Kuala Lumpur. Could be unrelated. In fact, chances are it's unrelated. If they wanted to come through undetected, they would've come in on a boat somewhere in Malaysia and driven here."

"Not everyone has the resources for a water entry. I'll wake Sage."

"No. I don't think you need to. I found a small tracker inside Sloane's shoe. You know those cloth things she was wearing with the grassy woven sole?"

"Yeah."

"After we got the call, Sloane said she had nothing with her other than the clothes on her body. So, I found those shoes and dug a knife into them. Bingo."

"Shit. I checked her for jewelry…didn't think about the shoes."

"Yeah, well, Sloane's determined to get to the bottom of this. She and I are boarding a commercial flight to Los Angeles, then we're going to take a private plane to the Caymans."

"Run that by me again."

"You're taking Sage back to Asheville on the flight tomorrow, as planned. They shouldn't have any way of locating you and Sage. But be alert."

"And what exactly are you planning on doing in the Caymans?"

"Sloane wants to get her stuff. Her laptop. And…" I let out a loud sigh, letting him know I'm not totally on board with this plan. "She believes if she can get on her work server, she can figure this out. She wants to access that report she was working on. See who else accessed it. Look at it again to see if that could be what kick-started this. She's as confused as we are about why someone would come after her. Why they'd keep her alive."

"If they're killing over data, it's no longer accessible."

"I'm aware, bro. But she's determined. And I can see it from her side. What's she going to do? Run from all this indefinitely? Plus, she's worried about her boss. Wants confirmation that she's okay. Reason dictates her boss is involved, but Sloane swears she wouldn't be."

"Dammit." Frustration drips in his huff. "Sage is going to want to be there."

"Sloane mentioned that. She said we couldn't tell Sage the truth. Suggested we tell Sage about the men, so she knows to be careful, and that we moved her out of the country tonight as a safety precaution. She says we should tell Sage that she's flying to DC, and that she'll meet up with her in Asheville soon."

"I don't mind that plan."

"Figured you wouldn't." Sure, he promised Sam he'd take care of both sisters, but he's in love with only one of them.

"What about you? Is Arrow sending someone to join you?"

"Still working on that. Spoke to Jack about an hour ago. He says there are other parties interested in this, and to do whatever we need to do." Of course, Jack's also committed to finding those responsible for Felix's death. We all are.

"Did he say which parties?" Knox's question comes through hushed and laced with frustration.

"Interpol. CIA. They want whatever information Sloane can gather. Did you know that Sam Watson met with Jack Sullivan?"

"Jack mentioned it to me once. He was considering a gig with the CIA and wanted to gain insight from Jack."

"Right." I force the fact Knox didn't mention it to me earlier to slide off my back. "Well, it's not unusual to consider all options. But do you think that's why Jack's so supportive of helping the Watson sisters? I mean, obviously, now Arrow is engaged. Felix's death guarantees we'll see this through to the end. But at the beginning? Do you think that's why he didn't hesitate to help Sage?"

"A man like Jack has so much money, it's beyond our comprehension. The man probably earns hundreds of millions of dollars in interest and dividends each year. He doesn't think like we do, Max. And he's also a good businessman. If he's got outside entities interested, he's either charging them or seeing this as a way to deepen relations."

Right. Sure, he'd bankroll us without outside interest, but he'll take advantage of outside interest if he can. Just like a good businessman. "Well, the boss man also shared with me he can't tell me everything that's going on. You can take the guy out of the CIA, but you can't take the CIA out of the guy."

"You'd think he'd want you to have all the information before you went out there." Knox's statement mirrors my thoughts.

"Agree."

"I'm sure it's some rank level, security clearance BS," Knox says.

"No doubt." The BS part is especially foul, though, when we're working for a private entity. "Well, you keep Sage safe."

"Want me to get your stuff from the hotel room?"

"Yeah. Thanks. I'd say I'd go back to get it, but I risk bringing a tail right to you."

My phone vibrates in my hand with an incoming text and emits a beep, something that only happens when there's an urgent text.

ERIK

Spotted Solonov's associates on traffic cams. Possibly headed your way.

Shit. And there's got to be a delay on that information. Unless maybe the source is Interpol.

"I gotta run," I say to Knox.

"I see that," he says, making it clear he got the text, too. "Get out of there. We'll be behind you tomorrow."

When I end the call, the nurse is wrapping up with Sloane. There's a bandage on the back of Sloane's hand that secures a large cotton ball over the IV needle insertion point. The nurse is probably in her mid-thirties, and her black hair is pulled back into a tight, rounded bun. Her English is solid. We haven't had any issues speaking English since arriving in this prestigious hospital.

"All okay?" I ask the nurse, wondering how quickly we can move. I'd like to get out of here and as far away from that disabled tracker as possible.

The nurse smiles and nods. Sloane swings her legs off the hospital bed, and her bare feet remind me she can't very well wear the shoes I decimated with my knife, and she'll stand out walking through the Kuala Lumpur airport in the tattered dress.

"Where can I get some clothes for Ms. Watson?"

"There's a shopping center nearby," the nurse answers with her back to me. She's writing information on a chart.

"Anything in the hospital?"

"The gift shop might have something. I believe they have sweatshirts, sweatpants, that kind of thing. But I don't believe you'll find shoes here. Maybe bedroom slippers." She tilts her head as if she's giving it serious thought.

"You okay coming down in that gown?" I ask Sloane. It ties in the back, and I'm not about to mention this to her, but I have a view of her spine and the top of her ass. My gaze catches on the divots along her spine and her noticeable ribcage. Christ, they must've starved her for the last several weeks. Hopefully, that IV loaded her up with nutrients as well as hydration.

"I can't go down like this. It wouldn't be appropriate."

Her statement doesn't exactly surprise me. I've got a sister, and I'm pretty sure Natalie would say the exact same thing. Trouble is, we've got two tangos in the wind. The nurse must sense my apprehension.

"I can stay with her if you like. The shopping center is just—"

"I'll go to the gift store. Where's that?"

"Main level. There's an information desk you can ask for directions, but it's around the corner from the elevators."

I come around to face Sloane. Her gaze is on the ground, making it a little difficult to get a read.

"You okay with that?" I ask.

It's not exactly my preferred plan, but we need to be quick. My other option would be to wait here with her until Knox made it over with clothes. Sage had already thought about clothes for her, and I'm pretty sure she has some back at the hotel. But I don't want to risk exposing Knox and Sage. And we need to get on the move.

"I'm fine," Sloane says. "I need to go to the restroom, anyway."

All right. She probably doesn't want me here for that. There's a thin panel bathroom door that does nothing to muffle sounds.

"I'll be right back," I say.

The nurse smiles brightly. "I'll stay with her. She'll be fine."

I don't waste any time making my way to the elevator and then locating the gift store. As I'm paying for an oversized sweatshirt with the words "Kuala Lumpur" down one sleeve, sweatpants with a hospital logo on the top right side, plain white socks, and silky slippers decorated with golden dragons, I read the name tag of the person checking me out.

A vision of the nurse flashes before me. No name tag.

My gut twists. It's got to be nothing. Solonov's associates would be men.

At the elevator bank, I stand around checking my phone for any updates, blending in with all the others waiting, but with every glance seeking a green arrow, I wonder if I shouldn't find a stairwell. But no. By the time I found a stairwell, the elevator would've arrived.

I shoot off a text to Erik, requesting details on the associates.

The elevator dings, and I, along with five others, shuffle on. One nurse pushes an elderly man in a wheelchair. She's speaking to him in Mandarin. A middle-aged woman holds the hand of a young girl. The girl is holding a small teddy bear and a balloon.

They were in the gift shop with me. And there's a man in scrubs, lost in the phone in his hand. He's wearing a name tag that identifies him as Hilmi.

When we arrive on the second floor, the nurse pushing the old man's wheelchair moves as slow as molasses. It takes every bit of self-control not to push her aside and shove the wheelchair into the hallway.

Forty-five seconds later, we're on my floor, but damn if it didn't feel like forty-five minutes.

I barge down the hallway, ignoring the greetings from the front desk. Sloane's suite door is closed, and I shove the door open, scanning the room like I'm on deployment.

Blood coats the tile floor.

Sloane stands over the nurse's body, a bloody scalpel in her hand. The nurse's eyes are open in surprise, but her eerie gaze tells me all I need to know. She's no longer alive.

"Are you okay?" I close the door behind me as I scan Sloane for injury.

"She told me I needed to come with her. I refused. She picked up a needle. It was self-defense. They aren't taking me again."

I nod, approaching slowly. She's still holding the scalpel, no doubt processing what happened. "It's okay. Sometimes death preserves life." It's a phrase I held to my heart over the years as a soldier.

"I know that," she snaps, holding the scalpel higher. "My fingerprints are on this." Is she in shock? "The scalpel was on a tray of instruments. If I could've put it through her eye, there would be less blood, but I didn't have the right angle. I like this scalpel better than any of Sam's knives. It slices easily."

"Sam taught you knife skills?" I continue my cautious approach, careful to steer clear of the pooling blood. We don't have the time to get caught up in an interrogation. We have a flight to catch, and the sooner we get to the airport and out of this place, the better off we are. If she's in shock, I'll have to ease her out of here.

"He wanted to teach me to shoot guns. But I don't like guns. I refused. I will not touch a gun. He taught me how to use knives."

"You want to give that to me?" I'm close enough now. The shopping bag is in one hand, and I hold out the other arm for her to hand me the weapon.

"Then your prints will be on it."

"How about I clean it? You get dressed." I glance around the room, knowing I need to buy us time. We need to be through security before they discover this body. If I put the body in a closet, maybe we'll get lucky and no one will discover her until after we're long gone.

"What about the blood?" Her gaze is fixed on the floor and the slowly spreading pool.

There are blankets near the sofas, and a container for used hospital gowns and sheets stands in the corner. Towels might be in the bathroom or a closet.

"You get dressed. I'll take care of it." Cleaning a scene isn't an area of expertise, but I've picked up a thing or two over the years from some of our more covert operations.

"Did you get me shoes?"

"Slippers." With a glance at the body on the ground, I say, "More like fleece lined silky socks. She was right. That was all they had."

Sloane twists the scalpel, placing the handle in my palm, and bends down next to the nurse's feet where she unfastens the dead woman's shoes. "I think she's about my size."

Who would've thought it? Sloane Watson is a cutthroat badass.

CHAPTER 6

Sloane

I killed someone.

But I had no choice. She was going to take me back to Cambodia. Or put me on a boat.

It's against the law to kill.

But not if it's self-defense.

The Bible says thou shall not kill.

The Bible also claims a man split a river with his rod.

But you know killing is wrong. It's the most wrong thing a person can do.

The blade went in so smoothly. She didn't expect I would fight back.

She underestimated you. Whoever is doing this is underestimating you. Just like Mrs. Jones when she told your parents you might need extra help. You proved her wrong.

I killed someone.

Killing is wrong.

I don't like the feeling in my chest. It's uncomfortable. I wish I could squeeze my eyes shut and make it go away.

"Sloane, are you okay?" Max's touch sears my shoulder, and I flinch. I don't want to be touched right now. "We need to get going. This woman wasn't working alone."

In order to leave, I need to get dressed. There's a stainless-steel railing on the bathroom wall, and I use this for balance as I change. More fingerprints. But I stayed in this hospital room. My fingerprints will be everywhere.

When I exit the bathroom, the white floor tiles shine, and the air smells of cleaning solution. The nurse is gone. Max works fast. Or maybe I dress slow.

There's a knock on the door to the suite. Max steps in front of me as the door swings open.

"Ah, you're ready to go," this nurse says, sounding surprised.

She's wearing white shoes that match mine.

"Oh, a nurse came and removed her IV. I think we're ready to go, unless there's any paperwork?"

"I'm supposed to be discharging you. Who came in?"

"I don't remember her name. Do you Sloane?"

I'm a horrible liar. I don't want to be a good liar. Lying is wrong. Instead of lying, I shake my head, which is still lying, but it's not verbalizing a lie. There is a difference.

"Is she feeling okay?" The nurse's question to Max offends me because I'm standing right here and she's asking him. I hate it when people do that. People used to do that to Sage all the time, and I don't know how she remained calm.

They are speaking to each other, and I interrupt. "I'm okay."

My gaze returns to the window. Green grass and leafy trees adorn the golf course. It's warm outside. I won't fit in with everyone else in the airport in my sweatshirt and sweatpants, but I am cold. Freezing.

"I'd like to get her home so she can rest." Max lies easily. "Are we good to go? It's my understanding our company handled payment?"

"Yes, yes. You may leave. I wonder who came by. You're my patient."

Her tone is playful, not irritated. If it were my lab, I'd be indignant. She steps closer, as if she's going to touch me. I step away and accidentally bump into Max's arm.

"Thank you for being so good to me. I will never forget you." I heard Sage say that to someone at a hospital once. It made the nurse happy. It's a lie, but if a lie makes someone feel good, then it is acceptable.

Max and the nurse speak as we leave, but I focus on the exit. In one of those closets is a dead body. If they find her before we leave, will they come after us? Will I be in prison for a long time? How does Malaysia handle internationals who commit a crime? I doubt statistics are readily available. If I had a phone, I could search.

But I have nothing. How am I going to get through customs?

I peer up into the bright sun as Max opens the back door of a waiting sedan.

"I don't have any identification," I tell him.

"We already handled that. The US Embassy sent documentation. It pays to have connections."

"Sage is my only connection." What connections is he referring to? I had my brother and my parents, but they died. I have William, but he doesn't know me well. We have sex. Had sex. We haven't communicated since he moved away. Most people annoy me. If I spent enough time with William, he would have grated my nerves.

Max places a passport in my hand. It's my passport. It looks like my old passport, except the pages are crisp and new.

Max talks to the driver, and I look out the window. I want to ask Max what is going on, but the driver can hear. Max types away on his phone. There are many people like him who get obsessed with their phones.

It doesn't take long before the car approaches the airport. The covering over the departures deck reminds me of a series of circus tents with stunningly curved plank boards on the ceiling. The architecture is memorable. Luxurious. Much like the hospital. I think I would have liked Malaysia if we'd had time to stay.

But time is something we don't have. I need to figure out what is going on. Who have I angered? Or threatened? The most obvious would be the source of the transplant data. But when I was reviewing study results and comparing variables, I didn't pay close attention to the source. It wasn't a relevant factor. But that's the information we need. It has to be.

I also need to confirm Dr. Kallio is okay and they don't have her locked away somewhere.

Max leads the way. His hand heats my cold one. The security line isn't a long one, and we don't have luggage, so we're through the line rather quickly. Signs in multiple languages hang throughout the airport, but English is omnipresent. Bright, colorful advertisements for shopping and restaurants within the airport abound.

"We should go to a restaurant that serves with knives. We can carry knives on the plane."

Max stops and pulls me to the side, out of the flow of pedestrian traffic. Travelers pulling wheeled suitcases continue speeding past us. Many wear masks, but not all do.

"We're going to be okay." He lightly touches my arm. I don't flinch, but I also can't stop looking at the veins traversing the back of his hand and his short, clean nails. "They won't do anything at the airport. We're safe. Do you hear me?"

He pulls me flat against him, and his body heat warms me like a wood stove on a cold winter's day. "Christ, you're cold. Do you want to get some hot tea?"

The furnace dims the sharp effect of cold. The tip of my nose seems icier, so I press it into the nape of his neck. He wraps his arms around me, holding me tight.

"We can stand here for a minute. You don't need to be afraid.

Do you hear me?" Obviously, I hear him. His lips are quite close to my ear. "The Kuala Lumpur police are working with Interpol. They located and picked up Solonov's associates and are questioning them now."

"The nurse?"

"We don't know who she was. We're working on that. But we're safe."

He smells musky. There's no hint of cologne. William wore cologne that made him smell like my grandfather's pipe. An odd mix of leather and apple. I prefer Max's mild scent and warmth.

"I don't understand what's happening. Why are they still coming after me?"

"That's the question. We'll find the answer."

He sounds confident. I'm good at discovering answers and solutions. Together, we'll solve the puzzle.

"Thank you."

"For what?"

"For holding me." His grip tightens. "You're warm."

CHAPTER 7

Max

We find two leather armchairs in the SilverKris Lounge, an area only first and business class Singapore Airlines fliers can access. I've never given much thought to what it's like behind the lounge club doors at airports, but I guess if I had, I would've expected a little more. The brown carpet and seating shows wear and tear, and the free food buffet isn't as enticing as the food options out in the general area.

But it's safer in here. From our chosen seats, I can see everyone who comes and goes. And we'll see on the screen when it's time for us to board.

A hum of differing languages surrounds us. Some I recognize thanks to military training, and two I'd need closer proximity to confirm.

Sloane slumps in the chair beside me, her gaze on the floor. I pull out my phone and log on to the VPN. I kick out a leg and lean forward, stretching the quad. I depend on my cardio workouts to lessen the aches and pains, and I'm off schedule and stiff everywhere.

"You want to grab a magazine or something to read?" She doesn't have a phone or any electronic device. She looks dazed, most likely because she's processing everything that has happened in the last hour.

The identification we're using is our real identification, which means now that we've passed through customs, depending on how powerful the people who want her are, they've either already been notified of our airport location or will be shortly. Still, it's highly unlikely they would come for us in the airport.

"I'll watch the news." There's a television on a far wall. The news isn't in English, but there are English subtitles running below.

"Suit yourself."

"There's a tropical disturbance brewing." The reporter points at an unformed tropical depression that may or may not grow into something, and they aren't yet projecting a path if it forms.

JACK SULLIVAN

Touch base before you board.

He sent the message to me within the Arrow company board. He could've texted. But he didn't. He chose the security of a firewall.

ME

In airport lounge. Boarding shortly.

JACK SULLIVAN

At LAX, you'll transfer to a private plane. When you arrive in Grand Cayman, look for a man holding a sign that reads Trafalgar party. He has everything you'll need and will take you to a secure location.

ME

Sloane wants to return to her apartment.

JACK SULLIVAN

Expected as much. You'll need your bags before going. And you can't stay there. If they aren't watching her apartment now, it won't be long before they will be. Get in. Search. Get out. And don't leave her alone. She may look for something she doesn't want to share with us.

He doesn't trust her.

Sloane appears to be intent on the news, which shows a man dressed in red with a sword spinning through the air. The English subtitle reads World Combat Games. Sloane appears to be intent on the screen, but she's too close for this text conversation if she can't be trusted.

ME

I'll check in when we connect in LA

———

The full moon lights the parking lot as Sloane digs around in the dirt near the steps to her place, searching for a buried apartment key.

Thanks to the time change and almost thirty-five hours of nonstop travel, the moon and the pervasive silence are the only clues to the time of day. My internal clock is useless. If it had been my call, after we shuffled through the door of a small villa, we would've crashed, ensuring we adapted to our new time zone, and planned this apartment intrusion for the next night.

But Sloane's wide awake. And she's like a dog with a bone. I recognize determination, so I didn't waste effort attempting to dissuade her.

True to Jack's word, luggage awaited us. We have clothes for our stay here, plus a full arsenal of handguns, ammunition, and a secure phone for Sloane, which she promptly turned off.

I offered to find what she needed, letting her stay behind where she would be safe and could rest.

Unsurprisingly, she didn't bite.

And after spending almost two days with this woman, I've noticed she eats little. Crackers and two plain bagels in thirty-five hours. All she drank on the plane was Coca-Cola. She refused any water. Full on grimaced when a bottle of water was offered.

She's not taking care of herself, and she's borderline obsessed with her work. On the way here in the car, I asked, aiming to emphasize this isn't a game, "Is whatever you're working on worth risking your life?"

All she said was, "Every choice bears a cost."

And I can't get that answer out of my head because it's a guilty person's defense. Did she remember more on the flight home? Tomorrow, when she's in the shower or something, I'll need to log a call to Jack. He needs to read me in on whatever the fuck he knows.

By the time we landed, Interpol had an update on the two tangos the local police back in Kuala Lumpur picked up. They hadn't actually broken any laws, but they managed to extract some useful intel. One, they'd been hired by the Wagner Group to retrieve Sloane. They weren't there to go after Sage, but they were aware of her. Turns out somewhere out there was a reward offered for Sloane with a much higher sum paid if she was alive. Our tech team finally found the post. Kairi back at HQ had been saying all along it had to exist. Now they're trying to track who posted it, but that might be damn near impossible.

"Got it!" Sloane triumphantly holds up a grimy Schlage key.

"You didn't trust a neighbor with it?"

There are twelve apartment units in this two-story apartment complex. She's been digging below a window of one of the ground units. Lights are off in all the units, there's been no curtain movement, but knowing someone could be inside watching us doesn't give me the warm and fuzzies.

She opens the door, and I lift my SIG from its holster. With one last scan of the parking lot, I push past her. She steps inside, and I position her at the door.

Per her description, it's a simple one bedroom. The front door opens into an open living area with a den and kitchen. There's a musty smell in the apartment, as one would expect from a unit that hasn't been lived in for over a month. But other than a stuffy smell derived from closed windows, it's immaculate. Nothing appears out of place.

The kitchen counters are bare other than a wood block holding a dozen knives. There are no canisters on the counter. No dish towel hanging from a knob. No photos anywhere in the den. The coffee table in front of the small, slightly worn sofa is bare, as are the two side tables that hold only lamps.

In the far corner, there's an odd-looking wooden sculpture. Stacked wood blocks covered in splintered divots and bright color spots in the center of the splintered wood.

Hanging blinds with a thin layer of dust cover the two rectangular windows on one wall of the den. They're folded closed, but moonlight streams through the cracks. Sloane stands against the entrance door, waiting for me to give the all-clear.

There are two white closed doors on the back wall in front of an area where a kitchen table would normally be located, and one stool beneath a kitchen counter.

As a military guy, I'm used to seeing barely decorated apartments. It's common for young single soldiers. Can't say it's what I was expecting from Sloane.

When Sloane drew out a diagram of her apartment, she explained the door on the left opens into a storage closet. The door on the right opens into her bedroom suite.

Behind the left door, there's a broom, dustpan, and a shelving unit with dry food, paper towels, toilet paper, and a large bag of generic dry cat food.

Behind the right door, there's a neatly made bed that would pass inspection on base. On her nightstand, there's a framed photo of Sloane, Sage, and Sam. Sage is a child in the photo, so I'm guessing the photo is an old one. There's a white desk pushed against one wall. A charger is plugged into the wall below the right side of the desk, but it connects to nothing.

I push the bathroom door open. Movement has me slamming the door against the wall and aiming at the shower.

A long centipede scurries across the tile and disappears down the drain.

Bathroom's clear.

I reenter the bedroom and bend to double-check the one-foot space beneath the bed frame. Clear. The closet doors are sliding mirrors.

In the moonlight, my reflection catches my attention. I look like a regular guy with a handgun checking his house after hearing a sound.

Using the end of my SIG, I rifle through the hanging clothes in her closet after scanning the floorboards for feet. The shelves above the hanging clothes hold a series of cardboard boxes. Neat lines of shoes fill every inch of floor space. Heels, flip-flops, two pairs of running shoes. All arranged in order from dark to light color, as are her hanging clothes.

Sloane Watson leads an organized life. Or someone came in and cleaned after she left.

I quietly step into the den and signal to Sloane with a thumbs up, telling her it's okay, and then I place my index finger over my lips to remind her we are to be quiet. I don't have a sweeper with me. Before we entered, I warned her that the place could be bugged and someone could be listening. Even if it's delayed, meaning someone checks the recording periodically, anything we say, we should assume someone might hear. In our case, if we can come in and leave no evidence that we've been here, the better.

She barely glances around the den as she brushes past me and pulls a chair from her desk over to the closet. She's a tall woman, so my curiosity rises when she stands on the chair and reaches up to the highest shelf.

A sliding glass door opens onto a balcony. The view out the window is of palm trees, shrubbery, and a street. Vertical blinds hang over the sliding glass doors, but they're set to open. I twist them closed.

She's wearing a black cotton tank top, black Lycra leggings, and a pair of light blue running shoes we picked up in the Los Angeles airport. The leggings leave nothing to the imagination. She's got long, lean legs and a firm, tight ass. Her shoulder muscles flex as they strain with the weight of the box she's pulled off the top shelf.

I tap her from behind, setting my leg against the chair for

balance to prevent the chair from tipping over. The weight of the box lies heavy on my arms.

Wordlessly, I place the box on the mattress. She returns the chair to the desk and lifts the box. Her slender arms strain with the weight. She jerks her head, indicating she's ready to leave.

I return the vertical blinds to their half-opened position on the off chance someone has been monitoring the place. She's already near the front door, but I scan the room one last time. I would've expected her to grab clothes, cosmetics from the bathroom, something. Natalie sure as hell would've been repossessing her cosmetics. Given my sister often places cosmetics on her gift list, I know what those little bottles and tubes cost.

But not this girl. All she wants is whatever is in that one box she kept on the top shelf.

"Clothes?" I mouth.

Her eyes widen, and she places the box in my arms. She kneels on the ground and drags out a suitcase and a black duffel from beneath the bed. She opens the suitcase and throws clothes inside. Given the state of her apartment, I would've expected more care with packing, but perhaps nerves are feeding her desire to get out quickly.

It's the drawer in the nightstand beside my bed that gets my attention. Lube. Vibrators. Three—no, four get tossed in. I don't bother to look away because she's showing no signs of embarrassment. *Well, then.*

With her suitcase packed and closed, we exit the apartment.

I reposition my handgun in my waistband in case we come across someone in the parking lot, place a finger against my lips, open the door, scan the area, and push it wider for her to pass through. As she steps past me, she lifts the box, insisting on carrying it plus the handle of her wheeled suitcase. I hoist her duffel.

She doesn't wait for me as I lock the door.

"Wait for me," I hiss.

She sets the box down on the dirt in the flower bed and shakes her hands like the box hurt her fingers.

Headlights approach, and I leap to her side.

Reggae music wafts through the night air, growing louder as a Jeep slows to a stop in a nearby spot. Thanks to the headlights, I can't see the vehicle's occupants.

My hand rests on the butt of my gun holstered at my waist. With one eye on the vehicle, I scan the area, and determine it's best if I shove Sloane behind me if they aren't friendlies.

The headlights flick off, and laughter replaces the reggae. It's a group of people partying, returning from bars.

A woman with long blonde hair looks our way. I push Sloane up against the building wall, using my back as a shield. If someone comes by asking about Sloane, like our own guys have done over the past month, I don't want anyone recognizing her.

Her eyes are wide. Scared. Lips close to her ear, I whisper, "Play along."

"Hey, you okay?" A feminine voice calls out.

I dip my head, aiming to cover Sloane's lips. Warmth covers my shoulders, and fingers dip into the nape of my neck. Thank god, she's playing along.

Her tongue slips between my lips. And fuck if that brief touch doesn't go straight to my dick. She tugs my hair, and my mouth opens. Her tongue tells me she's into this kiss, and fuck me, the girl can kiss. She tastes like mint with a hint of sweetness. There's no hesitation. She alternates between nipping my lips and kissing me so hard it's a fucking challenge to keep an ear out for the folks behind us. Her body rocks against my hips as she mewls.

"Get a room, you two." A low chuckle follows, and I hear a slap and a squeal as the guy corrals his female companion away, presumably to his apartment.

Their steps grow distant, and Sloane's fingers tap against my cheek. I lift my head, my breaths rapid and deep. Christ. That went from zero to sixty at lightning speed.

"I think they're gone."

She's right. I push off the wall and grimace when I straighten. My dick presses uncomfortably against my zipper, a reaction I need to settle pronto.

"Get in the car."

CHAPTER 8

Sloane

"Hey, Sloane!"

My little sister's face fills the screen. She's smiling so wide you'd think she discovered the cure for cancer.

"Happy to be home?" A burgundy red wall fills the screen behind her along with the corner of a framed black and white print. "Where are you?"

"We're at Jimmy's. Where're you?"

"Hotel in D.C."

The lie comes easily because I know it's best for her, but since I'm on a video call, I need to be careful with how much of the frame behind me she can see.

The truth of my situation starkly contrasts with my lie. I'm on a lounge chair with thick white cushions. A lap pool stretches the length of the deck, and then beyond the tiled pool rim lies the Caribbean Ocean. The villa Arrow rented for us is in the exclusive, touristy section off of Bodden Town Road. The only time I've ever been to this section is when Sage visited, and I drove down here to let her see where all the rich vacationers stay.

"Are you safe there?" There's worry in Sage's trusting eyes.

Max doesn't think we're safe. He wants to leave but has agreed to stay until we confirm Dr. Kallio is safe. I'm smart enough to know he doesn't really care one way or another if she's safe. The only reason his employer is funding our continued stay on the island is they're developing a plan for us to break into Origin Labs one night so I can access the server. They want to figure out who did this, too, as whoever is behind this killed one of their colleagues.

I can't help but believe this is all a big misunderstanding. The work I am doing is important, but the aim is to save lives. Killing over research that will help humanity is contradictory.

"We're safe," Max's voice cuts in.

"Where are you?" I ask, looking around for the growly guardian.

"Right here." He's sitting at a table behind me wearing shorts and a t-shirt one size too small. The material stretches over his shoulders and biceps.

"Can I have some privacy?" His presence disturbs my cognitive abilities. My thought processes simply don't run as smoothly when he's around, but especially since last night when he pretended to kiss me. Another lie, but it didn't feel like a lie, and that, in and of itself, is perplexing.

"I'll be right inside where I can see you," he says, and I glare at him.

That's not what I asked. I keep the phone close to my face so Sage can't see what he's wearing, but I don't break my expressive reprimand. His clothes are appropriate for island wear, but not for D.C. And if Sage sees all those muscles, she might see what I see, that he would be an appropriate cover model, and then I would risk her teasing me. She loves to ask about my sex life. Not that I have one these days.

"Hey, Max," Sage says from the phone.

"Hey there, Sagey Bean." He hardly knows her well enough to apply a family nickname. "Is Knox there?"

"He went on a run."

"Can you have him call me when he gets back?"

"Sure thing, Max." Sage practically sings her answer to him.

The glass door slides closed. The sunrays reflect off the glass at a sharp angle and distort the interior view, but I can still make out the shape of Max's torso. As I discovered last night, his very hard torso. Too hard. Like a brick wall.

"Where are you?" Sage asks.

"I just told you."

"Why is Max going inside?"

"I'm on a balcony."

"Is that safe?"

Are there even balconies on hotels in D.C.? I should've taken this call inside. "Sage, I want to hear about you. That's why I called. How are you?"

"Why are you holding the phone so close to your face?"

"Sage. Are you taking your medicine?"

"You know I am." She hates when I ask about her meds, but asking about her meds is a sure-fire distraction technique.

"Knox is still there. But he went running. Does that mean they think you're safe?"

"I'm at Jimmy's. And he's here. I'm safe."

"Where is Knox staying?"

"Jimmy put us up in his guest bedroom."

"Us? Sage…Max said something about that. Are you having sex with Knox?" My sister doesn't date. I tried to get her to have sex casually years ago because it's fun, but she's never shown any interest.

"I was planning on telling you but never got the chance." She grins, and her cheeks flush. "We're together. All of my dreams came true. I've never… Being with him is all I ever wanted. I know you're going to tell me it's all happened too fast, and it has, but I love him, Sloane. So much. I've never felt anything like this."

"What birth control are you using?"

"Condoms."

"Sage." I pointedly stare at the phone screen. "That's not an acceptable plan for you. The failure rate is too high. You need to see your gynecologist and ask for an IUD."

"I will."

Is she telling me the truth? She's smiling. Does that mean she's being truthful? I'm all for my little sister finally having sex. I like sex. But… "You could also ask the doctor about a hysterectomy. Or tubal litigation, I suppose."

"Sloane." She drawls out my name the way she does when she's complaining about something I've said.

"Sage. I'm serious."

"What if I want children?" My chest cinches.

"That is not advisable." The screen on the phone flits from her face to the beige fringe of an oriental rug carpet. "Sage. Be smart. If you want children, you can adopt. That's what Mom and Dad said."

"There's no reason for us to argue about this." Her tone is noticeably less bright. "I'll be careful. Knox said Max is going to stay with you during your meetings and then drive with you back here. Jimmy says to tell you he has another guest room. It's in his basement. I think you'd like it. He has a desk with four monitors, and he said it's all yours. He only uses it when he plays games, which isn't as often these days."

I don't want to dig deeper into this lie. "Is your classroom ready?"

"It was all done by the time I got back. The other teachers and Jimmy did it for me. Next week, I'll return to the classroom. I swear, it feels like these past few weeks have been the most surreal dream."

She's right. I long for my office in the lab. For my routine. Why did that man drug my water and lock me on a boat?

"What meetings do you have?"

Max didn't tell me this part of the lie.

"Are you interviewing for jobs there? Weren't you interested in an opportunity in the Richmond area?"

Job hunting. Yes, that works. "Yes, I'll be doing some job hunting." It's a twist of the truth. If all goes well, I'll be back at my old job, doing what I love.

"It seems to me Max likes you." She didn't even see him in his tight t-shirt, and she's teasing me?

"He doesn't. We kissed last night, and he's been mean ever since."

"You kissed!" Her squeal has me pushing the phone back, but then the scene widens and the glass doors behind my head enter the screen with the reflection of the Caribbean, and I bring it back up to my face.

"Tell me all about it." She's grinning again, beaming really.

"There's nothing much to tell." I think back to the way he pressed me against the wall and his plea to play along. And I did exactly what he said. I thought it was a good kiss. One of my better kisses, if not my best. "He's been terse ever since it happened. Snappy."

"Oh. Did you instigate the kiss?"

I roll my eyes. As if it matters who instigates it. I've come on to men and they've come on to me. In the past, every single time, the man became nicer to me. Max is different. He didn't like our kiss. He didn't enjoy kissing me. And that's fine. It's not like I expected he would want a relationship. I'm different, and I am absolutely okay with that. I thought we might have sex, but he's not interested, and that's fine.

"Sloane, don't take it personally. He's probably focused on the job at hand. You may be in D.C., but they still don't know who's doing all this. And he's the only one with you right now, right?"

A seagull squawks off in the distance.

"What was that?"

"The television. Can I call you later?" My thumb hovers over the red circle, and I recall the most important thing. "And Sage. Go to the doctor, okay?"

My sister is different, too, but differently. She needs to be careful.

After we share I love yous, because Sage always wants to say, 'I love you,' the call ends. I set the phone down, and a mechanical whir sounds.

"How's Sage?"

"She's considering having children."

"What?" Max's jaw drops, but then he recovers and resumes his normal beefcake facade. "I mean, I know Knox is pretty serious about her."

"She had a heart and lung transplant twelve years ago. It's a risk she doesn't need to take."

"Knox mentioned something about that. Look, I can talk to him—"

"It's not up to him. It's up to her. And she shouldn't be considering it."

"Well, sure, but they're kind of new—"

"It's not about them. It's about her. The doctors warned her."

"They told her she can't have kids?"

What did they say, exactly? Mom cried. She cried a lot back then. Of course, it all depends on how Sage is doing. She might be okay. I haven't been to any of her medical appointments in years. A dull throb behind my temple commences, and I rub over the tender area. "Adoption is the safest option."

"Well, look at that. Neither of you is choosing the safest option."

"What do you mean by that?"

"You're insisting on breaking into this lab. That's not safe."

The worst that would happen is they file charges for breaking and entering. Unfortunately, nothing on my old laptop's hard drives had anything of relevance. Also, none of my old laptops connect to Origin Laboratories. I'm not sure what they did with the laptop I left behind when I followed Anton Solonov out of the lab. If I could find my work laptop, that would be ideal. But the next best solution is getting on the network.

"Look at it from your sister's side." He pulls up a lounge chair. His shadow extends over my thigh. "Have you ever tried to do that?"

He's talking about empathy. I overheard Mom once on a phone call. She was telling someone I struggle with empathy. That's not true, though. I simply prefer to leave emotions out of any analysis. I find there is no struggle when emotions are removed from the equation.

Max releases a long-winded sigh as if I am paining him. "For some women, having children is important to them. It's worth some risks. But I can understand how you wouldn't want someone you love to take any risks."

Sam was a soldier. He risked his life. He was both selfish and selfless. Two opposing notions, each dependent on perspective.

"You know, Sage wouldn't want you here. She'd want the experts to handle it."

He's on that again. But they don't know what they're looking for.

But maybe he would be more empathetic with my purpose if I could show him. "Come inside with me."

CHAPTER 9

Max

Next to Sloane's feet is the cardboard box we lifted from her apartment. Her toenails, like her fingernails, are bare and cut short with rounded edges. I was there when the nurse discussed the nails with Sage, or more correctly, I was sitting in the background, observing.

Much like I am now. Jack told me to keep an eye on her because he doesn't trust she's been completely open with us. I'm doing what he said, serving as both security and investigator.

She's an interesting woman. Very different from my exes or my sister. She's direct. There's no guessing with her. She says her mind, and on the whole, that's a huge relief. This assignment would be a ball of frustration if I had to probe to find out what's bothering her.

The way she's treating that box, you'd think there were diamonds inside. If I hadn't prompted her, we would've left her place with only that box. What kind of woman needs to be reminded to pack make-up and shit? She's an enigma. Wickedly intelligent by all accounts. Capable of being involved in a complicated crime? Acting innocent? No. Jack Sullivan is off base.

When we extracted Sloane from the compound, she'd been clean, but her nails were dirty and jagged. Sage asked the nurse for clippers and a file. She wanted to take care of her sister, and cleaning her nails was something she could do as she slept. I'd asked if Sloane ever did Sage's nails, my thought being that if I snapped a photo, Sloane would get a kick out of the role reversal when she woke up, but Sage looked at me like the idea of Sloane doing nails was preposterous. She'd sort of laughed and then said no, not Sloane, and then she'd told me about how her mom did her nails when she'd been younger and in the hospital as a way to pass the time.

Sloane flips open a MacBook Pro. The only things in the box are laptops and a collection of chargers.

I don't think I've ever met a woman who is more my sister's opposite. If that had been my sister's apartment, I would've had to back our rental car up to the steps and load make-up, nail polish, picture frames, clothes, and every single one of those shoes. And Sloane's priority was her box of laptops that other people would've donated, but she kept.

Of course, I don't give away my laptops either. Security training covers all the risks.

While she's absorbed with her laptop, I shoot off an update to the team that I didn't find anything of interest in her apartment. I'm a little curious what's on the hard drives on her laptops, but codebreaking isn't one of my skills. If I see her enter a passcode, then I'll try it out on some of these others, but unlike Jack, my gut says we can trust her. If she possessed something that would help us, she'd let us know.

As it is, her long, dark hair shines beneath the incoming sun's rays. She tucks it behind each ear, but because she's hunched over, smooth, silky strands fall past her ears, refusing to be held back.

Last night, she threw me. The kiss threw me. I mean, sure, I kissed her, but I planned on acting. Pressing my lips flat against hers and hovering over her. Pretending. Playing it off like we were two lovers.

This case is too messed up for us to throw in sex, too. The villa we're in has two-bedroom suites upstairs. I took the one across from hers, insisting that our doors remain open. If she screamed during the night, I needed to hear her. Still, it wasn't the safest. This set-up isn't the safest.

If I didn't want Knox to chase this thing with Sage, I'd tell him to get his ass here.

But Arrow has two contract workers on standby, and if I need them, they'll get here quickly.

Jack wants me to get her into the lab. Let her get what she can off the server. Then he wants us to come home. But he's agreed we need to do some surveillance first. We need to better understand what we're dealing with at the lab. The hours. The security. See if anything's changed since we performed surveillance a couple of weeks ago when we first got pulled into this case, searching for Sloane.

Stella's currently scouring the island for a couple of nondescript cars we can rent. We need vehicles on the beat-up side that won't warrant a second glance. Maybe a little salt rust to underscore it's a local car. The plan is to park across the street from the employee parking lot, and we need a couple of vehicle options so we don't get burned with familiarity.

Sloane will spend the day watching who is coming and going. We'll gain her insights. Hopefully, we'll see this Dr. Kallio she's so concerned with. She'll see that her boss sold her out and let authorities take this over, supported by the information she compiles.

The speed of clicking keys slows and stops with a crescendo of one crisp clack. She pushes the laptop over to me. "See."

It's a live camera feed. She's logged in to a view of a hospital hallway.

"This is the ICU for the hospital where I interned one semester."

"They have a public camera?"

"No. I just remember how to access it. When Sage was there, I got to know a lot of the employees. The nurses and doctors were busy, but the security and janitorial staff had more time. Look down this hall. This is where people come when they've run out of time. I login sometimes so I can remember what it feels like. Sometimes I'll see family members crying. Pacing the hallway when either the maximum number of occupants are in the room or maybe they just need a break. Can't keep it together. My mom and dad were like that. They had their Sage-face, and then they had their hallway tear-streaked face, the one that came out when they thought no one was watching. Sometimes you'll see doctors and nurses running. Or you know there's a DNR if they don't run, they just walk. Over one hundred thousand people in the United States are waiting for organs right now. My research bent some laws, yes, but the reason is good."

"I get it." And I do. I'm a soldier who believes death can save lives. As much as we may wish for a black and white world, we fill our universe with shades of gray. "Why are you showing me this?"

"I need to tell you something." Her gaze lowers. She's looking at her nails, the keyboard, the black band on her wrist that alternates placement on her wrist and her hair. I don't know what she's looking at, but she's sure as hell not looking at me. That's her MO. I'm getting used to it and trying my damnedest not to read into it.

"Shoot."

"I don't like that word."

Won't touch guns. Also doesn't like any words associated with them? "It's an expression. Just say it. Tell me whatever you want to say."

She hasn't seemed to hold anything back yet. Is she about to cop to something?

"Don't get angry. Maybe I shouldn't." She stops speaking and places her hands beneath her thighs. Her knees bounce up and down. "No, I should."

She's got my curiosity spiked. I lean back, giving her more physical space. I've noticed when she's got a lot going on in her head, she does better when she's got plenty of personal space.

"Okay. I'm going to tell you because I think you need to know. As we work on this, you need to know."

"Okay." I soften my voice, doing my best not to scare her into shutting up. Jack Sullivan might've been right. She may be one we can't trust. But something tells me whatever she's struggling with is going to give us a shit ton of insight.

"In the compound, I know what they were having me test those people for."

"Okay." Yeah, I sound like a broken record, but her knees are bouncing like she's popped too many Adderall. In this moment, head bowed, shoulders caved in, she's flighty. Nervous. If I move too quickly, I fear she might fly away. And if she vanishes, the opportunity to figure this out and find the people responsible for Felix's death vanishes too.

She lets out a deep breath. "What they were doing had nothing to do with Origin. I mean, maybe they found me because of what I was working on. Or maybe they knew my personal history. But what was going on in that compound..."

"You can tell me. I'm on your side. Team Sloane all the way."

"You might not be once I tell you. What I did was wrong."

CHAPTER 10

Sloane

If he leaves, it's fine. I work better on my own.

"She excels in solitary sports, without a team. I love the idea of a dependable after-school program, and I agree with your ethos that they need physical activity after school, but I know my daughter. Sticking her in a gym with other kids will not make her happy. If you have a swimming program, horseback riding, fencing, anything that's more of a solo sport. I'll pay extra, but that's what my daughter needs."

Mom planned our activities on the car speakerphone. Her cell phone didn't work well within the hospital. Inside the hospital, even if she could hear the person speaking, most often they couldn't hear her. She had that conversation on my first week of an after-school program. What an awful, horrific program…after school. I forgave my parents for sticking me in it, only because Sam explained they didn't have a choice. They didn't know if they would be available to pick us up from school because of Sage, and Mom didn't want us to be home alone for too many hours. Not that they ever asked, but I would've preferred to be home alone.

"Whatever it is, you can tell me. I'm on your team. No one else's."

I blink, returning from a momentary memory flash. Why am I remembering Mom? Team. It's a trigger word.

"I don't really work well on teams." *But that doesn't mean you shouldn't tell him.* He's convinced Origins is involved, but if he knew everything, he wouldn't be.

"Well, that's okay. I excel at teams. High school football MVP. Military. As I'm sure you know from Sam, we're all about teams. I've got enough team skills for both of us. But it all starts with being upfront with each other."

And if you tell him, and he leaves, that's fine. You excel at solitary endeavors.

I ball my hands up, push my shoulders back, and say, "In the compound, I was checking for blood type, like I said. But I was also doing HLA testing." I pause. He's silent. "Do you know what HLA testing is?"

"No."

His answer does not surprise me. "HLA stands for human leukocyte antigen." I don't glance up to see if there's a flicker of recognition because there won't be. "Antigens are proteins on the cells in the body. Out of over a hundred different antigens that have been identified, there are six that have been shown to be the most important in organ transplantation. Except in cases of identical twins and some siblings, it is rare to get a six-antigen match between two people, especially if they are unrelated. A person can make antibodies against another person's HLA antigens. Antibodies can result from blood transfusions, pregnancy, infections or even a viral illness. Having one of these events does not mean a person will make antibodies, but they could. If a recipient has strong antibodies against a donor's HLA, the risk of rejection is high, and they would decline a donor for that recipient. Of course, kidneys are very successfully transplanted between two people with no matching antigens. But that doesn't hold for..." He is so silent, I risk a glance up. He's not getting it. "I was testing the people in the compound and recording if they would be suitable organ donors. I also tested for HIV, diabetes, and a few other things, although they didn't have the tools to test for everything they should have been testing for."

My knees bounce high of their own volition. It's as if I've lost bodily control. One sturdy, weathered hand with veins that split into a v settles over my knee. Tension eases and I close my eyes. Just say it. He'll either leave or he won't. "The people in the compound? Working on the computers? I created medical records for each of them detailing their compatibility for organ recipients."

"You believed they had your sister. You had no choice." Is he trying to make me feel better? What I did was wrong. Those people didn't have a choice. And while I don't want to think about it, my bet is they take more than kidneys. If they select one of those people based on the records I created, there's a good chance they won't survive. You can't donate your heart and survive. If that was an ethically viable option, I would've given mine to Sage long ago.

"They had records of people needing organs. I selected the best candidates from those I had tested. Two people. I selected two healthy people for organ harvesting." I squeeze my eyelids as tightly shut as they will go. "From a practical viewpoint, I can understand organ sourcing from those in society who are poorest. Especially if their families are compensated. If you take the emotion out of it, when we have displaced human beings who are struggling, it's a solution for all sides. But it's wrong. No matter how much I want the option, it's wrong. But I comprehend all the sides. Sage has already had one organ transplant. It's not unusual for a second transplant to be needed, especially since she had one so young, and she won't be top of the list. She's already had one. Worldwide, there's a massive organ shortage. And there are others who are simply denied organ transplants by hospitals that don't want to take the risk. And if you have money and you can save someone you love..." A dizziness hits me, and I have to breathe and put a hand to my chest. The movement is what I call pulling-a-Sage. "I could've refused. I did it willingly. And then those people... they were gone. Selected by me. And I kept looking at the others." Not really looking, hearing. Listening to them beg to leave. Cry. "I didn't refuse to do the work. Not at first. I selected two people to die."

"You didn't have a choice."

"There's always a choice." I expect Max to look at me the way Mom did after I was sent to the principal's office for screaming at the girl beside me in class when she wouldn't shut up so I could hear the teacher. I had been right. But also wrong. Hence the serious, disappointed look. I know better, and therefore I should be better.

But the lines around Max's eyes are soft, as is his forehead. His jaw is relaxed, and his lips aren't pressed together like he's holding something in. There's no judgement. His hand remains on my knee, warm and comforting.

"My reason for telling you all of this is to show you Origins can't be involved. There was no research going on in that compound. What they were doing in that place wasn't connected to Origins. It's not even connected to my research. They were simply determining which of their employees would be a satisfactory organ donor. And 'employee' isn't an accurate descriptor. You and I both know those people were modern day slaves. You can't count them as indentured servants because they have no plans of ever letting them go."

The warm squeeze over my knee heats the right side of my body.

"I heard those people. Heard their stories. Many of them responded to a job posting. The promise of a better life for themselves. They were promised a well-paying job that would allow them to send money back home. They lied to those people. But it took me weeks to stand up to them, and even then, I backed down."

I try so hard to be a good person. To do what is right. My parents would be so disappointed. It's good they won't ever know what I did.

"Sloane. I get it. If someone I loved needed an organ, I'd understand the other side too."

"I don't just love Sage. She's my responsibility. And she's my only person. I don't like most people. They annoy me greatly. Sage is my one person."

Which is also why it would be incredibly selfish of her to go against medical advice and have a child.

"I get it."

"Would you quit saying that? You clearly don't get it, or you wouldn't still be touching me. Places like that are the reason black market organ transplants have lower success rates than US records. They aren't testing for everything they should." A small voice nags that's not completely true. "That, and I suspect people who wouldn't be approved for an organ transplant seek these alternative options. You know, alcoholics, drug addicts, maybe people with a disease who just wouldn't be approved because in other markets, long-term viability is a factor in placement on the list. So, those factors also negatively impact success rates."

He's silent, and I bow my head under the weight of judgement. I can't stand it when other people do bad things, and yet I do bad things. I knew better, but I felt torn because I understood the why. That had to have been why they picked me.

"You said Interpol estimates they have around ten thousand people in compounds like the one I was in?"

"This one organization. Yes, that's what they're saying."

"Well, that's ten thousand organ donors. In the US alone, over one hundred thousand people need organs. The United States includes approximately four percent of the world's population. You can extrapolate that worldwide, the number of people in need of an organ in any given year is significantly larger than one hundred thousand. It's easy to understand why the black market for organs is a multibillion-dollar business. Obviously, I knew this. My research strives to find an ethical solution to organ needs. But when I first arrived in the compound, logic reasoned, it made sense. It's how the world works. The fittest, smartest, and most adaptable survive. But then I heard them. They had darker skin and needed showers, and they smelled, but the more I heard them, and got to know them, there was simply no justification. And yet, I kept testing them and updating their records."

His other hand finds my other knee. "Hey." His voice is soft. Dare I say, compassionate? Toward me?

"Sloane, you gotta remember who you're talking to. I killed people for a living. And I was damn good at it. I'm not one to judge. But I can see it's eating at you. And you've got to let it go."

With those words, with his hands on me, it's easier to breathe.

Sometimes it's harder to breathe around this man, but right now it's easier. It's a paradox. It should be one or the other. Not both.

CHAPTER 11

Max

Goosebumps rise along the silky skin of her legs. She shaves to just above her knee. The giveaway is the straight line below a smattering of golden hairs, twinkling under the sun's rays.

I should remove my hands from her knees because my dick has been steadily thickening. Given the context of the conversation, it's a completely inappropriate reaction.

Given I'm here for a job, and my boss spent a lot of money to ensure we have different bedrooms, I should back the fuck up and take what I just learned to the team.

I hear the brutal honesty in her voice. See it in her body posture. Jack Sullivan may be unsure he can trust her, but I trust her.

If she was hiding anything, it was the guilt from participation in what they were doing.

My gaze fixates on her thighs. She's sitting on the edge of the lounge chair. Her shorts have ridden up...and.

Christ.

Stop it.

I pat her leg. Touching her because she needs it. I sense that. Patting her like a friend because I need to get my head out of the gutter and focused.

"Don't be too hard on yourself. You were held against your will too."

I squeeze her shapely thigh one last time because I'm a masochist, and then I push back. My smaller head might be juggling the idea of crossing lines with her, but I won't. We need to find answers.

"So, I take it your logic is that Origins would never be involved in the organ trade, and therefore they couldn't be responsible for your abduction?"

"Exactly. Origins is first and foremost interested in research that delivers for its investors. I mean, most of the research conducted at the labs is related to anti-aging products. Skin-focused. My research is the one project that could one day—and realistically, it's not as far away as you think—lead to a scenario where we can grow functional organs."

"You dream big." Can't hate someone for having big dreams. If anything, jealousy stabs me. I've lived my big dreams. Climbing ranks, qualifying for Special Forces, a SEAL team, highlights of my life. I long for dreams.

"Yes. And no. A team at Mass Gen and Harvard Medical School used adult skin cells to regenerate functional human heart tissue. They infused hearts with a nutrient solution and allowed them to grow. After two weeks, the hearts contained well-structured tissue that looked similar to immature hearts. And… get this." The skin along her slender neck flushes. "When they shocked the immature hearts with electricity, they started beating." She cocks her head. "Why are you grinning? It's not funny."

"You're not even looking at my face. How do you know I'm grinning?"

"I'm looking at your face."

No, she's not. Her gaze bounces all around, but she's not a person who looks someone in the eye. "You're totally geeking out. I'm not knocking you. I love it."

"It's world changing innovation. Growing an entire human heart is conceivable. And, if we can grow them, we can create individualized hearts so transplant rejection will no longer be a side effect." Now, she looks right up at me, and this time she's the one who touches my leg, and her touch travels to my groin. She's got dark brown eyes with thick brown eyebrows that capture you, drawing you in. My heartbeat kicks up a notch above resting. Under her intense gaze, I'm the one blinking, shifting because my briefs are now uncomfortable, and I look away to the ocean.

There's a thin strip of sand and miles of jewel blue water. No one's on the beach. We're away from the hotels and the resorts. This job is a solar system away from my deployments in the Navy.

"Anyway, my old boss called my research a pet project. He was an ass."

"Growing heart tissue was a pet project? What did they hire you to do?"

"Organoid research. The heart tissue. But then the woman who hired me went back to the States, and the new investors started placing priority on financial returns. And I had to pick up the other project." She sounds incredibly bored with the concept. A loud sigh underscores her lack of enthusiasm. "We're trying to find the right dosage levels that won't bring on unwanted side effects for this anti-wrinkling product."

"Oh. What are the side effects?" I'm not a medical guy, but I've injured myself enough to know that sometimes medicinal side effects suck balls.

"Suppressed immune system. And then you can get all kinds of things, you know, like cancer."

"Yeah, I'd say that qualifies as a detrimental side effect."

She waves dismissively. "Whoever can get it right and get it approved for use is going to make a mint. I didn't want to work on it. I only came here to work on trying to duplicate the Mass Gen team's work, only I wanted to grow the heart to maturity. And here, no one's checking in on us. We can do whatever we want. I mean, there are international laws, but it's..." Again, she waves her hand. "Those laws are put in place by people who don't understand. Politicians who don't understand cellular behavior and deal in fear."

"How'd they talk you into working on the skin project?"

"Rapamycin. That's the project. My boss offered to triple my salary if I took over the project."

"Wow." I jumped ship for a better payday, but it didn't triple my salary.

"I said no. I told them to keep paying me the same rate, but to let me oversee both research studies."

"You did what?"

"They agreed."

Yeah, I'd imagine they did. Some suit did a giddy dance over having a sucker in their employment.

"That's another reason I want to break into the lab. I want to see what they are still working on. My project is everything to me. And it has nothing to do with what we saw in Cambodia. I understand why you suspect my employer, but there is no connection between what I was working on and what was going on back in Cambodia. The more I think about it, if I return, they'll hire me back. I can't imagine they found my replacement yet."

This little talk is rapidly getting away from me. "Hey. I hear your frustration. But you owe it to Sage to figure this out before you waltz back into the office. Anton Solonov didn't do this on his own. He's a for-hire kind of guy, and an expensive one. And someone wanted you kept alive. And whoever did all this used Sage to keep you motivated."

"I'm the most motivated person I've ever met. They wouldn't

need Sage to motivate me. And anyone who has worked with me knows that. I could show you years of performance reviews—"

"That's not what I mean. I meant in Cambodia. And something is off here. If your employer wasn't at all involved, why refuse to help your sister when she contacted them about you being missing? Instead, they insisted you fell in love and resigned. Play along with me. Use that big brain of yours." Her lips twist, and I know she doesn't want to hear me, but she does. I've lost the attention of those big brown eyes. They're looking up into the porch rafters, but she's listening. "Let's say your employer is totally innocent. They get an unexpected email from you, saying you resigned without giving notice. Is that something you would do?"

The lines along her lips deepen and a few form in her brow.

"Right. A committed employee like you would never resign without giving notice. You wouldn't willingly leave the research you love without knowing someone is carrying it forward. But let's say your boss is super busy. She just deals with your resignation, even if it doesn't sit right. But then your sister calls, saying you haven't been in touch. Did your boss know about your sister?"

"Yes." Her expression is not a happy one. I'd say it's about the same as my little sister's when I forced her to eat mud. "Given your research subject is so closely related to your sister, I'd bet everybody knows, right?"

No response. But then I remember something from her file. "And you don't have any social accounts, do you?"

"LinkedIn. I'm on LinkedIn. And I follow several scientists and organizations on Threads. But I forget to check in. I have all notifications turned off."

It's conceivable someone followed her on social. But our guys found little from her accounts. But they were looking for social connections. What if someone was searching for someone with her skill set?

"According to Forbes, the average person spent over thirteen hundred hours on social media last year. On average, we receive sixty-three notifications a day. By turning off notifications, you can save a significant amount of time, although no one has estimated the impact or conducted a research study."

"That's just rolling through your head, isn't it?" One big brown eye closes slightly, in a half-squint. "Facts and figures," I explain. "And you just like to say them out loud."

My phone vibrates. I'm expecting to hear from the team today. I check the screen and grimace. Ginger Moynihan. She's been calling me. We're in a project lull, getting our ducks in a row, so I might as well answer or eventually she'll check in with my folks.

"I'm gonna get this. But something's not right with your employer. For Sage's sake, we gotta figure things out before you go waltzing in there. You on board?"

She'd better be because as a two-man team, I can't add restraining her to my to-do list.

"Yes." Her chin lifts. Stubborn. Defiant. I'm not at all certain she's on board. Whatever man ends up with her is going to have his hands full. Maybe that's why she's single.

I step inside the villa and take a seat on the armchair facing out, so I can keep an eye on the dark-haired, stat-spewing scientist.

"Wazzup?" It's a cheesy greeting, but it's a relaxed one I concocted years ago after Ginger and I split and she insisted on staying in touch.

"Are you home?"

I scratch an itch on my jaw as I weigh my answer. She lives in San Diego. What does it matter? "No." I draw out the answer, bracing for whatever madness is about to spill from her two-timing mouth.

"I need to see you."

"Why?" Again, I draw it out. She's married. I doubt her husband has any idea she calls me.

"Zac and I had a huge fight. We're getting separated. It's over for us."

Given Zac is the guy she cheated on me with, I'm at a loss as to why she would call me. Silence falls on the line.

"Max?"

What the hell does she want me to say? "Okay."

"Can I stay at your place? I don't have anyone else to turn to. When do you get back?"

Fuck me. The sentiment plays on repeat in my head as I give her my address for god knows what reason. If luck falls my way, this little op will last weeks. If it doesn't, I'll be home and have to deal with my ex.

CHAPTER 12

Sloane

"Glad you made us get here so early," Max says. He sounds cross.

The parking lot is empty. Not a single car is in the lot. Same with the bike rack, although my bike had been the only user of the rusted metal bike stand contraption.

"Six-thirty a.m."

"What?" He pops the white plastic top off the coffee he purchased from a Texaco where he insisted we stop.

"That's what time I made it to work."

"First one in?" I really don't like his tone.

"Yes. But I was also the only one who was overseeing two projects."

"And when did others show up?"

I didn't pay attention. I closed my lab door and expected people to leave me to my work uninterrupted.

He breathes over his coffee. I tap my finger over the top of the white plastic coffee cup lid and jiggle my ankle. "How long do we have to sit out here?"

We're in an older, faded blue sedan with rust along the edge of the chrome bumper. I roll my window down and the stench of exhaust enters the car.

"Can you turn the car off?"

This car is so ancient there's an actual key you turn. I prefer bicycles for transportation. It's a better choice for the environment and there's really no need for a car on Grand Cayman, but even I have to concede that it's difficult to watch and remain hidden when perched on a bicycle seat.

He pulls on a silver lever in his armrest and his window glides down, then he finally turns the key.

"If we were in an EV, you could keep the car on. But not in a combustion engine. Especially an old one like this. Idling for more than ten seconds uses more fuel and produces more emissions that contribute to smog and climate change than stopping and restarting your engine does."

"How do you do that?"

"What?"

"Spit out facts and figures."

I lift the coffee cup and wipe the lip with my thumb. "I remember things."

Your daughter is very gifted, Mrs. Watson.

"I'd say so." He sips his coffee. He's angled so he can watch the entrance to the place. There's a 35mm camera sitting between us. He said he'd prefer to keep our phones off, but I can't help but wonder if that's because of the phone call he received yesterday. After he took that call, he fell into work mode and never snapped out of it. I do that sometimes, so I understand.

"Tell me something," I say because I have a sinking feeling I'm one of the few who showed up before our nine a.m. official start time, so we might as well fill the time so his annoyance with me doesn't grow.

"What would you like to know?" He's wearing sunglasses, and with his body turned away from me, it feels like he can't stand to be near me. He's not the first person to react like that to me. It's not a good or bad thing. It just is.

"Tell me why you left the Navy." If Sam was still living, I don't think he'd leave. Nothing made him happier than his job. My brother was like me in that way.

"Ah...well." He shifts in his seat, sitting up straighter, then repositions again, sinking a little lower so his knee rests against the dash. He's wearing tan slacks, a loose-fitting button-down shirt with the sleeves rolled up, and hiking boots. It's a strange outfit to sit in a car all day. His cargo shorts and t-shirts make a better outfit that show off his muscular legs, chest, and arms.

"The short story is I got a job offer I couldn't refuse."

"What's the long story?"

"You really wanna know?"

"We've got the time, right?"

"That we do," he says and sips his coffee. "Well, my team was changing. Again. Knox retired. Medical reasons. About as soon as I got the gist of a new team, chances are I'd be assigned to another location, another team, perhaps. And I mean, I guess that's all fine and dandy, but it's a young man's game."

"You're not exactly old."

"You'd think that, right?" He glances back at me and shoots me a grin that I feel between my legs. He's really too good looking. Too muscular. "But, nah. What we do? It's a lot of wear and tear on the body. Pounding the ground. Busted joints. Average length is six years, and I made it fifteen, almost sixteen."

"Isn't retirement at twenty?"

"You can retire at twenty years. But..." He knocks back the coffee cup, gulps it, smacks his lips, and lets out a sigh. "If I'm honest, I was burned out. Tired of the bullshit. When Knox dropped, he introduced me to this guy named Ryan. He's one of Arrow's founders. He'd been in my shoes, and now he's got this company, and they seem to look out for guys like me. Like him. We got to talking, and one thing led to another. They offered me a sweeter deal than I'd get if I clocked my twenty."

"You don't sound happy about it." I sometimes regret leaving my old job back in North Carolina. It's one reason I don't like change. Sometimes you change things, and it's not better, yet you can't go back.

"Meh. It's an adjustment, you know?"

"What was life like in the Navy? I mean, Sam told me some stuff. I remember one time he told me that for every fifteen minutes of 'hell yeah,' there's a solid ten days of 'what the fuck.'" The memory makes me smile. Sam was two years older than me, but he'd been my best friend. Well, him and Sage.

Max chuckles. He doesn't laugh often, but my lips stretch into a smile whenever he does. It's an automatic reaction, similar to how an acid and a base react when mixed. But that's a silly notion. If given enough time, he won't laugh around me, and if given enough time, I won't smile when he does. That's not true for an acid and a base.

"That's a pretty accurate assessment." Sadness coats his words.

"What do you miss the most?"

"The adrenaline rush."

"Is sitting in a parking lot not adrenaline-inducing enough for you?"

Another chuckle. And I smile.

"You realize we got here a couple of hours too early, right?"

"What gave you an adrenaline rush?"

"Jumping out of planes. Diving. Shooting guns."

"You can still do all those things."

"You're right." He bobs his head a couple of times. "That's another reason I took this gig. Not only do they pay well, but I still get all the toys. They prioritize being fit. It's a requirement. But they do it in a healthy way, mindful our joints have taken a beating already."

"But you still don't sound happy."

"Just wrapping my head around it, you know? I was a member of an elite team. It's…harder than I thought it would be to let that go."

"Once a SEAL, always a SEAL, right? That's what Sam said."

"Yep."

He lets out a long sigh and lifts his coffee cup once again.

"I could give you a blow job."

His head lurches forward and brown liquid coats the plastic top. He chuckles. And yes, I smile. Acid and a base. A reliable reaction.

"Wow." He wipes the back of his hand over his mouth. "That was unexpected. I mean, I never quite know what you are going to say, but that definitely tops the unexpected list."

"I enjoy sex and most sexual acts. I don't believe it's something to be ashamed of. It's natural human behavior. And it's great exercise. An orgasm will raise your endorphins, so you won't feel as sad."

"Okay. Well, wow. Good to know."

"I'm serious. And besides, I forgot to pack my charger for my vibrators. I mean, I still use my fingers for masturbation, but my orgasms aren't as strong. I don't know if it's the same for men. It's probably individual preference. Do you prefer to orgasm with your hand, someone else's hand, or vagina? Or do you prefer anal?"

There's a significant amount of dust in the air conditioning vents on the dashboard. The black plastic squares are probably hard to clean. It's easy to understand why car manufacturers evolved from this design.

As I stare at the dust, I become aware that he's no longer watching the building, but staring at me. I can feel his gaze, and my cheeks burn. That's not a good feeling. "What?"

"You are one-of-a-kind, Sloane Watson."

No one's ever put it quite like that, but similar remarks have been used to describe me my entire life. "I just say what I'm think-ing. The world would be simpler if everyone said what they're thinking. Honesty is an undervalued trait."

"I could not agree with you more."

"You're not going to answer me?"

"How about we table that discussion?"

"Until when?"

"Until I've finished my coffee."

He's been drinking forever.

"You know, I have to ask. How do guys usually handle it when you ask them direct questions about sex?"

I rarely have non-work-related conversations with men. But when I first talked about sex with William, my old boss, we ended up having sex in the lab. "I guess we usually have sex. Unless they're married. I would never do anything with a married man. Or someone who had a girlfriend. Unless they're in an open rela-tionship. Current estimates are that approximately one in five Americans have been in an open relationship at some point in their lives and approximately one percent of marriages are open relationships. Canadian research puts that figure at four percent. But almost ninety-two percent of open relationship marriages end in divorce, if you trust survey data. Even if the margin of error is ten percent, or even twenty percent, that estimated divorce rate would give one pause before pursuing an open relationship, right?"

He's silent. Rambling is a habit I should curb. My siblings never cared, but other people do.

"Sloane Watson. I think you may be my favorite person in the world."

CHAPTER 13

Max

It's Day Two of parking lot surveillance. Day Two of me sitting in a banged-up car sporting a nonsensical semi. She's not my type. I like them curvy and blonde. Admittedly, it's not her fault she's skin and bones. It's not like she starved herself on purpose. Although she should eat more. I'll have to get involved soon.

But the question is…why am I finding myself attracted to her? Why am I hyperaware of her physical presence? Why do I find her left-field statements to be so damn entertaining? I don't know what's wrong with me.

The biggest question is she's offered, but I've done nothing to engage. Normal Max would've taken her back to the villa and fucked her brains out. Hell, Normal Max would've moved that seat back away from the wheel, pulled out my dick, and said, "Have at it, baby."

She's not innocent. Clearly.

Yet she's different.

Her perspective on life is refreshing. She doesn't have a selfish bone in her body. There's no grand plan with her. Hell, she's not even focused on marriage and kids. It's just what you see is what you get, and maybe because of that, I feel I can really trust her. It's been a long damn time since I felt I could trust a woman. And maybe I want her to be able to trust me, too.

Maybe that's why I can't just bang it out with her. Because I like her too damn much. And I want to earn her trust.

Here I sit, my thoughts running wild as I stare at a parking lot in front of a non-descript one-story office building, listening to the subtle sound of her breathing and the tapping of her foot. Observing the pale skin of her exposed thighs and the sun's glint on the fine light hairs leading up to the short runner's skirt she's wearing today.

It's not like I want a relationship. And even if I did—which I don't—it's not something that's on the table. After we get this situation figured out, who knows where she'll end up? Her dreams aren't the dreams you stop because to do so would be monumentally selfish. It's best for humankind if she succeeds.

And what the hell? Why is my train of thought circling the future? That's not me.

I gave Knox hell for adopting a freaking dog after we left the Navy. What is up with my head? Next thing you know, I'll be following in my mom's footsteps with three cats shitting in a litterbox.

Yesterday, we played the back-and-forth question game for hours. Thankfully, sex never came up again. Unfortunately, her boss didn't show up either. Which, I will grant her, is thought-provoking.

Now she's really nervous something's happened to her boss too. And I'm coming around to her way of thinking. The tech guys have searched, and she hasn't left the island. Or at least if she did, she didn't go through customs.

Of course, Sloane being Sloane, has no idea where her boss lives, so we can't swing by and check out her residence. The tech guys are working on getting us a home address. The first place they checked was the employee files for Origins Labs since they hacked into that server a few weeks ago. There's no address other than her address in Switzerland. I could tell that Erik thought it was odd. I have faith in our guys, though. We'll have some intel soon.

Jack isn't thrilled with us doing old school surveillance. He's ordered some high-tech camera options to be installed near all entrances and exits to the Origins Labs. Once we get Sloane inside the labs so she can get on their server, which our guys still haven't been able to breach, she and I can head on our way. Arrow will monitor the cameras remotely. All we really want is an idea of who is coming and going from the building.

"So, tell me something," she says.

This morning, we got here at 7:45. Still, we've been sitting here for almost an hour, and we've seen three employees enter.

"I really don't remember much from my elementary school days," I quip, being a smartass. The coffee has yet to sink in, I'm sexually frustrated, and I didn't get my morning workout in two days running. My muscles and joints ache because I need my workouts to ease the old age pains and I'm off fucking schedule.

"That's not where I was going." Her bottom lip pushes out, and I want to pull her across the seat and claim that pout. Maybe ask to cash my rain check on that BJ offer.

A silver Lexus pulls into the parking lot and, instead of grabbing Sloane, I reach for the camera.

"Didn't you learn plenty about me yesterday?" A person in slacks, a pink button down and a navy tie gets out of the sedan, and I snap a few shots. We're across the street from the parking lot. Far enough away that someone would have to have excellent vision to see inside today's decrepit Town Car. The lens on the camera gives top notch distance vision.

The image in the viewfinder piques my curiosity only because the guy is wearing a tie, which stands out here. I show it to Sloane.

"That's Parker."

"Does he always wear a tie?"

"I think so. He works in billing."

"What's his story?"

She sighs like I'm causing her pain. "I'm not sure. I met him one day when we had a fire drill."

"What's his last name?"

"I never asked." Her elegant nose juts out a little farther as she strikes a defensive pose. "AP News shared survey data that showed two out of ten people have a close friend at work. That's only twenty percent of people. Eighty percent of people do not have a close friend at work."

"Got it. You don't know his last name. That's all you had to say."

"How old were you when you first had sex?"

"It's a good thing I drank all my coffee." I can't stop the smirk that I can feel twisting the corners of my lips. "You like to talk about sex, don't you?"

"No." She twists in the seat, looking out the window in the opposite direction of the parking lot we're staking out.

She's an odd bird with a specialty in off-the-wall commentary. But she's also right. We've got time to fill. "Fifteen. She was seventeen. What about you?"

"Nineteen."

"College?"

"Yep. He was sixty-two."

My mouth drops and now I'm not watching the parking lot either.

The corners of her lips turn up in amusement. She expected my reaction.

"He was my chemistry professor. I noticed he had an erection."

"And let me guess. You pointed it out to him and asked if he wanted you to do something about it?"

"Something like that."

Jesus, her professor must have thought he walked into an old-school porno set. "How long did this torrid affair with your professor last?"

"It wasn't an affair. He wasn't married. I told you I would never be with a married man."

"Right. So, how long did it last?"

"Not long. He was afraid we'd get caught. But he would come over to my apartment sometimes."

"He didn't mind your roommates knowing?"

"I didn't have roommates."

"Aren't you lucky. Rich parents?"

"No, not particularly." Her eyes glaze over, and I get the sensation there's a conversation going on in her head. Or a memory playing. Happens to me all the time, so I wait while keeping an eye on the beauty to my right and the entrance to the gravel parking lot on my left. "My personality is such that I do better in solo situations."

"Nah, I call bullshit on that. We're all stronger as a team. With a team, you got backup." Another car enters the parking lot. This one is a convertible Mercedes. The man getting out of it has bright white hair, pressed paisley shorts, and a polo shirt. I'd bet money he's a golfer. Sloane isn't paying him any mind. "Does he work with you?" I prompt, showing her the image in the viewfinder so she can get a closer look.

"I think he rents one of the office spaces on the ground floor in the back. I don't know his first or last name, if that's what you're going to ask me."

"Other than Dr. Kallio, was there anyone here you worked with closely?"

"No. I told you. I prefer to work alone."

"Well, you know, this is where the benefits of a team come into play. If you didn't work alone, you'd have other people you could get in touch with."

"Or they'd be missing, like Dr. Kallio."

It's true that we don't know where her boss is, but "missing" isn't a term I've agreed to apply yet. I pick up my phone and turn it on. Yes, I'm antsy. Yes, I'm breathing in a light, fragrant scent that I suspect is the soap Sloane used this morning in the shower, and I'd rather not think about why I am so aware of everything Sloane.

"Why aren't you married?"

There are no updates. And I'm officially stuck with twenty questions that, if I'm not careful, will stray into sexy questions that will turn my semi into a full hard-on pressing uncomfortably against my zipper.

"Why aren't you?"

"I asked you first."

I side-eye the bullheaded woman. I've been on ops where a team would've been able to listen in to this inane banter. Thank god this isn't one of those ops. "I'm not the type to get married. But you are."

"Who says you're not the type?" She sounds mystified, which is snort-worthy.

"I do. Pretty sure I know myself. Now, come on, what's your story?"

She's sexy as fuck, and she seems to like to fuck. And she said she doesn't cheat. That's three in a row for a win in my book. She opens her mouth, and there's a devious sparkle in her eye. Fuck. For once, I know exactly what she's going to say, so I stop her with my index finger. When it presses against those soft lips, I jerk back. For one, I felt that touch in my groin. Second, in a small space, touching isn't a great idea.

"Don't want to hear any more about excelling at solo play," I tell her in response to her adorably quizzical expression. "As for me, I almost got married." That would've been a mistake of epic proportions.

She says nothing, but the silence prods me to spill more. "Bought a ring."

"She said no?" Surprise rings her question.

"No." I twist my head. There was a time when this shit hurt. Now it just stings. "I'd been deployed. Came back. She found someone else."

Her eyes widen. "You walked in on them?"

"Shit, no. If I'd done that, I'd be serving time for killing the douche. No, she didn't meet me at the airfield, so I knew something was up. Twelve-month deployment, and at some point during that, she'd fallen in love. Didn't want it to play with my head, so she didn't tell me 'til I got back."

"That's awful."

"Was a pisser, that's for sure." Wouldn't have been nearly so bad if nearly every guy I was with overseas hadn't cheated on his girl back home. But not me. I'd been the angel. That part still pisses me off.

"I've never had a boyfriend."

"Really?" This surprises me.

"Not a real one. Sage and I sometimes share book boyfriends."

"You share them?" Intriguing.

"Not like that." Her eyelashes flutter, and she smiles. When the corners of her lips turn up, she drops her guard, the defensive one who claims she's a solo girl and doesn't like other humans. "But we talk about them. Sage is the only reason I read those mindless books." She lifts one long, lean leg and rests the ankle on her knee. "Now that Sage is dating someone, do you think she'll still want to read those books?"

"I can't imagine Knox would expect her to stop reading." Knox is a pretty good guy. If she's talking about the books I think she's talking about, he'd probably consider it a bonus.

"It's okay if she does. There are better ways I could spend my time."

Right. "Speaking of time, what do you say we clear out of here? It's pretty clear your Dr. Kallio isn't coming to work today."

"Do you agree with me now? Whoever hired that awful man probably got her, too."

"It's possible. We've got people searching for her. If they took her, chances are she's not on the island. Which means, once we get all our equipment in place, we'll get you inside so you can get on the server, figure out who accessed your report, and then we can head back to the States."

"I want my job back."

"Well, let's be certain your old bosses aren't behind this before you waltz in there. Got to be smart, right?"

"There's no way—"

"Sloane, we've been over this. Shit's not adding up. At this point, we all believe it has something to do with that report. Be smart. It's not just you. They went after Sage too."

Her lips press together. She nods.

"That report needs to be shared broadly."

She's not going to give up. But I need a break. "What do you say we get out and have some fun for a few hours?"

She looks suspicious. "Doing what?"

"We can rent a boat—"

"No." Her arms cross below her perky little breasts and the foot that had been dangling near her knee hits the floor mat. "I do not go on boats. I get severe motion sickness."

She also refuses to drink water from water bottles. I connected those dots and haven't pushed it. I've just been glad at the villa she'll drink tap water.

"Okay." I think about all that glorious salt water in front of our villa. "Snorkeling? Paddle boarding?" Her nose scrunches. "The sun is good for the soul." We need a break from this, and I need out of this car before her gaze falls to my crotch.

"Studies have shown that the sun provides many of the same benefits as a workout. And it gives your immune system a boost." That smile shifts into a devilish grin. She leans closer, and yeah, her gaze is on my crotch. "Of course, sex does the same thing."

Fuck.

My fingers curl into her hair, completely of their own volition. Glossy. Smooth. I could grab a fistful—

What are you doing?

Knox flashes before my eyes. Yeah, he'd want to kill me. And for good reason.

I release her hair, grind my teeth, and turn the key in the ignition, because yeah, we're in another oldie but goodie. It's part of the plan to keep from getting noticed. Never the same car and never one that's so nice it deserves a second glance.

"Let me teach you how to snorkel."

"The sun's rays are most damaging between ten and four. Which is right now."

"We'll use sunblock."

The devilish grin returns. "That could be fun."

CHAPTER 14

Sloane

Max was right. Snorkeling is fun. And I'm experiencing no signs of motion sickness. The sun is warm on my skin, and the salty air is invigorating. My mind feels sharper. I feel more awake and vibrant.

We walked into the water directly in front of our villa. The waves roll in smoothly on this section of the island, lapping the shore. There are sharp rocks partially submerged in the sandy ocean floor, but it's easy enough to sidestep them thanks to the crystal-clear water.

The view of the undersea world through my mask mesmerizes me. Small fish scurry below, flitting near, then zipping away.

If Max is bored, he's not letting on. He's a diver, meaning he goes deep. I'm guessing he, like Sam, has all the diving certifications.

Sam once told me they nicknamed Navy SEALs "frogs." Amphibians. He got a tattoo on his ribs of a frog with a gun and a dagger. It looked ridiculous. I told him. He ignored me. Or so I thought. About a year later, he had the strange tattoo removed.

A school of slender silver fish swims by, and I point. Max simply increases the pressure on my fingers. He can't smile. The plastic mouthpiece prevents smiles. The skin inside my mouth is drying, but I don't want to stop. The salty water coats my tongue, leaking in, probably because I'm not doing something right, but the sides of my mouth and around my lips need fresh water.

The black fins on our feet allow us to glide over the aquatic paradise with little effort. If it weren't for the mouthpiece, I could do this all day. Of course, breathing through the snorkel is loud, as is the water sloshing near my ears. Loud noises often bother me, but this is oddly soothing and rhythmic.

Sage would enjoy snorkeling. There's a meditative quality to passing over mounds of white sand, shaped in uniform patterns by current, and a sporadic thrill at a fish sighting.

Face down in the sea, it's easy to forget the outside world. I suppose this is why people choose to vacation on islands.

Max tugs at my hand. He's stopped. Standing.

The front of my fin sinks into the sand, and my knees buckle. Max's arm slips around my side. His skin is warmer than the water, and I lean into him. I didn't realize how cold I was getting. His mouthpiece dangles below his chin. He's smiling.

"You okay there?" His other hand lifts the mask, and there are deep lines across his forehead and cheeks where the mask created an airtight seal around his eyes and nose. "We're back."

My fins stick in the sand, and it's virtually impossible to straighten my legs, but next to him, I'm secure. His golden chest hair is slightly rough against my waterlogged skin, but it's…nice. My knees give, and the full weight of my body presses against him, causing him to stumble back.

"Sorry," I mumble through the mouthpiece.

Coordination is not a strength of mine. Sports and I are oil and water.

But he lifts me with one arm, supporting me with his strength. I'm tall, but he's taller, and he lifts me until my fins dangle above the sand and the water swirls around them. I spit out the mouthpiece, and with one hand, he lifts my mask.

"Why'd we stop?"

"We've been out here for hours. Your shoulders are getting pink."

I push away from him, not because he doesn't feel good. He feels better than I would've expected. I rather like being manhandled in the sea, which is another result I would not have expected. But pink skin means I'm probably already sunburned.

I lathered on SPF 80, but you should reapply every two hours. It's in the instructions. We've been out here for hours? How many? How?

Max moves gracefully through the water. It's like the fins are a part of his body. His deeply muscled and toned cover model physique, while appealing, troubles me. He looks like an amateur body builder, and it's conceivable he's using steroids.

My bathing suit bottoms ride up the middle of my butt, halting my progress. As soon as I can easily stand and the water laps my calves, I remove the fins, one by one, using Max's forearm as a brace. He didn't need a brace. He's an athlete. Possibly a doping athlete, but an athlete.

On the shore, I straighten my bottoms and adjust the small triangles that create the illusion of breasts. My skin prickles. It's the strangest sensation. I stop fumbling with the wet suit to scan my body, searching for a jellyfish tentacle or telltale pink skin. I lift my gaze and meet Max's.

He's staring at me with an expression I recognize. He's looking at me like he wants to have sex with me. But I've offered, and he's turned me down, so no matter how much I enjoyed this little outing of ours, I'm not offering again. Besides, I'm probably reading him wrong. Interpreting other people's intentions is not one of my strengths.

"Did you enjoy that?"

It's obvious I enjoyed it. I wouldn't have spent so long out there that I burned my skin if I didn't. Does he want me to say thank you?

I'm barefoot and step carefully, an eye out for sharp shell pieces jutting through the sand. Most shell pieces on this cove are bleached white, but some are a striped gray. Many are smooth, but some are sharp and hurt.

"You said you've never done it before."

"That was my first time." We reach the villa, and there's a spigot that's knee high. I turn it on to wash the sand off my feet and ankles.

"You okay?"

I take stock as the water streams over my prune feet. Nothing burns or hurts yet. The spigot water is cold, but the sun's heat overpowers the chill. I'm thirsty, but other than that, my muscles are relaxed, and a mild, tired sensation plagues my eyes. I haven't had that much fun in years. If Sage were here, she would thank him. He had to have been bored.

"Thank you," I say, stepping back from the stream of water. I also gather his fins and mask, because he did something for me. I should do something for him.

"How long have you lived here?"

"Eighteen months."

"And you never went snorkeling?"

I pause on the top step to the deck. "You're saying I'm foolish, right?"

Sometimes you miss the forest through the trees. Mom used to say that, and what she meant was that I'm foolish.

"Just saying it's a perk of living on an island."

He's saying I'm foolish. But, in my defense, I do important work. Lifesaving work. And it's not like I don't exercise. I ride a bike to work. Or I walk. And on Sunday I video chat with Sage. I pause at the stairs inside the villa. If I explained my perspective, it wouldn't do anything to make me look less foolish to him. I'm just different from other people, and many people don't understand that.

"I'm going to go shower," is all I say because there's no point in saying anything else.

Goosebumps light my skin, reacting to the cold air. In my apartment, I never turn on the air conditioning. I don't like air conditioning. I don't like how it feels, and it increases my carbon footprint.

At the top of the stairs, I shout down, "Can you please turn off the AC?"

"Sure thing." He's amenable. Nothing seems to bother him. That must be a nice way to live.

After I shower, shave, and slather my skin in lotion, I get dressed in a pair of shorts and a white, long-sleeve SPF shirt that should protect my skin from any more sun rays today.

When I return downstairs, Max is studying a computer screen. A voice radiates from the computer speakers.

"They installed the cameras at all entrances and exits, but they aren't wired. Battery-powered. And be aware. They've got security cameras too. You see this image?"

I step back and mouth to Max, "I'm going—"

"Wait guys. Hold on a minute."

He follows me into the foyer. I don't like speaking on conference calls when I'm not a member and I'm unaware of all the participants.

"Where are you off to?"

"Bike ride." His eyebrows furrow and his bulky arms fold

beneath his chest. "Just down the road to the stand where they sell papayas." I hold up some of the cash from the dresser upstairs. "I'll pay you back."

"Wait." He leaves and comes back with a circular silver disc. "Put this in your pocket. You've got your cell?"

I shake it in my hand.

"Keep it with you in case you need to call. Here." He takes my phone and types into it. "Now, you call me…this number…at the first sign of anything concerning."

"Sam taught me defense skills. And I'll die before I get into a car with a stranger." Again. The word rings in my head. Yes, doing anything with a man because he was romance-cover-worthy was inordinately stupid. Stupid is worse than foolish.

"How long will you be?"

I shrug, trying to estimate where we are and where the outdoor market is. "Thirty minutes? I was just going to take one of the beach cruisers sitting outside, since my bike is back at my apartment."

"Thirty minutes. Any longer and I'm coming looking."

As I approach the door, a deep voice asks, "You sure that's a good idea?"

Great. The conference call heard us.

The market is essentially an expansive tarp that covers multiple tables with fresh fruit from the island. Set back from the road, about fifty yards from the roadside market, is a small cinderblock building. Cars sometimes park in front of it, but I set my bike on the side in a shallow ditch that's closest to our villa.

When I arrive, there's a woman with strawberry blonde hair and long nails standing beside the coconuts. The ends of her pointy nails are a punch-colored pink, and the base is a milky white. On one nail, there are three diamonds clustered near the apex of the nail. Are those glued on, or did they puncture it like an earring? I can't imagine having nails that long. They would click on the keyboard when I typed and probably make it harder to notate.

"Do I know you?"

"I don't believe so, as I'm here on vacation." I reach for a papaya as I lie. The fruit is ripe. Slightly soft, but not too soft. Perfect. My stomach rumbles, and a slight shake befalls my hand, most likely a sign of low blood sugar.

"You look like a woman who rents from me. But they say everyone has a doppelgänger."

She's the woman who works behind the desk. I saw her once. She has a good memory. I don't remember her nails, and I'm sure if she'd had them before, I would've remembered them.

An older man with wrinkled dark skin approaches, and he takes my money for two papayas.

"How long are you here for?" The eclectic nailed woman picks up a papaya and squeezes, the same way I did.

"We leave on Saturday." Most people who come stay for a week. Saturday and Sunday are the busiest travel days of the week.

"Are you enjoying it?"

"Yes. I went snorkeling today."

"Nice. If you get a chance, go on a sunset cruise. Have you seen any of those? I have a coupon you can use. If you use it, I get a little money from it, but it's—"

"I don't like boats."

Gravel churns under tires as a car slows, rolling past us into the parking area to the side.

"Hope you have a good day," I say to the woman and step past her, watching the four-door car. I lift my bike off the ground and set the papayas in the basket. Just beyond the car, two men are talking. My body reacts like I'm in a movie.

I recognize one man. The markings on his back. Inverted triangles in a circle. An intricate pattern of lines partially obscured by a dingy white tank.

Anton Solonov's tattoos. Unmistakable. Unforgettable. He's talking to a man who is about a foot and a half shorter than him.

I grip the plastic handles on my bike and shove down hard on the right pedal.

Just go. Don't look back. Just go.

CHAPTER 15

Max

On my phone, I see the dot moving steadily in my direction. The second she left, I turned my phone on and watched the dot. Throughout the call reviewing schematics and floor plans, I watched the dot.

In theory, no one knows we're here. We flew in on a private plane and our identities weren't run through any database. We've been here for four days and have seen nothing remotely suspicious.

Still, when she left, my stomach twisted. I told myself to calm the fuck down. We're on a vacation island loaded with tourists. It didn't help that, as she was leaving, Erik asked if it was a good idea for her to go out on her own. Erik, the tech guy who lives behind a keyboard and monitors. The guy who has a team monitoring the handful of intersections and parking lots with surveillance cameras connected to hackable servers.

They haven't seen a damn thing. Nothing suspicious. Also, no Dr. Kallio, which is concerning.

The last time we came here, a mere six weeks ago, when Sloane first went missing, it had been a waste of time. The kinds of crimes that take place on this vacation paradise aren't the violent type. They're the type that forensic accountants find. This is one of the world's safe spaces to hoard the monetary rewards from crimes that take place in other countries. It's not a place known for crime.

Still, someone abducted Sloane once from this very island. I told Knox I'd keep her safe. Hell, not just Knox. The Arrow team is counting on me. Sure, it's easy to let your guard down when you spend the day out snorkeling. What the hell am I doing? I'm not here on vacation. I'm here on a job.

I scan the street, looking to my right, in the direction of the dot. She should be coming up at any moment.

And there she is. My breath comes a little easier.

Letting her go out on her own was a bad idea. A very bad idea. But she's okay. She's fine. I got all worked up for nothing. Damn Erik and his paranoia.

She's bent over the handlebars and pumping her legs like she's getting in max reps on a sprint.

Her mouth opens and she yells. I step closer, unsure what she yelled.

"Get. In…" The word gets muffled. She's out of breath. "Get. In. Side."

What the hell?

My hand automatically goes to my waist. I'm not carrying. That's something I will fix the moment we get inside.

I'm running to greet her. The two-lane road is empty. Far off in the distance, I see a van that looks like one of the resort shuttle vans. I scan the skies for a drone.

The bike hits the ground, and she charges into the house, the whole time chanting, "Get inside. Get inside. Get inside."

One wheel spins slowly, the bike flat on the ground on the path to the front door.

If someone's looking for that bike, it's a crumb trail right to our door."

She screeches from the doorway, "Get inside!"

"Close the door." It's a stern command.

I'm not leaving a calling sign to whoever spooked her.

Out of my peripheral vision, I see the front door close and lift the bike.

I could hide it below the deck. There's a gap on the sides, as the entire villa is raised off the ground in case of flooding. But it wouldn't take much investigation to find a bike stashed below the deck.

In six strides, I'm pushing through the door, the bike held in one hand, a trail of sand grains scattering behind me.

"Who'd you see?" She's standing in the hallway, eyes wide. She's fucking terrified. "What happened?"

I lean the rusted beach cruiser against the wall. It's not a suitable permanent location, as someone looking in through windows might see it. But it'll work for now.

My guns are upstairs.

"He's here."

"Who?"

"Anton Solonov. He's here. I saw him. I don't think he saw me. But he's here. He's here!"

"Okay. I need you to take some deep breaths."

"He's here!"

I move to the door and glance down the street again. There's nothing. No movement at all. Nothing in the sky except a commercial jet plane flying in the upper atmosphere.

"All right. Head upstairs." I flick the deadbolt on the door.

I'll get my guns and come back down, double-check all the locks. We got careless. Things felt too safe. Too easy.

She pauses on the stairs, looking down at me. "You're bringing the bike?"

"Yeah. If anyone's searching for this bike, I don't want it where a passerby might see."

It's a pretty standard beach bike, but it's bright pink with identifiable stickers and a brown wicker basket on the front.

"Go."

She resumes climbing the stairs. My facial muscles tense as I run through action items.

Get weapons. Secure the place. Call Erik. How did he get on the island without us knowing? Probably the same way we got on. How does he know we're here? He's a hired gun. Someone has him coming after her. But why?

I set the bike against the wall in the hallway between the two bedrooms and enter my room. The gear Jack packed for us is in carrying cases and duffels on the floor along one wall. I unzip one bag. Locate my Glock. Check the chamber. Load it.

"What happened?"

"What do you mean?" She's standing in the doorway, hands twisting around each other like she's warming them.

"Tell me exactly what happened."

"I rode my bike to the market, like I said. Just down the street. Where they're selling coconuts and papaya. And as I was leaving, I saw him. He was talking to another man near the small building that's on that road."

"You're positive it was him?"

"He was wearing a white tank. You know, what they call a wife beater. His tattoo. Over his shoulder. On the boat, when he took me, he walked around with his shirt off almost all the time. I'll never forget his tattoos."

"Lots of people have tattoos."

"It was him."

"Did he turn around?"

"No."

I stare at her, studying her. She's too scared to be telling me anything other than the truth. Christ. If he'd turned around, I'd be chasing a dot right now. Anything could've happened.

"Okay. This is what you're going to do." Her gaze locks on my gun as I tuck it inside my waistband. She's frightened. Focusing on a gun won't calm her. "You're going to sit down on the bed and breathe. Do you do yoga?" I can't decipher from her glazed look if that's a yes or a no. "Stretch. Breathe. Do whatever you do to calm down. I'm going downstairs and taking care of a few things. I just need you to know you're safe. We don't even know for sure he was here for you." That statement sounds as false to my ears as it probably does to hers.

"You're leaving?"

"I'm not leaving the house, okay? I'll be downstairs."

This villa has an alarm system. If glass breaks, it sends a silent alert to the alarm company, who sends the police. I check all the locks, including the sliding doors, and set the alarm. I flip several of the plantation shutters to block incoming views, careful to avoid looking suspiciously closed off.

This place isn't a safe house. It's simply safer than her apartment would have been. And it's located away from the more popular resorts on a high-net-worth street.

If he saw her, he's not chasing her. Either he felt he would make a scene during broad daylight if he did so, or he didn't see her.

I dial Erik. He answers on the first ring.

"Anton Solonov is here. Or at least, Sloane believes she saw him."

"Provocative." The sound of keys tapping fills the line.

"Does this mean he flew private? He hasn't popped up on any of your surveillance networks, right?"

"No. But he could've come in by boat, too. That's what Sloane said, right? How he left?"

"How would he know we're here? Who could he be working for?"

"I'm not sure. The guy's circulating with a Red Notice on him. He's got to be good at it to go years without getting caught. It's good we've got those cameras up on the Origins property. If he goes there, we might gain some insight."

"And if he doesn't?"

There's more key tapping. Erik has no more answers than I do.

"After you get what you need, plan on leaving. Whoever is after her has resources, and they don't seem to be backing down."

She said he was in a wife beater talking to a guy. Based on my experience, that doesn't sound like he was working, unless he's doing a little undercover work and thought dressing down would get more people to open up to him. But there's a significant segment on this island who would be less likely to talk to him dressed like that. "Is there a chance he lives here? Like, we're assuming he came here to get her, but is this where he hangs his hat when he's not working?"

The clacking of keys slows. "Let me check some sources. If he did the right people favors, they'd make a home for him there for sure."

"I'm not sure if this possibility helps us or hurts us."

"Me neither," Erik says under his breath. "I'm running all known aliases through for any connections. In the meantime, stay in the villa."

He's not wrong to be annoyed. We got lucky as fuck. He could've seen her. We could've run into him earlier today. The dial tone sounds, letting me know Erik ended the call.

Upstairs, I set out my guns and ammo, taking stock. Two SIGs, two Glocks, three rifles, two scopes, ammo, a NOD in case I need night vision, vests. I've got more than I need.

Across the hall, her bedroom door is cracked open. I push it wide.

She's leaning back on a stack of pillows, one leg straight, one bent, one palm flat on the mattress, the other hand holding something pink. Her cheeks are flushed, but the color is as likely from the sun as fear.

"You doing okay?"

"I don't know yoga. The best way I know to calm down is to have an orgasm, but I'm not sure I can get myself to do that right now."

"Did I just walk in on you—is that lube?"

"The vagina is not a rainforest."

I swear I never know what is going to come out of her mouth. She's not playing me. There's not an ounce of embarrassment. No attempt at seduction. Clearly. The description "straight shooter" comes to mind.

"What're we supposed to do now?" Her question holds a hint of a whine. She's still worked up.

"Hang tight. Rest. We've got big plans for tonight."

She nods and sets what I suspect is a small pink vibrator on the bedside table. Her shorts are on, so whatever she was doing to herself she was doing above her clothes. I like that she's not embarrassed at all. After my ex, I freaking love that she's a straight shooter. And I have to admit, I agree with her. Orgasms are a great way to relax, but right now doesn't feel like the time.

The mattress sinks under my weight as I join her, pressing my back to the headboard since she's using all the pillows, and stretch an arm around her shoulders to pull her into my side. She's so thin. Too thin.

"Why don't I go downstairs and slice those papayas and some cheese? Eating can also calm you down."

She nestles into me. The top of her head rubs my neck, and the side of her face grazes my collarbone. Her silky strands are smooth, and the tension that's been as tight as a rappel line ever since she yelled from her bike, maybe since the moment she left the villa, eases. Her slender form fits snugly against me, and I close my eyes, giving myself a moment to relax into this, to enjoy having someone close to me. I'm a snuggler by nature, and it's been a long time since I gave in to this desire.

"Why are you being so good to me?"

Her question rouses me from the temporary reprieve. "Believe it or not, I like you." Hell, she's right. She's all kinds of different. But it's refreshing. I mean, sure, I'm also attracted to her. Any guy would be. But I like her too.

"No. You like Sage. You're doing this as a favor to her."

I take a minute to think that one through. I mean, I volunteered to be here as a favor to Knox, but that has nothing to do with why I'm here now. Yes, I'm here because that's my job. But I wouldn't have climbed onto a bed to hold any other client. And until this moment, I've never thought of her as a client. Maybe because I'm well aware Arrow took this case on with no payment.

"It's okay. Many people are nice to me as a favor to Sage. Or Sam. Back when he was alive. Mainly in high school."

I nudge her chin up so she's forced to really look at me when I correct her. "Sloane, I'm here for you. You got that?"

She's not looking at me. My view is of her eyelids and long black lashes, her nose and a dusting of too much pink from the sun earlier today, and freshly licked pink lips.

The damnedest things come out of those lips. Lips I really want to taste. And so I do.

Once. Twice. So fast, so soft.

What I want to do is push her back onto the bed. I want to give her that orgasm to both calm her and to rock her world. I want to lose myself in her. Forget about our fuckups earlier today by immersing ourselves in the physical. Sink into her over and over again.

The tips of her fingers brush over my ear and along my neck. I'm so fucking hard. So ready to pound into her. Make her see the real thing is far better than any little plastic gadget. Better than her fingers.

That's what I want to do. But that wouldn't be smart. Not just because we're out of here tomorrow, but because this woman needs more than that. She may not realize it, but she needs someone to show her that sex can be more than just the physical act. And yeah, she may respond to the world a little differently, but she deserves to be treated like a queen.

I push up off the bed, ignoring the uncomfortable pressure against my zipper. "You stay here. I'll be right back with food."

CHAPTER 16

Sloane

He kissed me. It's all I can think of after he leaves the room. Four of my fingers lightly cover my still tingling lips.

His closed-mouth kiss, like one middle school kids share, circulated heat from my lips through my body with the same impact as my first kiss in fourth grade. And just like back then, he moved away as quickly as possible.

He returns with a platter of papaya, sliced cheese, bread, one bottle of water, and one glass of orange juice. Nausea rises at the sight of bottled water. I got incredibly sick after drinking bottled water. I know it's irrational to stop drinking bottled water. If it had been Sage or anyone else, they would push me. Tell me I can't afford to mark one more thing off my list of things I will eat or drink. But he hasn't pushed me at all. He's simply accepted it, probably because things don't bother him.

We eat together in silence. I'm not hungry, but when I push the plate aside, he says, "Is that all you're having? Have at least two more slices of cheese."

Cheese and bread are two of my favorite foods, so I don't fight him. I also like papaya if it's not too slimy.

After eating, I follow him into the other upstairs bedroom and watch as he checks and re-checks guns and other equipment. Sam used to like to tinker with his guns, too. I don't mind guns when they sit in a room. It's when they are loud that I can't bear them. The kick is jarring when shooting them, and depending on the kind of gun, the kick hurts. I also don't like the acrid smell. Sam understood guns would never work for me. But, like Max, I would watch Sam clean and prepare his guns.

Every time Max passes, he touches me. Lightly. On the shoulder. Or my hair. My thigh. My knee. Whatever body part is close.

All the touching releases too much oxytocin, pheromones, and dopamine. I don't need to test myself for it; I just know. A tingly, warm sensation affects me with every touch, no matter how light or meaningless. I'm far too cognizant of his presence. Of his movements. His breathing. When he swallows. Of his scent. And he doesn't use cologne. His aroma comprises soap and possibly deodorant or aftershave, yet I have this irrational desire to rub my nose along his throat and breathe him in.

But he hasn't tried to kiss me again.

And I won't make a move. Not again. I'm used to men who respond positively when I first suggest sex. And he's sending mixed signals. For all I know, he didn't like the kiss. We don't fully understand attraction. Research has found that it's a mix of hormones and that attraction means our bodies are responding favorably to the mix of the other person's chemicals. Reciprocation is not guaranteed. Based on the evidence at hand, it appears my body is highly attracted to the mix of hormones his body generates, whereas his body isn't as receptive to my mixture.

I wish he was like William. Nothing was confusing with William. The physical attraction had been evident, and we both agreed to act on it. He would make sure I orgasmed, then he would orgasm. If we were at the office, we would return to work. If we were at my apartment, he would leave. It was a mutually beneficial arrangement without confusion or nerves.

I don't recall being as affected by William's presence. That was an easier situation to navigate. Being reactive to a light touch is irritating. The chemicals my brain is releasing lead to poor decision making and thought processing. When he kissed me, all thoughts stopped. That's not a beneficial situation at all.

He zips a backpack. Sets it down. Then opens a suitcase of clothes. He takes out a black long-sleeved t-shirt and black cargo pants and drops them on the bench in front of him. He lifts the bottom of his short-sleeved tan t-shirt and pulls the material up his back, then over his head. The shirt tousles his hair, and his fingers brush through his scalp, settling the wayward strands.

I think he's forgotten I'm in here. I've been sitting here lost in my own thoughts, and he's forgotten me, but I can't break my gaze away from his broad shoulders and tapered waist. His back isn't as tan as his arms, and a faint tan line cuts across his biceps and around the base of his neck. His hands go to the front of his pants.

I sit back in the armchair and find my throat has tightened, making it uncomfortable to swallow.

"Do you have anything darker to wear?"

He turns, revealing his perfectly proportioned pecs and ripples along his abdomen. There's a smattering of darker hair below his belly button to the waistband, where his hand rests. I can't stop looking. I just saw him today in the ocean wearing a swimsuit. It's the same thing as boxers, which are undoubtedly what he's wearing below those shorts. Or maybe tight briefs. It's all the same thing, and if it wasn't for my body's pheromones—

"Sloane? Did you pack something that's darker?"

"Yes." I rush out of the room to change. Not because we need to hurry, but because I can't stop staring and my mind isn't functioning as sharply as it should.

When I exit my bedroom, I'm wearing a dark purple long-sleeve lightweight sweater and a stretchy black miniskirt that falls to mid-thigh. I'm not sure the two colors match, but he said to wear dark clothes, and most of the summer clothes I packed when I moved to Grand Cayman are light color combinations, like sand, gray, or light blue. Years ago, I concluded that monochrome outfits save time, so I buy outfits that are the same color, top and bottom. I sometimes buy dresses, but they aren't as practical for biking.

"These are my darkest clothes. Are they okay? And I have leather sandals downstairs."

He blinks, and I follow his gaze to my legs. They are quite pale, almost luminescent. My face and shoulders are pink, but the sun didn't seem to touch the skin on my legs. "I have some lightweight tan pants. Do you want me to change?"

"Do your sandals have heels?" His voice is low and growly. *What an odd question.*

"No. I don't wear heels. They are terrible for your feet. Also, with my height…" I shrug. "I have a rule against impractical items. Heels are highly impractical. I would probably trip and fall—"

"What you're wearing is fine. Let's go."

———

Origins Laboratories doesn't have a security team patrolling the grounds. This is what the Arrow team has concluded. I told them they didn't, but they insisted that they might have made changes since I've been gone.

The plan is to wait until Arrow overtakes the stream of the one camera by the front door. They'll replay the footage from the night before, which consists of views of the parking lot with palm fronds swaying gently in the breeze in the background.

In the messenger bag slung over my shoulder, I have flash drives to copy the files I need. I also want to find my hard drives.

Every Sunday, I backed my research up on the hard drives as a safety precaution. In theory, yes, the cloud is a secure storage location. But multiple storage locations are safest, and I know people who have lost significant work on the cloud.

"You ready?" he asks.

I've been avoiding looking at him because his black shirt is made of something akin to Lycra, and it clings to every single curve of his muscular form. It's not fair how good looking he is. Men like him belong on covers of books or in movies, not out and about in the real world.

"Do you remember the plan?"

It's a simple plan. "Of course."

Yes, he flusters me, but not so much I can't remember his rules. Watch for his hand signals. Be quiet. If he tells me to stay with a stop sign hand signal, I stay. If he motions for me to go with a wave of his hand, I move. Get in. Get out.

If we find them, I'm allowed to take my laptop and hard drives, but nothing else.

Our dark clothes ensure we don't stand out, but there's a nearly full moon overhead, and it's a clear night. We blend into the shadows, but someone could easily see us. Darker clothes don't make us invisible.

The hope is there's no one here to see us. The cameras are hijacked. Although I'm not sure anyone watches those, anyway. As I told the Arrow team, I'm fairly certain those cameras are more for after-the-fact review, as in if there's any theft, someone can review them later to determine who walked out with lab equipment. And in the eighteen months I worked there, nothing was reported stolen. We aren't one of those labs dealing with highly addictive substances.

If someone notices something is missing, and looks at the tapes later, thanks to the tape hijacking efforts by Arrow's tech team, they won't see anything except two identical nights, and it would take someone with astute observational skills to notice that two nights are identical.

When we first arrived, Max parked up the street. He left me in the car while he scoped the property. And now he's back at the car, opening the door for me, confirming my readiness.

There's no one out here. It's a business district, and all the businesses are closed. It's just the two of us. He holds out a gloved hand for me, and I take it. Oddly enough, the leather between us does little to soften the prickling sensation.

He's got a gun in a holster on his waist and one strapped in a shoulder harness. If I looked harder along his legs or crotch, I might find more guns, but I won't stare at him. To do so risks distraction.

I pat my shoulder bag with my ID card, pocketknife, throwing star, and three sharp, flat blades. I, too, am prepared.

There are two men with Arrow covering us tonight. They have comms with Max. They're positioned on opposite sides of the building. If anyone approaches, they'll notify Max through his earpiece. He'll give me a hand signal, and no matter what I am doing, I am to stop and follow him.

We cross the street like two normal people crossing the street in the middle of the day. Because that's what makes sense. If anyone is out and about, there's no need to look like we're thieves in the night running from cops.

Max approaches a side door with a basic lock. There are no cameras on this side entrance, but the reason the team selected this door for entry is the ease of picking the lock. Shrubs line this side of the building, and the prickly leaves stab my back.

Max's cargo pants drape over his glutes, but I can't help but think if he wore jeans, he'd be sumptuous. His gluteus maximus is so well-developed that even a gun holster doesn't detract from his yummy factor.

He fumbles with a brown suede cloth, rolling it and placing it into a pocket in his pants, then gives me the waving hand motion. Just in time. Standing around looking at him simply doesn't work well for me in my current pheromone-overloaded state.

In the narrow hallway, I lead. The lights are off in the building, but thanks to the moon outside, there's enough light I can easily find my way through the halls. I push into my lab and frown at the pristine state. The counters are clean. As is my desk. It's as if I never existed. My work never existed. What did they do? Throw everything away?

I rush to the biosafety cabinets and am instantly relieved when I see the incubators. They didn't throw out the tissue samples. I itch to bring a sample to a microscope, but that's not why I'm here. And I'd need light, and we're keeping the lights off.

The pen drawer in my lab desk is empty. In the file cabinet to the right of my chair there are hanging file folders, but none of the papers I stashed. The only thing I stored in these folders were receipts that I never got around to submitting for expense reports. Why would someone take those?

They wouldn't. It was mostly trash. I frantically move the hanging folders, most of which I never used, looking to the back of the long, unwieldy drawer.

I can't see a thing, so I shove my arm to the back, face planted to the top desk drawer until my fingers touch plastic. I grip wires and tug.

Thank god. When I stored my hard drives here, I hadn't been trying to hide them. The lab desk simply didn't have any drawers that would hold the drives and the long wires. The sight of the orange plastic and silver sided rectangle has me grinning. If I can't find my laptop, I've got my research.

As I'm stuffing my messenger bag with the hard drive and the wire, I remember I hadn't downloaded that Sunday. Which meant the report that theoretically caused so much trouble isn't on this hard drive. Frock.

I push up off the ground. Max holds up his thumb. Then flips it down. Then up. The gesture questions if I've gotten everything I need.

With a quick shake of the head, communicating that no, I do not have everything I need, I scan the room. There's no sign of my laptop. If they took my receipts and invoices, whoever packed up my lab obviously took my laptop. Where do they store former employee belongings? In a storage room?

The only storage rooms I remember had shelves holding supplies. One storage room on the second floor had a small square table that William and I made use of more than once.

Is HR in a different building? I think they are. If only I'd paid closer attention to colleagues' names and functions.

"What is it?" We agreed to not talk in the building, but here Max is talking, breaking his own rule.

"I need to go into the building next door."

"No."

He's being assertive. But his response is logical. They haven't hijacked the security cameras for the other buildings. Although it's quite possible there are no security cameras in that building. It houses offices and maybe storage rooms. What would someone steal? Paper. No, they have computers in the other building. People steal computers.

"Ready?" Again, he's violating the stated rules.

This space has been cleaned, but maybe not the others. And what about Dr. Kallio?

I leave Max behind. We're clearly the only people in the building. We pass the lab with the stacked guinea pig and rat cages, and Dr. Kallio's office is next. My breaths pick up, and I'm sure my heartrate hits the eighty percent zone, but none of that matters. I need to find out — and turn the knob.

Her stuff is here. Dr. Kallio's stuff is here. Or at least, someone is using the space.

There's a laptop on a desk. Plugged in. I flip it open and pull up a stool.

The screensaver asks for a username and password.

I'll never figure this out. There's movement in the doorway. Max.

I pull open the long, flat drawer that runs along the desk. It's identical to my lab desk. Huzzah!

This is still Dr. Kallio's space. Taped to the bottom of the drawer is a list of passwords in her crisp, easily deciphered handwriting. She once told me she keeps a laminated list of passwords in case something happened to her unexpectedly. I always thought it was a rather morbid way of looking at life.

The question is… are any of these passwords for her laptop?

I scan the list, looking for something easy. Something a person wouldn't mind typing in repeatedly all day.

There's one password combo that fits. Her email and the password newday321.

Huzzah! I am in.

Max raises his handgun. The movement catches my eye.

The screen before me lights.

I search her app bar. Find the icon for the Origins server. Click.

"We gotta go." Max's voice is hushed, but he's supposed to use a hand signal.

I hold up a finger to silence him. I follow rules.

Think. What can I do so Arrow can access this server after we leave? The gun wielding muscle man probably won't let me sit here long.

I can't, can I? You can't just save access.

A tiny green light glows on the zip drive I've stuck in the laptop's side.

The data is too extensive to transfer.

"Sloane. We've got to go."

He grips my arm.

I yank it back. *That's not the plan.*

"Sloane, we've got company."

I can't think. Between Mr. Muscles and pressure…

Frock.

I lift the laptop, drive and all, shove it into my messenger bag, push the stool back under the desk, and give a hand signal. One index finger pointed out, following the agreed to rules.

CHAPTER 17

Max

"Security entered front door. Hold."

My fingers clamp around Sloane's elbow, holding her close.

Someone from Erik's tech team breathes heavily into the speaker relaying static.

"Rounding the corner," a female voice says into the comm.

Sloane steps forward, and I jerk her arm and give a quick shake of my head.

"Turned onto the far hall opposite side of the building. You're good to go," Erik announces in the comm. I adjust the earpiece, as it's rubbing, and respond, "Oscar Mike." Yes, we are on the move.

With my pistol raised, on the ready, and one hand on Sloane, we exit the building, hurry through the parking lot, cross the street, and reach our car. I don't waste any time locking the doors and starting the ignition.

"Who the hell was that?" I ask the team.

"Whoever it was wasn't in uniform. You must have triggered an alert when you entered."

Obviously, the team is right. There were no wires. No lights. Damn if I know what we did that triggered any kind of alert.

"Matteo and Brooks are hanging back. We'll let you know if anyone follows. He's still in the building. Move."

Matteo and Brooks are the local contract guys.

"I got a laptop," Sloane announces loudly. "They cleared out my office."

I shoot a glare her way. We're in the car, but she doesn't need to freaking shout.

"What?"

The woman tries my patience.

"You don't need to shout. They can hear you." I take out the earpiece and hand it to her. "Here. You carry on the conversation."

She describes what she got, and perhaps most importantly, what she didn't find. As I drive us back to the villa, I scan our surroundings, searching for any headlights or movement.

"Ask them if they got a photo of the person coming into the building." If he wasn't security, maybe Sloane will recognize the person checking up on us. There's no way someone entering that building at one a.m. is a coincidence. The guy had to be checking on us.

"They didn't," she answers. "They can hear you." She gives me a meme-worthy smart-ass expression that I would caption 'When the guy sitting next to you is a complete moron.'

I roll my eyes at the attitude she's spinning. "When you check the tape, send us a screenshot of the guy."

I pull into an unoccupied house two doors down from our villa. Our villa has covered parking, but just in case someone saw our vehicle and goes hunting for it, I don't want to lead them straight to our door.

With her hand in mine, we take a side path to the beach and follow the jagged shoreline to the path leading up to our villa.

Do I need to hold her hand?

Probably not. Then again, if anyone sees us, at first glance, we'll look like a couple strolling along the beach late at night.

She speaks to the team as we walk. "Yes. Okay. Yes. Do you want to speak to him? Okay." There's a break where she's listening. "Bye." She pulls the piece out of her ear and tells me, "The guy who entered the building left. He walked to an apartment building nearby."

That's why we didn't see headlights.

"No one followed us. They're calling it a night. They'll follow up in the morning. Oh, and they said I probably won't be able to access the databases outside of the firewall, but if they can get their hands on the laptop, it might be just what they need to get in. So, we did good."

As we approach the villa, I scan the area. No headlights, no soft purr of a combustion engine in the distance. Palm fronds waft below the moonlight, and cricket chirps mix in with the soft pulse of the surrounding turquoise sea. All clear.

When inside, I don't let go of her hand until I place her against the wall and tell her to stay. Room by room, I clear the place.

Adrenaline pumps through my veins with the fury of a stormy, turbulent ocean. There's no way I'll fall asleep.

When I return to her after clearing the villa, she enters her bedroom and I enter mine, setting aside my weapons, one by one.

A light glows in the hall, beckoning me. A silent siren.

From across the hallway, she sits on the end of the bed, her bare feet flat on the floor and knees spread to each side in an unfeminine stance that gives me a view straight up her thighs. A silver laptop sits beside her, but she hasn't opened it. She's staring at it.

Her dark, silky strands fall haphazardly around her shoulders.

"Something wrong?" I ask from the doorway. With her legs open like that, I've got a view of a slip of white panties that I assume are cotton. I shouldn't look. But I can't help but take her all in. Thighs, panties, perky little breasts.

"He's right."

"Who is?"

"I grabbed the laptop, but I won't be able to get what I need if we're not on the network."

"Erik will figure it out."

"You have an erection."

My palm flattens against the protrusion snaking up my pants, reaching the top of the waistband. She's direct. And correct.

"Is it adrenaline?"

"That plays a part." Her fingers glide over her thigh, inching closer to the apex. She leans back on her other hand, and the angle sends those perky nipples skyward. "Do you have any idea how fucking sexy you are?"

"I didn't think you wanted me."

"Why would you think that?" I'm sure every man who sees her wants her. She's not my type, but I'm flexible. I'm a man, after all. If humans weren't flexible with our preferences, our species wouldn't be on the verge of overpopulation.

"I suggested sex. You weren't interested."

"Never said I wasn't interested. I said we shouldn't."

"Why is that?" The tips of her fingers reach the seam of her panties, and the pad of her finger rubs up and down. Fuck, she's hot. My palm presses hard down over my dick, up along the tip, giving it some much needed pressure.

She moves the lining of her white panties to the side.

And holy fuck.

Her finger slips inside her glorious, silky, pink pussy. She shifts on the mattress, and that finger goes deeper.

She pulls it out and slips it between her lips, sucking it.

My breaths are so fucking shallow it's a wonder I'm standing.

"I'm wet."

"I bet you taste good."

She pushes up off the bed, that finger on her lower lip. Her skirt falls back in place, covering what I imagine is some very damp cotton.

And then she replaces my hand with hers. The tip of her nose traces along my neck and her hand explores the outline of my aching dick.

Christ.

If she keeps on like this, I'm going to spin her around, press her up against this wall, slide those panties to the side, and thrust deep inside. Fuck her hard.

I cup the back of her head to angle her and press my lips over hers. She opens, and my tongue slips past. The combination of our tongues and teeth clashing with her hand on my dick makes me lightheaded. Dizzy. Out of breath.

And then her bare hands are on me. Circling me. Stroking me.

Holy fuck.

My eyes roll into the back of my head. I break the kiss, gasping for air.

I shouldn't do this. But why the fuck not?

If there was a reason, it's sure as fuck not coming to me right now. She has just the right pressure, the right movement.

"Is this what you want?" I somehow manage to ask.

"Yes."

Her grip strengthens, and my knees nearly buckle.

"Are you sure?"

"I'd say the evidence at hand supports my statement." Christ, she's got one smart mouth on her.

My restraint snaps. I spin her around and lift the shirt until it gets snagged near her armpits. "Raise those arms." It's a growl. And yes, my dick whimpers from the loss of her touch, but the shirt goes flying.

Her breasts are bared to me because she's not wearing a

fucking bra. Fuck if my mouth doesn't water. One hand goes to her throat, locking her in place against the wall, while the other dips to her panties, dipping inside to test those waters. And fuck me. She's fucking drenched. She squirms on my fingers, getting herself off.

My tongue laves one nipple, sucking the peak into my mouth, and when my teeth apply pressure, she gasps.

"Ahhhh." The sounds out of her mouth are a mix of moans, sighs, and high-pitched pleas.

Finally. She, too, is at a loss for words.

I have two fingers deep in her channel, and my thumb circles her clit. Her knee bends, pressing into my leg. It's as if she'd fall to the ground if I didn't hold her up.

I move to her other breast, and just as my lower teeth scrape her tender skin, she detonates on my hand, quivering. I lift my head in time to take in her closed eyelids and open mouth. The look on her face is one of pure bliss. Uninhibited, flushed, and wild. She's the most gorgeous woman I've ever laid eyes on.

Her arms encircle my shoulders, and my mouth claims hers again. Only this time, the kiss is slow. Easier. And fuck, I want her. I want her so badly my body aches with need.

She lets out a loud sigh and rests her head against the side of mine. Her breaths slow, and her fingers tousle with my hair. Her eyelids blink open, and I get a good look at her dark, sated irises. The tip of her tongue laps her bottom lip as the rising and falling of her chest slows.

"I want you inside me." The words are so soft, I'm uncertain I heard her correctly. Then her fingers wrap around my cock, which at this point pulses with need. "Please."

"I don't have a condom." My forehead presses against hers. The truth aches in my chest. Because damn if I don't want to slide into her, to feel her as she comes hard on my cock.

"I do." Once again, she lets me go, and my poor dick whimpers at the loss of her touch. She saunters over to the black duffel she took from her apartment and digs into it. She pushes off the floor, holding a familiar square packet, and grins. "Sam's emergency go bag."

"Your brother packed condoms for you?"

"No." She shakes her head, grinning, and that black skirt falls to the floor, along with those white panties. "He packed license plates, cash, and alternate identities." This doesn't surprise me, as he did the same thing for Sage. He must've been mixed up in some scary shit before he died. "I figured an emergency bag should have condoms."

"I really like the way you think." That's what I say, but I'm plastered to the wall, all focus on her, sauntering to me, condom in hand. She's so fucking hot, I'm frozen. Taking her in. She is too thin, but fuck if I'm not mesmerized by those long legs and her flat stomach and the peaks of her nipples that punctuate the slight curves of her breasts.

And then she's before me, within touching distance. "Take off your shirt."

This is one time I do not mind a bossy woman. I do exactly as she asks as she tugs on my waistband.

I throw my shirt across the room, and she kneels before me. My pants and briefs are around my ankles. She works on my boot-laces, and I let her, lifting a foot when she tells me. I grip myself and stroke, all the while watching as she strips me of my unnecessary clothes.

Her palms flatten on my thighs, and she rises...only she stops, mouth hovering over my dick. I'm holding the base of my shaft, and her tongue traces up my flesh.

Every ounce of oxygen leaves my lungs with her ascension, and when her mouth takes my crown, I fucking gasp.

My balls tighten.

I let her hot mouth take me, suck me, move up and down. For a little while. What she's doing feels so fucking good. I don't want her to stop. Want her to do whatever she wants. I can let her—my lower back tightens. That's it. That's the signal. Any more, and I'll blow. I pull her off.

She grins. It's the grin of a woman who knows she gets to call all the shots. And she's fucking right.

She tears the condom using her teeth. Somehow, I swallow.

Her brows come together in concentration as she rolls it down my shaft, and her fingers test the reservoir, ensuring there's room for me to unload. She's a fucking pro.

"Ready?" she asks.

And boy, am I ever.

I spin her up against the wall again, kicking my shoes and whatever else is on the floor out of the way. With a bend of my knees, I position myself at her entrance. She lifts one leg, and I loop my arm beneath her lithe leg and rock into her. She's tight. So fucking tight. Gloriously tight.

I have to pull out and push, stretching her. Forcing her to take me.

"Breathe, baby." Maybe she's too tight like this, standing. But then she breathes, and those eyelids close, and she relaxes in my arms. And with one last thrust, I'm balls deep, as deep as I can go.

I have to stop because it feels too fucking good. *She* feels too fucking good.

And then we're rocking together.

She comes against the wall, eyelids closed, moaning. Her muscles grip me and I slow, watching her in wonder. When her eyelids flicker open, a slight smile on those lips, I kiss her. I'm still deep inside her, but this deep, long kiss feels more intimate. She breaks the kiss with a gasp, and I pull out, then spin her, placing her hands on the dresser. I dip, pressing my lips to her back and taste her salty skin. "Hold on," I whisper.

"Like this?" She looks over her shoulder, ass out. Eyes sultry, lips glistening, skin flushed.

"Just like that."

I drag my tip between her folds. She stretches, reaching for me. Like she wants to impale herself on me. If that's what she wants, I'm a giver.

I slam into her. Over and over, slapping her impertinent ass until it pinks. With each pop, she groans and demands, "Again."

She's a fucking goddess.

I'm close, but I want her to come with me. I reach around and massage her, then pull back and slap that bundle of nerves. And fuck. She pulses around me, milking me. And it's too much. I lose it. An explosion. A climax like no fucking other.

Perspiration drips down my forehead. Keeping her ass against me, she collapses on the dresser, arms braced across the wood. My chest stretches across her, hovering over her damp skin, still pulsing out my release.

Gripping her hips, I hold her to me, skin on skin, mind blown. We didn't even make it to the bed.

CHAPTER 18

Sloane

"Holy shit. Damn. I haven't come like that in…" His deep, breathy tone assures me he enjoyed that as much as I did.

He slips out, and I close my eyes, breathing deeply to slow my heart rate. His rough, warm skin soothes the tender parts of my ass. The dresser is sticky beneath me, and the hard edge digs into my hip bones. I need to go pee to avoid getting a UTI.

I push off the dresser and, on wobbly knees, make my way to the bathroom. The door closes with a loud bang that makes me jump. I turn the shower on before sitting on the toilet, just in case he's still in the bedroom. I don't want him to hear me pee.

Showered, lotioned, and teeth brushed, I pause for a moment in front of the rectangular mirror, taking stock of my flushed skin and resting heart rate. That was fun. And healthy.

The orgasms he gave me were far more powerful than the ones my battery-operated devices give, or that various lab partners over the years have given. Orgasms provide stress relief, something we both needed after breaking and entering. Maybe he'll want to do that again before we leave.

I swing open the bathroom door and freeze. The light from the bathroom spills into the bedroom, so it's not like I can't see. I just don't know what to do with what I'm seeing.

I assumed he would go to his bedroom.

But no, he's in my bed.

I should not have assumed. He didn't shower, so he's in my bed with sweat-dried skin. *Ew.*

"What're you doing?"

"Waiting for you."

"Did you shower?"

"No."

Yuck. "Well, I guess I can sleep in the other bed." Although that doesn't seem quite right. This is clearly my room. My duffel bag and suitcase are right here.

He pats the mattress where he's pulled back the cover and sheet and there's space. He spreads his fingers as he pats the sheet, and I zone in on the two fingers that were recently inside me. And then a visual of him using that hand to stroke himself hits, and my hormone levels rise above a healthy range.

"Come on, beauty. It's going to be daylight before you know it."

He pushes up on his forearm. In that position, his bicep flexes, and his pecs stretch. The sheet drapes over his muscled abdomen.

"What's the matter?"

"I don't sleep in the same bed with other people." I like to sleep on the same side of the bed every night, and I like for the sheets to be cool, crisp, and clean.

"You've never...you know what? I'm too exhausted. Get your skinny ass in bed. After what we just did, I'm going to hold you, and we're going to fall asleep. We can dissect everything tomorrow."

My eyelids are heavy. I am tired. The adrenaline levels from earlier have clearly declined, although I remain suspicious of my hormone levels. I let the towel drop to the floor and slide a leg against the cool cotton, then shift so my other leg fits. A palm flattens across my waist, then rough skin presses into my hipbone and I'm tugged across the bed into a wall of muscled heat.

He settles the sheet over me, and I roll onto my side, facing the wall, on my side of the bed. He inches forward, placing his long body next to mine once again.

I let out a frustrated sigh. "Are you a cuddler?" I've read about those people.

"Not necessarily, but after I fuck the brains out of someone, I do like some skin-on-skin time. Especially when I want them close in case we do it again."

"Again? In the same night?"

"Yes."

Something warm presses onto my shoulder. I think it's his lips. My arm drapes over my breasts protectively as I assess. I do kind of like him near. He doesn't smell like I thought he would. Well, he doesn't smell bad. He's got this manly scent, and there's still a hint of sex in the room.

The rough pad of a finger glides down my ribs. It tickles, and I squirm forward. Now, that, I do not like.

"Damn, girl. We've got to get some meat on those bones."

"I'm not usually this skinny. It's because of—"

"Shh." The sound is indistinct and, well, soothing. "Shush. I know exactly what it's from. And if you can't tell, too skinny or not, I'm still very much attracted to you. I don't remember the last time I wanted someone so much." His fingers tangle in my hair, and cool air tingles my neck. Warm, soft lips press over the sensitive skin, and my thighs squeeze together. If he wasn't lying behind me, I would press my fingers into me and make myself come. "I have a feeling you could gain fifty pounds and I'd still want you. Still think you were the sexiest thing. It's that mouth. The best kind of unexpected."

I don't have any idea what that means, but... "What you're experiencing can be explained."

"Yeah?"

He nuzzles below my ear, and I close my eyes, reveling in the sensation. His chest radiates heat, warming my back, his arm comes down along my side, and his fingers slide between my arm and chest. Those fingers twist my nipple. *Oh, my. I like that.*

"You were saying?"

Right. I was. "God, you can be distracting."

"Right back at you."

I let out a huff and try to get my brain to focus on the scientific explanation instead of the physical evidence at hand. "When you're physically attracted to someone, it's a sign that your body's chemicals and hormones are aligned. More research is needed, but it's conceivable that one day we could submit a blood sample and find a list of chemically compatible subjects."

"If you ever get around to creating a match making service based on this premise, I recommend you hire someone else to handle the marketing."

"Are you making fun of me?" His fingers tweak my nipple again, and even though he's behind me, I let my fingers drift between my legs.

"I would never."

He nuzzles my neck and shoulder. Something thick and hard presses against my back. His powerful thighs curl up beneath mine.

"And when you have a physical reaction, especially like the kind we had..." The tip of my finger presses into the top of my fold, and it feels... I squeeze my thighs to increase pressure against my finger and in turn on my clitoris.

"You were saying?" His teeth clamp down on my earlobe.

"Dopamine is released. It's the body's reward."

"Huh. So, each time my dick slips inside you, our bodies release dopamine." He's pumping his hips against me, and combined with my hand, it feels good, especially with his palm warming my breast. "So, every time we fuck, we get a dopamine hit."

"Not a hit. More like a surge."

"Surge. I like that word."

"The surge of dopamine is released by the nucleus accumbens," I'm panting now, and my breaths are coming faster, "which is a cluster of nerves near the hypothalamus."

"Sloane?"

"Hmm?"

"Can you reach for that condom that's on the dresser?"

I blink my eyes open and see the foil pack.

"Yes."

There's something about Max that has me chanting that three-letter word over and over during the night.

———

Light pours through the windows. I listen but hear nothing. Max's side of the bed is empty. I run my fingers over the rumpled sheets, and they're cool to the touch. He's been gone for a while.

I throw on a t-shirt and long pajama pants. In the doorway, I listen. The door is open to the bedroom across the hall. The gun cases and Max's bags are still in there.

"Hello?" I call.

"Hey, beauty." Max's deep intonations travel up the staircase, and my muscles instantly relax. My body moves forward of its own accord. "Get your butt down here. I've got breakfast for you."

Out the back windows on the ground floor, the ocean twinkles bright slivers of yellow and white. Rolls of water lap the sand. There are no waves in this protected cove. It feels almost like you could walk from the sand onto the sea and continue walking all the way to the horizon. Which is silly; obviously, you can't.

"Coffee?" Max asks, causing me to blink away the bright sun and focus on him. He's bare-chested and wearing worn jeans that are slung low on his hips. The faded denim is one sexy notch above the worn cargos he's been wearing. And those bare feet on the tile floor—

"How do you take your coffee?"

"Ah, sugar."

"No cream?"

"Well, do we have almond milk?"

"No. I used it all in this protein shake, which I want you to drink." He pushes forward a glass with a thick, greenish brown liquid in it. *Ew*. "Drink it. Your body needs it. High calorie, high protein."

"Why do you say my body needs it?" I'm not sick.

"After the night we had, you need replenishment." There's a sizzling sound and a burning scent. He holds a spatula out and turns his attention to a pan on the stove. "Plus, you need to gain some weight."

I sniff the liquid. Then glance at the black coffee. Then dip my tongue into the greenish-brown shake. It's sweet. "It's not bad." But that color. And it's a little grainy. "What did you put in here?"

"Mango. Bananas. Kale. Lots of protein powder."

"Vegan protein powder?"

"As a matter of fact, yes, it is vegan."

My stomach rumbles as if to yell that yes, it is starving. I loop my tongue into the goop, but it's like dipping my tongue into cold sand.

He scoops a ton of slimy eggs onto a plate. *Ew*.

"This is a scrambler. Are you vegan?"

"Sometimes."

"What does that mean? If you're in the mood?"

"No. If I like it and it's not gross."

He looks at me like I'm not making sense. It's been a long time since I had to spar with anyone over my food choices.

"Do you eat eggs?"

"If they're not slimy." The ones he made have a slightly yellow runny stream. I am not eating those.

"Well, I also made blueberry oatmeal. I noticed you hadn't eaten meat that I've seen, so in case you were vegetarian..." He opens the oven and removes a bowl of mush with blueberries sprinkled across the top. "What's that face?"

"No one makes food for me."

"Why?"

"Well, I'm particular with food."

"Yes." He pushes the bowl of light brown mush closer to me, along with a small ceramic dish filled with an amber liquid that looks a lot like syrup. My gaze travels from his golden, oh-so-happy trail up his tight abdomen to his plentiful pecs, and I glimpse a smirk. A really sexy smirk.

"If you keep looking at me like that, I'm going to be tempted to bend you over the kitchen table, and I can't do that because you need to eat."

As if my stomach can hear him, it growls, and this time, it's so loud Max hears it, and he chuckles. "Eat. I was going to surprise you with breakfast in bed, but you're here."

The stool legs scrape the tile as I pull it out. Syrup covers the taste of anything. This, I know from experience. It can even make something that's a little too slimy palatable. And...it works. I can eat this.

"What was wrong with the smoothie?"

"Too grainy."

"Ah. I get that. My mom and sister don't like it when I put too much powder in it either. Next time, I won't use so much."

For several minutes, we eat silently, as if neither of us has eaten in days. When the hunger is satiated, I push the bowl of oatmeal back and reach for the coffee mug.

"So, what's the plan for today?"

"I've got a call in an hour with the team to review logistics. I think we'll fly out tomorrow."

"Why not today?"

"Well, that private plane we flew in didn't stay here with us. It's a company plane and they're scheduling the return to pick us up."

"We can fly commercial."

"We'd rather not send your identity through customs, so we aren't going to do that."

"I have some alternate passports in that duffel. I could use one of those."

"You know, we haven't really talked about it. Did you think it was odd he created alternate identities for both of his sisters?"

"He was cautious." I push away from the kitchen and jog up the stairs to grab the laptop.

"We also have weapons. Can't easily fly those commercial," he says as I'm halfway up the stairs.

When I return with the laptop and the list of passwords, Max is at the sink washing a pot. "I should do that, right? You cooked." Those were the rules at my house.

"Nah. I got this."

"Thank you." I open the laptop and set the passwords aside to see what I can access without being on the employee network. He slides a plate of cubed cheese my way. I'm not hungry, but I do like cheese. I pop one in my mouth and tap on the laptop.

"Don't go accessing anything from here." He adds green grapes to the plate of cubed cheese.

"What? Why?"

"You're not protected. If they're looking for you, you could lead them straight to our door. Let's wait. Let me find out from Erik what we should do."

"If I can find that report, we can share it. If you're right, and all of this is over keeping that report hidden, then sharing it means there's no reason to come after me."

"Who would benefit from that report not seeing the light of day?"

It's a question I've pondered. "I know you think it's someone at Origins Labs, but I think it might be the investors. My report showed that a viable alternative could significantly improve black market transplant survival rates. Maybe some investors have more to gain from existing options..." But that makes little sense. The circular debate goes nowhere.

"You realize your boss has to be in on this, right?"

"She's not." My response is immediate.

"It's the only thing that makes sense. She's the one you mentioned the report to."

"But I accessed databases from multiple sources and had to login with my username to do so. If anyone was monitoring those databases, they'd know who accessed it. Just like last night. Someone knew we had entered that building. And besides, if you knew Dr. Kallio, you'd agree with me. She's trustworthy."

"People can surprise you. Even people you think you know well. But there's no point in arguing. The only thing that will change your mind is evidence. I get that. I've been there."

My big toenail is bordering on too long and needs to be clipped, and I can't stop looking at it. "You know, you're wrong about Dr. Kallio. And she's still missing."

"True. Once we get that laptop to our team, they'll discover all the secrets on it."

"Isn't there a way we can use a VPN or something so no one can trace us?" If I could get on—

"I'll ask the team."

He disconnects his charging phone and turns it on.

"You charged it down here?"

"This morning when I woke up, it was dead. I got a little distracted last night."

"We probably shouldn't have done…you know, what we did last night."

His attention is on his phone. I'm not sure he even heard me. Or maybe he did, and he agrees. We each live by our own rules.

"Well, look at that," he says. "Anton Solonov went through Heathrow customs using an alias. Picked him out with photo recognition on a delayed screening."

"Huh. Where do you think he's going?"

"Who knows, but he's no longer here."

"Maybe they aren't looking for me after all."

"Don't forget what happened in the hospital." My gaze falls back to my too-long toenail and the tile. His tone feels like a reprimand. "I'm not trying to scare you. But we've still got to be smart." He wipes down the counters with a rag. "I'm gonna go move the car from the empty villa down the street."

"Do you think we could stop by the market? Buy some stuff for lunch, if we're still going to be here? We're out of fruit." They had stocked the villa with basic nonperishables, most of which I don't like, but fruit is my favorite. And cheese. And pizza. I feel antsy. What I really want is to get on Dr. Kallio's laptop. If I can see that data once more, maybe something will jump out at me. "It's just right down the street."

"You want to get out of here?" he asks, hands pressed on the counter.

"Some fresh air."

He pinches the bridge of his nose. "After my meeting, we'll ride bikes down to the market together. Or we'll take a car to a real grocery store to hunt for your favorite foods. Together. We'll get more cheese."

"I like pizza."

"I can work with that. As for now, if you want fresh air, we've got a nice stretch of sandy beach right out our back door."

He's right. We do. But first, I need sunblock.

CHAPTER 19

Max

When I get back from moving the car, Sloane's gone. Stepping out on the deck, I scan the beach and find her off in the distance. She pulled her dark hair up in a ponytail that sways back and forth with each step. She's in a clingy long-sleeve shirt, which I'd bet is an SPF shirt, and running shorts that set off those long, lean legs. The woman has one amazing set of legs.

She's not a heels kind of woman, but damn if she wouldn't look hot in towering heels and thigh-highs. That vision has me readjusting myself as I step back inside.

But Sloane won't wear heels. She's far too practical. Serious. And funny as hell without meaning to be. A guy can never know what's going to come out of that one's mouth. And now I'm grinning, just remembering—Do you want to have sex?

Yeah, surprising. If only all women would be so straightforward, the world would be a better place.

My phone buzzes, and it's a reminder of another reason I steer clear of relationships and why I shouldn't be standing around the kitchen like a dope thinking about a woman. Her legs? Fine. The behavior fits with any guy on any day. Quirky personality? Nope. That's sucker land. Thinking about a woman's personality is a blaring warning sign.

GINGER

I'm all settled in your place. Thank you so much for letting me crash here. Do you think you'll be back soon?

I choose to ignore the woman who branded me a sucker. Besides, I might not be in the military anymore, but I'm away for work. She'll assume work is keeping me from responding.

I flip open my laptop and login through our secure VPN. Erik isn't a fan of video conferences, so it's a group audio call. I have to say, if a similarity in preferences is any sign, it's conceivable I'll be right at home on the tech team. I need more training, but one thing my time in the military taught me, it can all be learned.

"Hi. It's Stella here."

"Hey, Stella. It's Max. No one else has joined."

"Great. I'm just popping in. I'm still working on scheduling the jet to pick you up. Both of our company jets are in use this week. I'm fairly certain I've got everything worked out, and one will arrive to pick you up tomorrow afternoon, but I'm still waiting on confirmations."

"No rush. We're good here."

"Is that villa nice?"

"Very."

"Trevor's birthday is coming up. Do you think he'd like it there?"

"Ah..." I glance out the window at the relatively flat sea. No waves mean no surfing. "I mean, this place is luxe. There's snorkeling right out your back door. But you'd need to get on a bike or drive to go do anything else."

"So that's a no for Trev?"

"Probably. But maybe not. It's not like he can't get to activities. At the airport, they had travel fliers for all kinds of stuff…you know, paragliding, scuba. This place has all your normal island shit."

"Erik here."

"Jack here." Jack Sullivan isn't normally a part of our team meetings, but he's shown an interest in the Watson case from the beginning. He said he only met with Sam once, but I'm beginning to wonder if there isn't more behind his involvement.

A few others from the tech team announce themselves.

"Max. We got identification on the man who entered the building last night." Typical Erik, he doesn't bother with any kind of intro or summarizing who is on the call.

"Is he a Solonov associate?" That's really my biggest concern. That there are more hired guns on the island.

"Local security guard. Employed by Wright Security, a small security company that installs security systems. No record. Our best guess is that you guys triggered an alert, and he was called to check it out. He never called the cops. And no alert went to the police station. He lives in an apartment nearby, so maybe the alert triggered someone who checked their employee database and sent him because he's so close."

"Wouldn't a typical security system automatically notify the police?"

"Possibly. Depends on how it's set up."

"So, your risk assessment would be…."

"We don't think he's anything to worry about. But I think that building has a security system that we didn't identify, so I wouldn't go back in there. Do you have that laptop?"

"Yes."

"And that's the only thing you took?"

"Yep. We'll get it to you when we're Stateside."

"Can you get in it?"

"Well, we have the username and password for it. And Sloane grabbed a password list from a drawer."

"Snap a photo of that list and send it to me. Turn the computer on. I'm going to walk you through how to let us take over that device."

"Remotely? You can do that securely?"

"Yes, we can. Keep it plugged in."

"Sloane wants to find the report she created."

"We'll find it."

"You think that's the key to what's going on?"

"That's Interpol's theory. They'll help us figure out what we're looking at. They want to see which databases she used to source her data."

"How's Knox and Sage?"

"Stella dropped off the call." Erik can be a jackass. Like he doesn't know how they're doing.

"Jack here. No signs of concern. Sage returns to work Monday, I believe."

"Thanks, Jack."

"No problem. Keep your eyes open and keep Sloane safe. We still don't fully understand what's going on here."

"Copy that." An understatement if there ever was one.

The call ends, and I get Erik set up on the laptop. Watching him take over feels a bit like handing over the reins to another team, something I'm hardwired to take as a failure. But he's working with technical resources I don't possess out here with a couple of phones and a laptop. I tell myself it's the same as handing it over to a reconnaissance team.

Out on the deck, I scan the beach and see the tall, dark-haired beauty strolling slowly along the beach. I dial Knox and kick back in a chair, happy to keep my eyes on her.

"Hey, man. I hear you've made progress." Laidback happiness oozes from the guy. It's in his tone. There's a smile there I can hear.

"Keeping tabs?" I ask.

"You know it."

"And things there?"

"Spent a couple of rough days with Sage salvaging what she can from her house. It's emotional for her." That sucks. I forget sometimes that she didn't escape this ordeal unscathed.

"Fire destroyed everything, huh?"

"It did a number. I know we determined the goal of burning her house was to flush her out, but if you consider the fire intensity, you'd think they were set on eliminating evidence."

"She taking it all okay?"

"Eh, I think losing her parents' and Sam's stuff hit her harder than losing anything she owned. But she's at the school today."

"Jack said she was going back Monday."

"Nope. She's been back for a couple of days."

"And are you patrolling the school grounds?" The idea of a protective Knox hanging out in a school parking lot all day has me grinning.

"No. She teaches at a fancy private school that has security on the grounds. I hung out there at first, but based on the reports I'm hearing, the heat is off. You agree with that assessment?"

"Yeah. I do." It's a fair assessment. "We're out of here tomorrow, if Stella can secure the plane for us."

"That's what I heard. A couple of other jobs are taking priority. Plus, we're in investigative mode on this one. But I'm not actually working today."

"Oh?"

"I'm house hunting. We're crashing at Sage's buddy's house, and I'd like for us to get our own place."

"No shitting?"

"Nope."

"Good for you, man." Never thought I'd see the day Knox got serious enough to move in with someone. But with a guy like Knox, I suppose it all comes down to timing. Those first few years, he witnessed so many relationships combust with the weight of distance, mine included, he pretty much refused to go down that rabbit hole. But now, there are no tours on the calendar. He's done with all that. We're done with all that.

"It feels good. Right. How're things there? Is Sloane driving you crazy?"

She steps into the swirling water up to her calves. Her back is to me, and she kicks a leg, sending a foamy spray through the air. She's like a kid playing around on the shore, oblivious to anyone watching her.

"Nah. She's not so bad." She's staying strong, all things considered. She's not the only Watson to lose something important. "She's clinging to hope she can return to work, but I'm not sold that's the case."

"Sage told me her work is everything to her. How's she handling it?"

"All right. She still believes once we clear this up, she can safely return."

"Sage wants to talk to her."

"I'll have her call her."

"She's not with you?"

"Took a walk on the beach."

"Is that safe?"

"I've got eyes on her."

"Do you, now?" I snort at his innuendo. Well-deserved innuendo, as it stands. "Nah, in all seriousness, man, don't go playing around with her. She's Sage's sister. I don't want things getting awkward years from now."

"So, it's like that, is it? Already doing long-term planning?"

"It's exactly like that. And you're family to me, so don't go making the holidays awkward."

"Aye, aye, Captain."

"Fuck off."

We end the call, and I throw the phone down and fold my arms behind my head, kicked back to watch the slender sexpot meander along the secluded shoreline.

She's not really my type. With each day that passes, the thought feels more like a barrier I'm constructing.

But it's not bullshit. I go for blondes with serious curves. I've always loved a full rack. But there's something about her. Like now, just watching her, I'm totally turned on in spite of those barely there tits. She's not trying to be sexy; she just is. Maybe that's what it is. She doesn't doctor anything. Her words, her face. What you see is what you get. Compared to Ginger and the frog hogs who followed her, she's refreshing.

If she ever found someone else attractive, she'd tell me. She might explain it with an in-depth tutorial on chemistry and pheromones, but she'd tell me.

Knox doesn't want me messing around with her because he's worried we'll cross paths in the future and it will be awkward. But, you know, I don't think it would be with someone like Sloane. Things get awkward when someone doesn't come out and say what they're thinking. If something bothers Sloane, she'll tell you.

She washes her feet at the spigot and doesn't seem to see me until she's climbing the steps.

"How'd the meeting go?" She lifts her sunglasses and blinks to adjust her eyes to the shade.

"Good," I tell her as my gaze tracks down those slender legs to a smear of sunblock above her knee that needs to be rubbed in.

"Still heading out tomorrow?"

"That's the tentative plan."

"What're we going to do until then? Market?"

Those shorts of hers are flimsy fabric, the kind our high school girls' soccer team wore. Short enough to reveal the smooth curve of skin where thigh blends to ass.

I push up off the chair, stalk toward her, and pop that fine tush. She squeals, and I smooth my palm over her, just like I did last night, letting my fingers trace the seam of her panties, because yes, her shorts are that short.

"Get inside. I'll show you a few things we can do."

CHAPTER 20

Sloane

The warmth of his skin on my sensitive, sun-kissed flesh affects me like a light switch. My mind goes from contemplating how to salvage my research to wanting him inside me posthaste. Night and day. Positive and negative. Acid and alkalis.

There's no rush. We have time. But we aren't patient. The urgent need strikes us both. He lifts me, and my legs wrap around his waist, and he stumbles and falls backward onto the outdoor sofa.

For a split second, we laugh. Light and carefree. Because we're acting like teenagers. But then his palm caresses my cheek while his thumb explores my lip. And I look down into bright blue eyes.

My chest seizes. My core cinches. Everything slows.

Because of how we fell, I'm straddling him. My hips, ever so slowly, undulate over him.

We sit there, in the breeze, shaded from the overhead sun by an overhang. I'm locked. Frozen. Stuck, looking directly into watery hues. I should look away. But I can't.

A pressure on the back of my neck urges me closer. And I blink. My gaze falls to his lips. My breath flows faster.

There's no soft brush of lips. No, it's as if our mouths meld instantaneously. His fingers glide along my sides.

I lift, separating our torsos just enough to tug on his shirt. Skin on skin. It's what I want, and we break apart long enough to remove the irritating garments. He palms my breast, and I tilt my head back, loving the contrast in sensations. His rough skin. The salt breeze. His heat.

"God, you're sexy."

His words are breathy, like maybe he's also having trouble breathing.

"I want you." I reach between us, fumbling with the button on his shorts. The need pulses. And as if my body has superseded my brain, my core clenches over and over, leveraging Kegels to ease the urgency.

The tips of my fingers brush the smooth head of his crown, and he groans.

I'm airborne, and my back bumps against the stiff cushion. My shorts and panties are brushed to the side, and his finger plunges inside me. I cry out, not from the intrusion, just the surprise.

He pulls his finger out and sucks on it. I whimper and squirm. The grin on his face couldn't be any sexier. He's really too gorgeous to be real.

"You are so ready for me."

"I told you. I wouldn't lie to you."

He sits back, and I lift a leg, rubbing my calf and foot over his ass, urging him to move. And he chuckles.

I stop. Confused. What's funny? I'm not trying to be funny.

"No, you wouldn't lie to me."

I don't understand, but then he frees himself, and I'm mesmerized as he wraps his fingers around his length and strokes. Up. And down.

Over and over.

And then his broad, massive body shadows mine. His heat. Those wide shoulders. I lift my knees, thighs spread, and his tip pushes into me as his lips hover over mine.

Then he freezes. His eyelids close.

My hips buck up, begging for him.

"Christ." He dips his head, and his rough, unshaven cheek scrapes mine. "Condom."

"It's okay." The tips of my fingers dig into his shoulder blades. "I have an IUD."

"Yeah?"

His Adam's apple flexes. He rises, resting on one forearm as he nudges my chin upward, forcing me to look into those oxygen-hogging blue depths.

"Yeah?" he asks breathlessly, like it's hard for him to breathe too.

"Yes. Please."

And then his tongue plunges into my mouth as he pushes inside, stretching me. Filling me. This. It's exactly what I wanted.

My fingernails alternate between scraping along his sides to his scalp. The force of his hips moves us. With each thrust, the light-weight sofa scuffs the floor.

"God, you feel so good." His mouth is by my ear, his breath hot and heavy.

The weight of his body is intoxicating. It's both sheltering and a complete and total frocking turn-on. The absolute best part is how his body rubs against me, creating divine sensations.

"Christ, I don't want to ever wear a condom again."

My thighs clutch his hips as my muscles contract. My toes curl.

"Don't stop," I gasp. "Right there. Keep on. Right there. Harder. Harder."

The blood vessels in his neck expand. His skin flushes. I grip him, nails digging into his skin. On the verge. So close.

An animalistic sound escapes from him. And I feel him pulsing deep within me. And all of that…all of him…pushes me over.

My eyelids close as an orgasm spasms through me.

His thrusts become erratic. Sloppy kisses rain down along my cheek and neck, and then one big, heavy man collapses on top of me. My legs and arms wrap around him, and I giggle into his neck.

Perspiration dampens his skin and the hair along his brow. He lifts his face inches from mine, and my thumb brushes over his eyebrow.

"Something funny?"

He's still inside me, and I'm clinging to him. And yeah, he's talking to me. It's weird. Super weird. But I also kind of love it.

"Nothing," I answer. "I kind of love this." The admission makes me feel like I'm exposing myself, which is an odd emotion since I can't really be more exposed than I am without clothes on, and he's seen me naked.

"Kind of?" He thrusts up playfully.

"My shorts are still on."

"Hmm." The rumble vibrates from my throat to my chest. "So are mine."

He pulls out and readjusts us so his back is to the back of the sofa and I'm lying below him. He adjusts both of our shorts, in case someone walks by on the beach. Of course, I'm not wearing a top.

My arm covers my breasts, and he moves it, shaking his head in reprimand as he nips my finger.

"Don't cover those."

"They're not really much to look at."

"They are to me. And they're mine."

It's a ridiculous statement. Logically, I know this. My body is not his. But those words deliver a thrill. A warm, gooey, illogical, all-encompassing thrill.

"And I can't seem to get enough of them."

He dips his head and swirls his tongue around a nipple. My

back curves, stretching into his touch. He lifts his head and smirks, cocky and sated. The cool air envelops the wet skin, and I roll into him. I let my head rest on his shoulder and breathe into relaxation.

He cups my breast and tweaks the nipple while his other hand caresses my butt. He likes to touch me, and my body responds every time.

"I enjoyed that." It feels like a confession.

"I could tell."

My teeth grind down on his chin.

He lightly slaps my ass, then palms it. "In case you couldn't tell, so did I."

We should talk about something. About the case. About my sister. Something.

"Everything's good for tomorrow?"

"Should be. Waiting for some confirmations."

"What confirmations?"

"Stella didn't say. I'd imagine it has to do with air traffic control. We're on an island that sees plenty of private planes come and go. Plus, the jets are in use, so maybe she's confirming pilots."

His phone vibrates on the table. "This could be confirmation."

He stretches to grab it from the floor where it must have fallen.

I'm a tall girl. Gangly. But, next to him, I'm miniscule. He collapses back against the sofa, and I let my fingers wander over the curves of his muscles and twirl the smattering of golden chest hair. He stretches an arm out so he can see the screen, and I read it too.

GINGER

I bought you a plant and some throw
pillows to brighten up the space.

The photo is of a beautiful blonde taking a selfie on a sofa. To her side is a neon pothos plant, and there's a bright yellow pillow behind her, but what my gaze catches on is her cleavage. Cleavage covers approximately twenty percent of the photo.

"Is that your girlfriend?"

"Ex." The phone clatters across the coffee table. "Ex-girlfriend. We broke up four years ago. She's married."

"I meant ex. Obviously. You wouldn't cheat on someone else. I wouldn't be with you if..." I let out a sigh as my index finger swoops along his thick bicep. "She's really beautiful."

"On the outside." He sounds sad, so I lean forward and press my lips to his throat.

"What did she do to you?"

"Well, we were living together. I was spending a lot of time on missions. You know what they're like, right? Sam ever tell you?"

"You mean you can't call? Or tell anyone where you are."

"Right. Well, I returned home from being overseas. And she met me at the door with a ring on her finger. And it wasn't a ring I gave her."

"Oh. She's the one you mentioned. The one who cheated on you."

"Believe it or not, she tried to deny that she cheated. But, like, how do you go from living with your significant other to being engaged to a different person without some lines being crossed?"

"Right." I relax against him and let one leg drift between his. "I'm sorry she did that to you." I close my eyes and see her cleavage. "You know, maybe that's why you're attracted to me. I'm her opposite, you know? No boobs, and she has huge ones."

His fingers spread across my butt cheek and his lips brush across my forehead. "I don't know about that. I'd say that with you I discovered I'm very much into barely there, hot as fuck breasts. And it has absolutely nothing to do with her." His fingers leave my butt and trail along my hip and to my ribcage. "But I can't deny I'd like to see you gain a little weight."

"I'll try." He's not the first person to harass me about my eating habits. As if on cue, my stomach rumbles. "But we need to go to the market."

"Can we just lie here a few more minutes?" I tilt my head up at him and scrunch my nose in question. "I'm a cuddler, remember?"

"A big teddy bear." I say it like I'm annoyed, but I smile into his chest. For once, I don't really feel like getting up either. I trace his muscles. He's really, really muscular. "Do you do steroids?"

"None of the bad stuff."

"Why would you take any of it?"

"I guess you could say I've always had an obsessive personality." His fingers comb through my hair. "I start a hobby and I dive deep. In the military, you've got to be strong and fast, so it doesn't work to bulk up. After I left the military, some of the muscle builders in the gym kickstarted me on some stuff. I've always been one to focus on the protein."

"That's why you're so into food?"

"I've been an athlete most of my life. Always into food. Supplements. Have played around with performance enhancers here and there. Truth is, a lot of the guys do a little something."

"Isn't that against the rules?"

"It is. Mostly it's overlooked. But we got this new CO, and he was gonna be a stickler."

"So that's part of why you went ahead and left?"

"Part of it. Not all of it. It was the right time. Do you think less of me?" His thumb brushes softly over my shoulder. I don't know enough about it to have an informed opinion.

"No. But I want to research it. Will you tell me what you're using?"

"You don't trust me to do my own research?"

"I just…I might see something you don't. I always double-checked Sage's doctors. You don't mind, do you?"

"No." He presses his lips to my brow. "I think it's sweet, actually."

Is it sweet? Double-checking medicine and medical advice is wise. Doctors are human, and all humans make mistakes. And Max isn't even a doctor.

He taps my nose. "What are you thinking about?"

I blink, bringing myself back to the moment. I should be thinking about our next steps. "Now that you've been to the lab, has your team developed any other theories as to who could be behind this? Since it's clearly not my lab."

"What exactly did you see that eliminates them from suspicion?"

I give that some thought. "Lack of evidence. And even though Anton Solonov was on the island, he never went to the labs."

"A guy like Anton is a skilled assassin. He's not going to visit the workplace of someone who hired him to chitchat."

"I just can't see anyone I work with doing this. They're scientists. I mean, yes, admittedly, some of our work will ultimately be used for skin care, but our efforts will benefit humankind."

"Tell you what. Let's agree to disagree on this one."

"That's what you said about pizza."

"Exactly. You call it a nutritious meal, and I call it a snack. At least you aren't vegan. Then we couldn't share a pizza."

I don't like vegan cheese either. The texture is like dairy cheese, but it's the aftertaste that gets me.

His lips curve into a smile, and my gaze travels up to his blue irises for the briefest of seconds. And then he's kissing me again. Slowly. And all arguments and thoughts flee as I melt into him.

CHAPTER 21

Max

Sloane is a nymphomaniac. All my life I've dreamed of finding one, and I found her. Last night she blew my fucking mind.

My cock is sore from all the fucking we did yesterday, and last night, and the night before that. Blissfully, blessedly worn the fuck out.

Yet, somehow, he's painfully engorged and ready to go again. Of course, I know the how. I'm entangled with a leggy bombshell, and my throbbing erection is perched between her ass cheeks.

I'm in deep with this one. It's clear as day. Because instead of coaxing her awake, I'm lying beside her, luxuriating in her soft skin and powdery scent. My arm's asleep with a million tiny needles pricking it, but I refuse to move because she's sleeping comfortably. My nose is buried in her silky hair, and I just want to stay like this forever.

So, yeah. In deep. I've had girlfriends before, and I recognize the signs.

Her eyelashes flutter and her nose crinkles. Those long legs straighten and stretch. The movement caresses my needy dick.

I'd like to wake up like this every single day. Yet another sign.

Christ. Knox worried about me making it awkward for Sloane on his so-called family holidays. What about for me? For the rest of my life, when I see her gorgeous, lean legs, I'll remember how they feel pressed against me in bed. I'll remember how tight her pussy is. How she has to stretch to take all of me, and how fucking good it feels when she does.

If I were to run into her in the future with some punk brainiac on her arm, I'd be the one stumbling over myself. Bashing down the desire to strangle any fuckwad with her. It's not a good thought. But it's definitely in the realm of realistic because I can be one jealous bastard. Jealousy isn't an emotion I enjoy. The insecurity that drives it isn't a good look, and it's one I do my best to avoid.

Her hips undulate slowly, and the movement feels glorious.

"Do you always wake up like this?" I hear the smile in her words as I nibble her earlobe and my hand wanders along her torso to cup her breast and tease her responsive nipple.

"With you, I'd say chances are good that's a yes."

"I'm sore." She says it softly and with great thought.

"So am I." I press a kiss to the back of her head and on the side of her throat. "And I need to go for a run. We've got a lot to get done—"

She twists on the bed, but that's not what stops me. It's her fingers wrapped around me. Her firm grip makes it hard to swallow. Hard to think.

And then her mouth. Holy fuck.

I roll onto my back and scoop up as much of her hair as I can, moving it out of her way, both out of care for her and as a totally selfish fucking measure because I want to watch.

She cups my balls and massages them as her hot mouth moves up and down my shaft, alternating circling her tongue around my tip and licking me up and down. Blood leaves my brain when she takes me wholly in her mouth. She can't take all of me, but what she can't take, she keeps in a firm, studied grip. And when I say studied, I mean it's like she's watching my every reaction, learning what I like, what I don't, and adjusting as she goes.

"Babe. That's incredible. You'd better… I'm gonna…" I tug on her hair, warning her. She doubles down, taking me deeper, and that's it. Game over. It's all she wrote.

I'm spasming in her mouth, hips gently thrusting, draining every bit of yet another mind-blowing release.

She swallows some, but I continue, and there's a milky white mess all over my abdomen. I pull her up to me, intent on giving her a thankful, sloppy kiss, but she pushes away, wiping at her messy mouth.

"That's kind of gross," she says. Her nose wrinkles, and then she's gone.

"Sorry about that." I did kind of warn her.

I watch her naked, gorgeous backside plod into the bathroom. I should get up and clean myself, but I'm too light-headed. Too out of breath. Too overcome.

I hear the toilet flush, then the sink, and force my legs over the bed. When she exits, I point at the bed.

"Get back in that bed."

"Aren't you up?" she asks as I place a hand on the bathroom doorknob.

"I will be." I nod in agreement. "But after that, I want some morning minutes with you. Just holding you before the day begins." I pause and wait. Her gaze is on the floor. "Sloane, can you give me that? Five minutes. Fresh breath. A start to the day holding each other?"

"You were…" Her skin's flushed, and maybe she's a little perturbed, but she waves a hand at me and says, "Go. Five minutes."

After taking care of all the things—cleaning myself, brushing my teeth and taking a whiz—I return, naked, to the bed. She has a sheet pulled up to her armpits, and she's lying back on a pillow, watching the television. It's on mute, but it's a news station, the BBC, I think, and there's a scroll along the bottom of the screen that she's reading. It's an announcement about a new drug being approved by the FDA.

I climb in beside her and pull her to me.

"We're going to have a busy day today." Yes, it's stating the obvious, but we've got to pass the awkward to get back into a cuddly groove somehow. "Erik said you're going to D.C.?" She nods, curling into me, and I know this is what we need. A little more time. "What's in D.C.?"

"Langley. I lived in D.C. briefly. I'll stay with a friend. Handle some things. Once your team clears it, I'll reach out to Origins and explain what happened so I can get my job back. Or, if you're right and they're somehow involved, I'll look for a new job."

She sounds down. Her calf slides back between mine, and my thigh rises to hers. Looking for a job, I get. Transitions suck, so I also get sounding down about that. But… "What things need to be handled at Langley?"

"Jack Sullivan recommended I meet with some people there. Plus, a guy from the NSA. Logan McDowell. They want to hear more about what I experienced in Cambodia."

"And what, exactly, did you experience?" I know the highlights. Saw the outside of the compound. But she said they didn't hurt her.

"It's not so much, I guess, what I experienced, but what I was doing. I mean, you know, lots of governments know about the compounds. And they have questions. And the blood testing I did. I guess they want to ask about that."

"Why would you need to meet with the CIA about that?"

"I suppose it's an international concern?"

"Are you nervous?"

"No." It's a weighted negative. My arm curves around her belly, holding her as close as possible. "But they're going to ask me questions. And it's going to come out that I knew what they were doing, and I participated."

I tilt my head back on the pillow, shifting beside her.

"You didn't take anyone out of that compound."

"I told them who would be the best matches."

"You didn't have a choice."

"There's always a choice. And I suspected they didn't really have Sage. But I kept conducting the tests and updating profiles into a database. They branded identification numbers on the people. On their arms."

"You didn't have a choice."

"I kept thinking that what they were doing wasn't so bad. Not really. Because those people didn't have good lives. If they ended up in that compound, they were all out of options. At least there, they got food and a place to sleep. Many of them were immigrants. Not only without homes, but without countries. And, if their organs—"

"Don't say it." I swallow. As a man trained to kill in battle, I understand the minimization of human lives. She shrinks down into the mattress, heavy with guilt. And dammit if I don't feel guilty. Telling her she can't speak, as if she's in the wrong. "I understand the logic. One life to save another life."

"It's not ideal. But it's today's reality."

"Do you think the US government is going to get involved? Shut down the compound? Did Jack make it sound like that?" He hasn't said anything to me about Sloane having these meetings with government goons.

"I don't know. But…I've been thinking a lot about what I found. The source fields I matched. I think someone used the people in those compounds to test something. Maybe someone out there is still using those people. That's why my data showed a much higher prevalence of cancer in organs originating from Asia. Someone was doing it, but not my lab. That's not what we do. It would be a company paid to administer testing."

"There are companies that do that?"

"Oh, yes. In theory, these third parties don't suffer from business interest conflicts. Most companies conduct tests on human subjects in China or India where the regulations are laxer. But it's time consuming. I think someone out there was doing broader initial tests in Cambodia. Probably years ago. It's all about speed to market and innovation, but maybe someone needed to do larger scale dosage testing?" She bites at the corner of her lip, her glazed eyes looking like she's deep in thought. "But if my theory is correct, Origins isn't involved in my abduction. We don't do that kind of market testing. What I'm doing is innovative, but it's a long-term project. It won't reap financial benefits for possibly decades. This makes more sense to me than anyone from the black-market organ trade wanting to block my report."

"But you wanted to submit your report for peer review. It definitely seems like someone wanted to block you from doing that."

"True. But not my lab. I identified a cancer cluster. I wasn't aiming to be a whistleblower. The purpose of the data I was collecting was to reinforce the benefits of our research. And I wanted to speak to the investors in their language, looking at it from a financial perspective. I was laser-focused on my project. But the more I think about it, I think I uncovered something bigger. Much bigger. And maybe peer review would invite those who focus on researching cancer clusters. But if I'm correct, the one piece that makes little sense is why keep me alive?"

My thumb brushes across her nipple. Lightly back and forth. She shifts her arm and squirms, but I don't want to be pushed away, so I palm her breast and still my hand. "You sound sad, so I'm going to repeat myself. None of this is your fault. Even those people who went missing. You didn't take them. Nothing happening in that compound falls on your shoulders."

"There are quite a few reasons to feel sad beyond guilt."

"Okay. Let's hear 'em."

"One, I don't have a job. And all the research I've spent years developing is not progressing. No one is working on it. I couldn't locate my files."

"If it's anywhere on Origin's servers, Erik's team will find it."

"Fine. Even if they do, I don't own it. The company does. I've got to find someone else to fund my research. That's a lot. A ton of work."

"I can see that."

"Can you?" She rolls onto her back and looks up at me with troubled, dark eyes. "Because if you could see it, you'd let me go back to Origins and ask for my job back. I'm not great with people. Selling investors on my research isn't something I can easily do. Finding a spot on a research team is possible but it would take so much time. I want my old job back, and I swear, it doesn't make sense for them to be involved."

"I get your theory. You could very well be right. Maybe after your meeting with the intelligence goons—"

"That's what Jack Sullivan said."

"When, exactly, did you talk to Jack?"

"He called yesterday. When you were in your meeting with the team."

Fascinating.

"So, I'll go to D.C. He asked that I meet with them. He asked for my patience. To let all of his resources look into this further." Her chest rises and falls dramatically. "For Sage's sake."

"You've heard that a lot, huh?"

"I have."

"That's got to be hard."

"No." Once again, she tilts her head, looking directly at me. "I'd do anything for her. That's why I tested all those people. That's why I did what they asked. Because while it breaks some people's rules, they're still saving lives. And someone out there loves those people. Just as much as I love Sage."

"But it's…" She's got to see that ethically what's going on there is all kinds of wrong. Harvesting organs from captive people shows an unconscionable disregard for human life. But that's why she's torn. She's feeling guilty because she knows it's wrong, but she'd do it for Sage if forced to make a choice. "Are you worried about Sage?"

"Right now, she's healthy, but if she lives long enough…"

"She'll need another transplant."

"And my research—"

"Won't be done in time."

"Probably not."

"Did you get contact information? So you know who to call if the day comes and you need—"

"No. I don't believe any of the men on the ground had any idea what I was doing or why." She's probably right. They hired mercenaries to run security. "But if we're ever desperate, I have a better idea now of how it works."

"They wanted you alive, but it doesn't sound like they wanted you for your knowledge. Not that you aren't all kinds of skilled, but they weren't using you for that. Not really."

"There was a building on the far end of the compound with a small casino and a brothel where both the guards and the workers could spend money. I overheard one of them mention they get one day off a month. But whoever put me there set me up on a different schedule from the other workers. I mean, I didn't get a day off, but I slept away from all the others. In a private room. I was definitely treated differently, but I don't know why. Do you think the men Jack's asked me to meet with will believe me?"

I think she might be in for a long interrogation, is what I think.

But I press my lips to her shoulder and hold her tight. "Is worrying about that meeting what's making you sad?"

"Oh. I didn't finish my list."

"No?" I let my teeth sink into her shoulder.

"Today is the day we have to say goodbye." She doesn't want to say goodbye either. An idea crystallizes.

"I don't know about that." My chest feels lighter.

"Yes. You'll go back to LA, and I'll—"

"We'll go to D.C. together."

"What?"

"Yeah. I'll let Jack know." There's no way I'm letting her go through a CIA interrogation without support. If not in the same room, I'll be counting the minutes and doing everything I can to ensure those fuckers don't put her through the wringer.

CHAPTER 22

Sloane

Four long canvas bags, five black duffels, and my navy wheeled suitcase line up in the hallway like an orderly row of beakers. Max's bag, another duffel, remains upstairs. After he showers, he'll change and finish packing.

Our plan is to stop by my apartment, pack up anything I want to keep and either ship it or carry it on the jet with us, get lunch, then head to the tarmac to meet the Sullivan corporate jet.

A sense of finality comes with packing up an apartment. The plans center around my not returning here. It's frustrating. I liked my job. It was perfect for me.

They keep telling me once they have more answers, I can return to Origins. The plan they've put into place, however, doesn't align with their words. Whoever did this to me came after Sage too, so I have to be cautious. Whether I agree or not doesn't matter as much as erring on the side of safety for Sage.

After I meet with the government agencies, I'll update my LinkedIn, which is my only social media account, and my resume, and begin the job hunt.

Or, in an ideal world, the men I'm meeting with will have answers. And everything will be clear, and Origins will ask me to come back and work for them, and I can resume my research. But I saw for myself the empty lab where I'd worked. I'd been the only one who pushed to keep my research going.

The stillness in the villa has me expecting someone to knock and announce housekeeping is here and ready to clean. Which is nonsensical, given we're not in a hotel. But it feels like a hotel. It's not a lived-in house. We're not on a schedule. I don't have a purpose. It's like an extended vacation and I'm antsy to get back to my routine, even though I don't have a routine to return to.

Max won't be back for another two hours, as he's doing his long run this morning. A swarm of zombies would have to be nipping at my heels before I'd ever run for hours, but it's his thing and it's a gorgeous morning.

Before he left, he fixed me a smoothie with no trace of sandy protein residue. It's been a long time since anyone cared enough to adjust recipes to arrive at something I liked.

For my part, I researched the steroid he's taking. It's not the worst of them, but I don't like the risk. And there's truly not enough data or research available on long-term health implications, but users do record it eases aches, and I can't help but wonder if that's part of the appeal. I'll do more research, but I'm hopeful I can talk him into transitioning off it. He might be lifting with body builders, but he's not one of them. He doesn't need to be a hulk of muscle.

I step out onto the deck and am greeted by the shrill cry of seagulls and a swooping pelican off in the distance, splashing into the water. My feet sink into the smooth, white sand. The tide is going out, but it's left behind shallow tidal pools, and I meander along the ocean's edge, letting my feet splash in the water.

As I pass the villa two down from us, movement on the deck

catches my attention. There's a man in sunglasses sitting in a lounge chair with what looks like a mug in his hand. He waves, and I return the gesture. I continue farther down this stretch of beach than I've walked before. Past the curve of the shoreline, the villas are built closer together. Up ahead, there's a hotel. Judging from the abundance of matching umbrellas and lounge chairs, it's a luxury hotel.

Voices carry on the beach. There's a Jet Ski zooming by. It's interesting because once you round the bend, the waves are substantially larger. Kids are in the water, and laughter and shouts mix with the crash of the waves.

It's a cheerful scene. But it's also crowded. I prefer our secluded cove.

If Sage were with me, I wonder which she would prefer? There was a time I could count on her to want exactly what I wanted, but that's not the case now. We don't have a time scheduled to talk to each other. We used to hold a weekly video chat every Sunday at five. When I get back, we'll need to get our recurring video call scheduled.

My palm rubs over my belly, attempting to soothe the uncomfortable sensation growing there. A sharp shell digs into the bottom of my foot. One-legged, I stand, checking my sole for a cut.

"Sloane? Is that you?"

There's no blood. I set my foot down and turn to the familiar feminine voice. And dress pants. Gray—no, putty-colored slacks I recognize. And dress shoes. But no suit jacket, just a white silk shell. Dr. Kallio dresses nicely when she's on the beach.

"Sloane? What're you doing out here?"

"I'm staying…" My arm lifts, pointing in the direction I came from. But… "What're you doing out here?"

"I had a business meeting." She gestures behind her to the hotel. "We were sitting outside on the veranda, and I thought that was you. But I figured that couldn't be right, because you left the island. Are you back for good? How's married life?"

My fingers lightly tap my thighs through my dress. Her shoes rest above the sand, but if she comes closer, her shoes will sink in.

"Sloane? Your email shocked me. I didn't expect that from you. I had to clean up—"

"I didn't get married. I didn't resign. Someone else sent that email." I want to apologize. It's on the tip of my tongue, but I will not apologize because that would make me look guilty, and I'm not guilty. I didn't do any of this. This is not my fault.

"Are you serious?" She steps closer, and I was right. Her pointed toe sinks in, and the sand rises over the shoe almost to her skin. "Why didn't you call? Where did you go?"

"Someone abducted me. I just recently made it back here."

"Sloane." Her hands fall to her waist. In fists. "Wow. You've got quite the creative mind, don't you? Whatever. I won't fight you. But for the future, let me give you some helpful advice. If you want to resign, it's best to give your two weeks' notice and to do so in person."

Those fists fall to her side, and she steps back onto firmer sand.

"But I didn't..." I step closer to her. She doesn't believe me, and I need her to. "I promise. I didn't...I was drugged and taken away on a sailboat."

"Seriously?" She's standing on the asphalt for the parking lot for the oceanfront hotel.

"I promise."

"And you're just hanging out here on the beach?"

That does look bad. "I..." How do I explain? Damn Max and Arrow for telling me I couldn't go back into my office. "I just made it back a couple of days ago. And Max said that I shouldn't—"

"Max? Is that who you married?"

"What? No. He's this..." What is Max? "My sister was worried. She knew I'd never resign. And she hired some people to help find me. They did, but they didn't want me to go back to Origins. Not yet. They're still trying to figure out what's going on."

"You're serious, aren't you?"

"Yes."

"Odd occurrences have been happening. Someone broke into our lab two nights ago. They stole my laptop."

I look back down the beach, in the direction I came from. She's talking about me. I stole her laptop. And I don't know what they found. It's some of what I'm supposed to review with the CIA and NSA.

"Sloane, are you telling me the truth?"

"Yes." The pearl necklace she so often wears isn't there. In its place is a necklace with an emerald pendant surrounded by diamonds.

"Well, come back to the office with me. You owe it to me, at least. I had to pack up your lab—"

"You have my work?"

"Of course. I'm interviewing someone next week for your position, but I'd much rather have you. You did the work of two people."

She's right. I did. I'm damn proud of that, too. Sand coats my feet. "I'm barefoot."

"My car's right here. How about I give you a ride to your place? You can get your shoes, and we'll go back to the lab. I mean, are you still interested in working for us?"

"Yes." That's exactly what I want. It's what I've wanted all along. "They said you might be involved."

"In what?" She sounds angry.

If I were her, I'd be angry too.

"Who is they?"

I don't know how to answer her.

She releases a frustrated sigh, and I bury my toes in the warm sand.

"Sloane, who is 'they'?"

"The people who helped find me. They work with the United States government." I'm not sure how to describe them. How would Max describe himself?

"Look. Let's get out of the sun. We'll talk about this at the office."

CHAPTER 23

Max

Fuck, I'm winded. A year ago, I could've done five miles without feeling it in my lungs and knees. And my time is for shit. Maybe Knox is right. Beefing up, as he calls it, has a downside.

It's the discipline of muscle building that I love. The concerted effort fuels the meditative quality of reps. Losing yourself in the clink of iron. Witnessing results from the sweat. But bulk takes a hit on cardio. Or maybe it's the one-two combo of getting old and bulking up.

Shut that fucking voice down. At thirty-eight, I'm hardly old. But I chose a career that does a number on joints. Jumping out of planes, time on the mat, maneuvers in the ocean, hours pounding pavement, it all takes a toll. There's no denying that.

The screen door slides open with a dull, grating sound. I look down and realize I'm about to track a shit ton of sand through the villa. So I backtrack, leaving the door open, to remove my shoes and socks. Sweat pours down my temples, and I swipe at the salty stream, but not before some burns my eyes.

I slap the sides of my shoes against the deck, but it's not good enough to get all the sand off. A plastic bag to pack my running shoes in would be ideal. I glance through the open door, searching for Sloane.

I like our new plan. It gives us more time to flesh out what's happening between us. Knox confirmed the other day he's relocating. He's still working out the details with Arrow, but he'll continue on their payroll one way or another. And, given I'm seriously considering a transition to the tech world, I could work anywhere. Or I could choose security as planned. The options aren't as open-ended with security, but there are options.

"Sloane," I call as the cool tile floor meets my sweaty, bright white feet. A tan line caps pale and slightly wrinkled skin. After being ensconced in damp cotton for hours, I imagine my feet smell pretty ripe too.

I carefully place my shoes on the table and turn to head upstairs. The bags and suitcases sitting by the door catch my attention. There's something off, but I can't put my finger on it.

An uncomfortable sensation pings in my belly. I ignore it and tug off my soaked shirt, charging up the steps.

"Sloane," I call again, turning from the landing into her bedroom. My suitcase is open, like I left it. My toiletries are in the bathroom. None of her stuff is here, but she probably packed it all up. But where is she?

"Sloane?" I call, moving into the room across the way. I packed up my gear before heading out on the run.

After one quick loop around the villa, it's apparent she's not here. But she said she was going to go for a walk when I went on my run. She must've packed and then gone, so she'll be back soon.

I charge up the stairs once more, shower, pack, and return downstairs.

"Sloane?"

Outside, I scan the beach. There's no sign of a tall, dark-haired woman with incredible legs.

Inside the house, I go to the computer bag. With my computer, I can check in with the team and also see exactly where Sloane is, maybe meet her out on the beach.

But, as I lift bag after bag, there's no computer bag to be found. Odd. It was a black messenger bag. I packed my laptop and the laptop we lifted from…

Christ. This is not good.

I find my phone and check it. There's a missed call from Erik. I return the call, and he answers on the first ring. That uncomfortable gut sensation intensifies.

"Sloane and Dr. Kallio entered Origin Laboratories. Sloane did not appear to be under duress. You know what's going on?"

A slight dizziness overtakes me, and I back into the wall and rest against it. Has she been playing me this whole time?

"You saw her on video?"

"Forty-five minutes ago. Found out five minutes ago. We got an alert about one of our trackers moving and someone on my team checked it. I'll be addressing the delay." He sounds annoyed, and also completely unaware that my emotions are all over the fucking place and I'm having a very hard time following. "Any idea what she's doing?"

God, I'm such a fool. Not once, but twice. Two fucking goddamned times. Any idea, Max, that she was stepping out? Nope. None, because I am a goddamn motherfucking idiot.

"Max? You still there?"

"I'm here. And no, I don't know what the fuck is going on. I went for a run. She should've been here when I got back." I run my fingers through my wet hair and pace along the pile of luggage, taking stock. "Her wheeled suitcase is still here. So is her black duffel." I squint, bending to confirm the luggage tag on the duffel is indeed hers. But her pocketbook isn't here. That held her identification. She'd need that to fly commercial.

I blink. This is Sloane. Get a hold of yourself. "She really wanted to go back and talk to them about her job. Maybe she decided to do that?" My gut doesn't settle down with the words. I don't know what the fuck to believe. "Do you have cameras inside the building?"

He doesn't. I know exactly where the cameras are. And so does Sloane.

"No. But she hasn't exited. I've got four watching the cameras now. We'll know the moment she leaves."

"She took Dr. Kallio's laptop with her."

"Doesn't matter. We already have access within their walls."

"Did your team find anything?"

"Nothing that jumped out to me as relevant. But we shared what we found with a few interested parties. They haven't gotten back to us with any updates."

"It doesn't make sense." I pace back and forth, down the hall, trying to piece it together. "Sloane seemed nervous about the D.C. meeting. But if she's been in on it…why play us?"

"What was she nervous about?"

"Looking guilty. And yes, I recognize it looks like she fucking lied to me." My little oh-she-may-have-gone-back-for-her-job looks like the cry of a desperate man wanting to believe he didn't get played.

"Stay on track. She was nervous because…" He lets the request for more information hang there, a dead weight on the line.

"She willingly worked with those fuckers in Cambodia. Yes, they threatened her with Sage. But she did it willingly. Even gave them the names of two matches, and it sounds like they took those people."

"And? She was afraid they'd file criminal charges? I'm not following."

"Maybe? She didn't say that…but…" Who the fuck knows? "Why would she play us?"

When Ginger cheated on me, the why was pretty fucking

simple. I was gone a lot. She didn't like military life. And boom, a suit-wearing prick offered her a nice big diamond ring. But why the fuck would Sloane lie to me? Was she full of shit when she told me her theory that some third party is involved? Or is this just about her trying to get her job back? Am I jumping to conclusions, or have I been played?

CHAPTER 24

Sloane

"Sloane, if you're willing to come back, I'll cancel the rest of the interviews. I'd much rather have someone working for me who I know and trust. I'm sure if I explain to our board what happened, they'll let me re-hire you. I mean, if you get some documentation to back your story. Do you think you can do that? You're not making this up, are you?"

The conversation plays over and over in my head. The cab driver pulls up to the front of the villa, and I realize I don't have any money.

"Oh, let me run in…" I can borrow some from Max.

"It's okay, miss. Don't worry about it."

"No. I'll pay you. Just give me a minute." He's a dark-skinned man with a peculiar pattern of moles around his cheeks, and perched on his head is a red, yellow, and green hand-knit cap. I peer forward, looking for a meter that tells how much I owe, but there isn't one.

"They paid for your fare."

"Who did? Dr. Kallio?"

"Your employer. I'm on their payroll. They pay a monthly fee, and we respond to pick up calls."

"Oh. Well, thank you." After I get out of the car, I close the door and then remember the tip. I wave to catch his attention and tell him I'll bring him a tip, but he's already pulling away.

Headed back into the villa, my mind brims with all I need to do. I'll need to get my bags back to my apartment. I won't need to fly today. Will the CIA and NSA still want to meet with me? I suppose they will…but could we maybe do a phone meeting? It's a voluntary meeting, so a phone meeting should be fine.

The front door of the villa doesn't twist open. It's locked. Of course it is. It automatically locks upon closing. When I left with Dr. Kallio, I didn't grab the keys.

I rap my knuckle against the solid wood door. I press my ear against the wood but hear nothing.

Maybe Max isn't back from his run. Or maybe he's in the shower.

It's not a big deal. I can get in from the back. I didn't lock the sliding glass door. My feet sink into the sand on the side of the villa.

"So. You came back." I stop, frozen by the sharp anger. Twice today. Two people have been angry with me. First Dr. Kallio, and now Max.

I should look up and face him. People appreciate it when you look them in the eye, and it's an important thing to do. But I can't force my gaze higher than his shoes. Brown slacks fall over worn hiking boots. It's an odd combination that isn't seen often here on the island.

"I ran into Dr. Kallio." I walk around to the steps because I have a lot to do. My gaze remains trained on his dusty boots.

"Really. Tell me all about it."

He blocks the door with his body, crossing his arms like he's blocking me from entering.

"I was walking down the beach, and she had a morning meeting and saw me over by the hotel that—"

"Cut the crap, Sloane. Don't fucking lie to me."

"I'm not." I close my eyes and place my index fingers on my thumbs, acquiring my bearings. "You were wrong. All of you were wrong. Dr. Kallio offered me my job back. If I can prove I was abducted, I get my job back. They weren't involved at all. She was mad at me. Like you are."

"You gave her back her laptop."

My eyes snap open, and I look straight at him. "Well, of course. It's hers." On my side hangs the messenger bag. It dangles off one shoulder below my hip. I lift it and offer it to him. "Here's yours. I didn't take it out. I just…I was barefoot when I ran into Dr. Kallio, and when we came back to get my shoes—"

"Did you go to the office to meet her?"

"No. I was walking along the beach. Where we decided it was safe for me to walk. I went a little further down and she was there. There's a hotel and she had a meeting there. She saw me and came out and spoke. It's a good thing. She wants me back. If we had left, I wouldn't have known that. She would've hired someone else." He has to see this is a good thing. He shouldn't be angry. I should be angry. Arrow's advice almost ruined my career.

"You are one fantastic actress."

"Ack—"

"I just can't figure it out. What did you gain by pulling Arrow into this little scheme?"

"It wasn't…I didn't…"

"Right. You're totally innocent."

"What exactly do you think I did?"

"I don't fucking know. All I know is you lied to me!"

"You're shouting." I dislike it when people shout. "There is no reason to shout."

"Right." He paces the front porch. "And so, what now? You go back to work here? I get on a plane this afternoon. It's all done. Is that the plan?"

"Well. Yes. I will probably return to work as soon as tomorrow. This afternoon, maybe. If I can get…what kind of proof would I provide? Would Arrow write something for me?"

"Are you for real?"

"Yes."

"Did they pay you off?"

"My annual salary isn't any of your business."

"Right." His hands rest on his hips, and his elbows jut out to the sides. "You've still got meetings in D.C. you need to attend. You've raised a lot of questions with some powerful worldwide entities."

He's right. I did. Or someone did. The person who hired Anton Solonov. But… "Why are you so angry? I never lied to you."

"You didn't? Really? Now you're staying. One meeting with Dr. Kallio and everything is right with the world?"

"I never thought she was involved. That was always Arrow's theory. Never mine. And you wouldn't let me talk to her. And now my theory is proven correct. My employer had nothing to do with what happened to me. You and your team will have to go back and develop new theories. Because you were wrong."

"And what happens to us?" The bite is missing from his words. I suppose he sees I am right.

"I need to finish my research. I'm too far along to walk away from it. You're like Sam. You'll be fine." Sam was always fine.

My chest stings. I rub my sternum in the same way Sage does. Why is he being mean? When William left none of this anger existed. And it's the same really. I am here. William left. Now Max is leaving.

He swings the front door open, bends down, picks up a bag. A click sounds. The trunk. He's loading the rental car.

I bypass all the luggage and head up the stairs. Putting no thought behind it, I reach for my phone. I normally keep it turned off because I don't like to be interrupted. I hate ringtones. I squeeze the sides until it comes to life. I open it to my contact list. My favorite. The sole star. And press her name.

"Sloane?" She sounds so far away. My lips curl up on their own, as do my nose and eyes, and everything gets blurry. My nostrils burn.

Kids scream in the background. She's at work. "I'm sorry. I shouldn't have called."

"What? No. I'm so glad you did. How are you? You're flying back today, right?"

"You're at work." I shouldn't have called her at work. I hate it when people call me at work. I tell everyone to text first. It's not appropriate to take personal phone calls during work hours. Sage and I schedule our calls to ensure we do not—

"I'm at recess. Hold on. I left you a message. I wanted you to call me." Sage lowers the phone. I can tell because her words sound more distant, but I still hear a muffled, "This is my sister. Do you mind if I take this?" And someone with a high-pitched joyful voice says, "Oh, go right ahead. Tell her we all say hi and for her to come visit."

"Okay. I'm back. Now, tell me everything. I called you, but Knox said you can't have a phone on where you are in D.C. and that Max and you have been very busy."

We have been busy but not doing work. An image surfaces of Max holding me in bed, and a sob escapes. I hold a hand over my mouth, then pull it away because my face is wet.

"Sloane? What's wrong?"

"I don't know why I'm crying." I sniffle again. I hate this. I hate feeling like this. I hate my face crumpling and… and… losing control. This doesn't happen to me. Not often. Not like it used to when I was a kid.

"Ohhh. Sloaney Baloney."

"Don't call me that." I clean the bottom of my nose with the back of my hand then wipe it on my dress. *Gross.*

"What's wrong? What happened?"

"If you call me that, I'm going to call you Sagey Bean."

"I won't call you that again." She sounds happy. Like she's smiling. And she should smile. She deserves happiness. I want my sister to be happy. "What's going on?" And now she sounds concerned and my tears free fall. It's… "Sloane, just…start from the beginning. Is this about something that happened in D.C.?" I hate I lied to my sister. All these Arrow people told me that's what I should do, but lying is never right. How could Max think I would lie to him?

"I'm actually in the Caymans. I'm not in D.C."

"I know. Knox told me. I was playing along because, well, I don't know. I'm out here on the school grounds, and it just seemed…"

I let out a loud sigh and sit down crisscross apple sauce in the middle of the floor. My dress makes a big tent, and I curl over and bury my face in the material. My muscles in my back stretch to the point of pain, but I don't care. The physical pain is worlds better than this nonsense going on inside me.

"Sloane? What's going on?"

With a huff, I sit up, squeeze my wet eyes shut, pull my knees up to my chest, wrap one arm around them, and say, "I was right. All of you were wrong. Dr. Kallio isn't involved. She was interviewing replacements for me until she found out I didn't run off and get married. Which is stupid, by the way. Who would do that? And why would she believe I would resign via email? That's just stupid. But she offered me the job back. And now Max is angry. At me." Tears leak through my lashes. I can feel them, and it's not at all a positive sensation. Or there aren't positive and negative sensations. It is a sensation I do not want to repeat. That's what I mean.

"So…you're going back to work for them?"

"Yes. It's excellent news." A sob breaks through, and I swipe my nose on my palm. "I can resume my research. My job. It's all here. I don't have to start over."

"Are you going to be going to D.C.? Or was that never–"

"Arrow wanted me to tell you I was going to D.C. They said you would insist on coming with me here if you knew the truth."

"That's what Knox said. But he also said you'd be going–"

"I needed to get into the lab. I wanted to find the report that I thought caused all of this because I can't let anything bad happen to you. That's why I came here."

"Did you find what you were looking for?"

"Sort of. And I suspect I know why someone came after me. Maybe. I have a theory."

"Well, why—"

I open my mouth to explain, but all I see is Max's crossed arms, and tears gush uncontrollably.

"Sloane. Honey. Why are you crying?"

"Max thinks I lied to him. But I didn't. I lied to you, and I'm sorry about that. I shouldn't have, but they told me it was best for you."

"It's okay. I know you'll always do what you think is best for me."

"I will. I love you Sagey."

"I love you too, Sloaney. Whatever is wrong, it's going to work out. I'm glad you called me."

"But you're at work and it's not scheduled—"

"Sloane, if I can't answer, I won't pick up. But your calls are always welcome. You hear me? I'd talk to you every day if you were up for it."

"Really?" More tears tumble down. It's just…wow. Maybe I'm ovulating. This level of emotion is not a normal reaction. Other people do not react like this.

"Really. And I'll ask Knox to talk to Max. We'll find out what he's upset about. I can't imagine he thinks you lied to him."

"It doesn't make sense, does it?"

"No. It doesn't." A loud screech pierces the line, and Sage, in her teacher voice, says, "Maddox...you know the rules. No jumping from the top of the monkey bars."

"I don't know how you deal with loud children who don't listen."

She laughs and I sniffle. "That's...they aren't... Ah, Sloane, now may not be the best time to tell you, but I have news."

"Oh?" I sniffle. Changing the subject is good. What's going on in my head is not.

"I'm engaged!"

"To who?"

"Knox!"

Oh, right. Of course. Knox. Max said they were in love. "Are you happy?"

"Sloane, I've never been happier. I've been so eager to tell you. I'm so glad you called."

"I'm happy for you. You know, I only want you to be happy."

"I met with my cardiologist. He says there's no reason I can't have a child."

I close my eyelids and breathe in. Count to three. Why would she take that risk?

I don't understand it, but I don't have to understand everything. That's what Mom said.

"Adoption is always an option." We've been telling her that since she was a kid and asked an adult if one day she could have kids. "There are many types of families and not all parents are biological ones." I say it in the same voice I used to read to her in.

"I know, and I can't really explain it, but I just want to have a child. It will feel like maybe all I've gone through will be worth it if I can give someone else life." She's referencing that someone else lost a life to give her organs. I know this because it's bothered Sage for years. But that person was already dead. It's not like she killed them.

My gaze rises to the ceiling. Sage is all I have. Why would she risk her life? "You don't have to have children for your life to have value."

"I know that."

"Sage, you're my everything. How can you not see how valuable you are?" And again those damn tears flood and my snot secretions increase.

"Sloane." She says my name with a sigh. "I love you, too. Please try to understand why I want this. Why it means so much to me."

"The doctor said it's okay?"

"Yes."

"And he's a good doctor? With a good rating?"

"Yes. One of the best cardiologists in the state. He's been my doctor for years."

My gaze rises skyward, and I breathe in and have to clean my nose again with the back of my hand. Life's too short not to take risks. It's a line from a romance book I once read, and it comes to me out of nowhere. "Then you should go for it."

"Well, we'll see. This is all so premature, but I'm telling you because you're my sister and you're my everything too, you know?"

"Max says that Knox is crazy about you. He told me he was going to stay in Asheville for you. I'm happy for you, Sage." My voice cracks on her name, and it shouldn't because she is happy. I've always wanted her to be healthy and happy.

"Max might stay there for you if you asked him."

"No. Max doesn't love me." And dang it, the tears fall all over again. Snot fills my nose. I need tissues.

CHAPTER 25

Max

My phone vibrates in my pocket. I ignore the blasted device and slam the trunk down. The hinges soften the slam, which only increases my desire to ram my fist into the car. Or the windshield. The side of the goddamn villa. Anywhere.

My phone vibrates again. I whip it out of my pocket, ready to explode on whoever is calling me yet again. *I'll call you fucking back, asshole.* The words are right there, waiting to be unleashed on whatever unsuspecting prick is calling.

And it's my mom.

I take a few breaths, stare at the ocean beyond the dunes, exhale deeply, and pick up. "Mom."

"Max. Hey, honey. Did I catch you at a bad time?"

I swipe my hand over my forehead and lean back against the car, facing the villa. "Nah. It's as good a time as any. What's up?"

"Is something wrong, honey?"

"No, Mom. I'm sorry, I'm just… The project here is wrapping up. I'm preparing to head out."

"Oh. So, you're heading back home? To Ginger?"

"To—No. I'm not headed back to her. How did you even know she's at my house?"

"Well, she called me. She wanted to check to see how you were doing."

"She called you?"

"Don't be mad at her. She was worried about you. But you say you're not going back for her?"

"No, Mom."

"That's good." In the background I hear my dad say, "Riva, what're you doing?"

"I'm not doing anything. I just…I think it's best that he not get involved with someone going through a separation."

My head falls back, and my gaze lifts to the sky.

Dad says to Mom, "Riva, don't meddle."

"I'm not meddling. He said he wasn't going back to her, anyway. And I'm his mother. I'll never stop worrying. Worrying differs from meddling."

"You called him. He's out of the country on a project."

"He said it's a good time. It's a good time, right, sweetie?"

"Yes, Mom. Tell Dad I said hi."

"I'm so glad you're not going back to Ginger. I like her. She's a very nice young woman, don't get me wrong. But you two were not right for each other—"

"Riva!"

"All I'm saying is she's not what you need."

"Mom, you don't have to worry. I promise you. I'm not interested in Ginger."

"Good. She's not what you need."

"Riva!"

"What do I need, Mom?"

"You need someone who challenges you in a good way. You've

always liked a challenge. And you need someone who sees past your football fame or SEAL team persona. You need someone who is real. You've got a big heart. I mean, I'm your mom. But you always put your guard up if someone is into you for anything other than you."

"Riva, for god's sake, just let him tell you about his day and hang up the phone."

"He asked me." She's speaking to my dad, and I can't help but grin. It's surprising Dad hasn't picked up a handset to join in the conversation. "The fact that you let Ginger stay at your apartment shows what a big heart you have. You'll never turn your back on someone, no matter what. What you need is someone who will do the same for you."

"Thanks, Mom. I'll take it under advisement."

The call continues with her giving me updates on her neighbors, my cousins, and a couple of people from my hometown I don't remember. I halfway listen because I'm evidently a glutton for punishment. But at the forefront of my thoughts is Sloane.

Do I think she lied to me? No. If I take a beat, and give it consideration, it's not in her chemical makeup. She's straightforward, and I like that about her. She doesn't care at all that I was in special forces. I doubt she watches football, and if I told her I turned down a pro football career, she wouldn't look at me any differently. And she has a big heart. She'll do anything for her sister. Even when she knows it's wrong.

When she falls for someone, that person will be a lucky son of a bitch. Because she loves with her whole heart.

Meeting up with Dr. Kallio felt like a gut punch. Blindsided me with a wicked jab. But, hurting me wasn't her intention. Apparently, we were wrong about Dr. Kallio. If we'd been right, she wouldn't have let Sloane go. She wouldn't be rehiring her.

After the call with Mom ends, I press Erik's name.

"Erik," he says over the faint sound of computer keys clicking.

"I'm calmer now. She's staying. Should I stay?" There's a private jet waiting for us.

"No. Come on back. You can go to the debriefing in D.C."

"Is she safe here?"

"We've got two contract guys close by. They can get to her fast if needed. Let her go back. Spread that report of hers far and wide. I'll keep a team monitoring the building."

"Should we maybe get our contract guys to watch her?" The clicking of keys continues. He really pounds his keys. "It's…it'd be safest right?"

"Jack says he'll get Stella on it. Matteo will step in today."

"What about at night?"

"I don't know. Reach out to Stella. Maybe they'll have her stay in the villa."

I don't particularly treasure the idea of someone else taking over the room across from hers, the room I stayed in initially, but it's safest. Erik ends the call. I'll touch base with Stella later. My brain feels a little numb after riding a wave of fury.

Inside the villa, the hallway is cleared except for Sloane's bags. Since she's staying, I left all her stuff in the hallway. I can't exactly leave without saying goodbye, so, calmer now, I trudge up the stairs to find her. I hate goodbyes.

When I reach the landing, my hand falls to the railing for balance.

Sloane sits in the middle of the bedroom floor, face blotchy and red, and a roll of toilet paper beside her with spent tissues littering the floor. Something inside my chest cracks. Not only does she have a big heart, but when she cares, she cares deeply. She might not easily show it, but she does. The evidence is all around her.

At least, that's if she's crying for me. For us.

The floor creaks under my weight, and she glances up. Her face crumbles, and she puts her hands over her eyes.

In a flash, I'm on the floor beside her, pulling her into my lap.

"Shh." I soothe her like I would a child, and she buries her damp face into my neck.

"I didn't lie." Her voice cracks, and she sniffles and then shifts and rubs her nose on my shirt. I don't even mind the snot. I just hold her, rub her back, and kiss the top of her head.

"I know."

"You do?"

"Doesn't mean I understand at all what's going on. But I believe you."

"Sage is going to have a kid." She picks up a tissue and presses it against her cheek, absorbing tears.

"Is that why you're crying?" Am I that big of a fool?

"Yes. No. Maybe." Her arm snakes around my middle and curves around my back, up to my shoulders, and I find myself embraced in a fireman's hold. And damn if it doesn't feel good to have her cling to me. "I'm happy for her, I guess."

"Does Knox know she's pregnant?"

"Oh. She's not pregnant. She just checked with a doctor to make sure she…you know, with her heart."

"And the doctor cleared her?"

"Yes. I mean, I'd prefer she take no risks. But I understand it. And I don't know why I'm so emotional. I really hate being this emotional."

"Well, we had our first fight."

"I don't like yelling, and I don't like fights."

"Me neither."

"I don't want you to be angry at me. I feel like I should say I'm sorry, but I don't say I'm sorry unless I have a reason to be. And I don't think I have a reason to be. I haven't done anything wrong."

"Shh." It's meant to quiet her sobs, but the low rumble soothes my ruffled heart, too.

"I would never do anything to hurt you. You know that, right?"

I take a second to reflect on her question. "Yeah, I do."

I lift her chin, forcing her to give me those glistening, tear-filled brown eyes. "Ditto, ya know?"

She sniffs. "I'm not ready to say goodbye to you."

She looks me right in the eye when she says it, and that crack splits wide open. I'm done. Sure, I've got a plane this afternoon, and there's a lot to figure out, but it's not going to be goodbye forever.

My lips fall to hers as I cradle her against my side. Her fingers thread through my hair, and all the anger from earlier, all that loaded frustration and hurt, morphs into something bigger. Something that was there earlier, but I just hadn't accepted. Warmth effuses from every pore. It spills out of my split heart. I've felt this before. It's love. I swore I'd never fall again, and yet here we are.

The bed is all of four feet away from us, and we're both completely undressed before I even think about moving us to it. But the hardwood floor digging into my knee hurts like a mother, and I lift her up to the middle of the bed.

I take it slow. Kissing her with all the love I feel inside. Licking her. Adoring her. Bringing her to orgasm with my fingers, my tongue, and then, finally, sinking inside her.

It's slow, languid, and perfect. I love this woman.

It's on the tip of my lips to say it, to tell her as she quivers below me. But then my body convulses, losing control, releasing everything into her and robbing me of thought and words. It's when I collapse beside her, kissing her, lifting errant strands off her still swollen cheeks, that I admit it. "I love you."

She smiles. It's a timid smile. I only get a glimpse before she rolls into me and buries her face once again in my neck. She drapes her body over mine, and I swear I could stay like this forever.

"I've never loved anyone before. I don't know what it feels like. But I read about it in books. The ones Sage and I read. I believed it was fiction, and even if it was real, it wouldn't happen to me. Because I'm different."

"I'd take your different over anyone else's normal any day of the week. Never doubt it."

"You don't have to say that." She presses her lips to my chest and nibbles. I pinch her ass, and we settle down, holding on to each other.

"You know, I think I fell for you because of your differences. You're refreshing. Honest. Dedicated. Passionate. And not like anyone else I've ever known. It takes work to get close to you, but it's the most rewarding work I've ever done."

"I think I love you, too."

"Yeah?" She presses her lips to my throat. I'll take that as a yes. "Well, it's a good thing, because I don't plan on letting you go."

"You're not going back?"

"No, I have to go back. The plane's scheduled. There are still a lot of open questions. Someone did this, someone with a lot of financial backing, and we need to find out who. But I'll be back." My hand wanders from her hip back down and cups her bare ass, and I squeeze. God, I love this. It feels so fucking right being here with her. "I suppose we're going to have to lay out some ground rules for long distance."

"Long distance?"

"Yeah. But luckily, it's not such a long flight."

"And maybe you could move here? Sage said it might be an option."

"You talked to Sage about me?"

"Knox is going to ask you why you think I lied."

I chuckle. Knox will probably be some kind of peeved that I ignored his warning about future family gatherings. Tough shit.

The pad of her thumb circles my nipple, and her thigh rubs over mine. This is heaven.

Her company may not be responsible for her abduction, for

coming after Sage, and for Felix, but I don't buy for a minute that no one within her company is involved. Maybe her direct boss isn't in on it, but someone is. Was. They may not have a reason to come after her now that we've accessed her servers and have the data, but we still have reasons to find the guilty parties.

I don't want to think about it anymore. I just want to hold her. She's mine. In this moment, she's all mine.

CHAPTER 26

Sloane

"Do you want to shower?"

Max's suggestion sounds nice, but there's so much to do. How will I validate what happened to me? How do I prove I was drugged, abducted, and held against my will? I have witnesses for the rescue part.

"Hey, there, beautiful girl… where'd you go?"

He tilts my chin, forcing me to take in all the glory of recessive genes. "You have beautiful eyes. Did you know that?"

His calloused hand glides over my hip and down to my behind. I like the rough feel of his skin. He playfully takes a fistful of my right butt cheek and smacks me. "I think I'd prefer a more manly word. But for the record, I'm a big fan of your dark eyes. There's nothing like that moment when you first look at me, directly at me. I feel it right here."

He finds my hand and places it over his sternum, between his bulging pecs. We're standing in a room naked. Well, I found my underwear on the way to the bathroom and put them on, but otherwise, we're naked.

"This is so unusual," I say, flattening my palm over the curve of his pec. He tilts his head, and that maddening grin spreads. "You make it hard for me to think. You distract me."

"Isn't that a good thing?" He lifts my hand from his chest and sucks the tip of my index finger into his mouth.

"We have things to do," I remind him. He's got a flight, and I need to move back into my apartment.

"What's unusual?"

What's he… Oh, I said this is unusual. He's asking me why I said it. "I'm not used to this." I stop touching him and scan the floor for my clothes. "With William, and…" My shirt's crumpled against the wall, and I bend at the waist to reach for it. "We would just have sex and then get on with it. With our day. You…you want to…" I stumble, both with my words and into the wall.

"I want to what? Hold you? Make love? Over and over? You walk around in only your panties and yeah, I'll never get enough."

I roll my eyes because I can hear the tease. With my bra in hand, I search the room for my sundress. Maybe I should shower and put on a more work-appropriate outfit.

He steps closer, and while it is tempting to just fool around and waste the afternoon in here, we can't. I hold out a hand to stop him, because I know it won't take much for him to make me forget all that we have to do. "You have a flight this afternoon, right?"

He glances at his wrist. It's one of those that scuba divers wear. I recognize the dial because Sam had one like it.

"Yeah, I guess I do."

"And I've got a letter to write." I point at the bathroom. "Go get your shower. Now." I use my stern voice and face, the same as I'd use with an intern.

He tugs me into his arms and gives me a sloppy, wet kiss. Haze clouds my brain, but thankfully he listens, and just as quickly, he pops my rear and disappears into the bathroom.

"You like my behind, don't you?"

He grins over his shoulder. "I love that firm ass of yours. And those mighty fine legs, too."

My gaze follows his down my body. Barely there boobs, but like Mom once said, some men are leg and ass men. I wonder if there's a gene for that. It would be interesting to find out, but it would be hard to derive the benefits of such a study.

The rushed sound of pouring water enters the room, and it has the effect of washing away the Max haze. I find my clothes, twist my knotty hair up into a low bun, and locate my old laptop.

By the time Max returns, his skin dewy, smelling like a fresh fragrance-free bar of soap, I've finished the letter. It's a highly unusual letter, but I'm not sure what else I can do to prove the truth of my story. And I want my job back. I've invested my career in cellular regeneration research. We're on the cusp of something great.

I spin the laptop to him so he can read what I've written:

To Whom It May Concern:

This letter is to confirm that Anton Solonov abducted Dr. Sloane Watson. He illegally transported her to Cambodia against her will.

The Arrow Tactical Security Team rescued her from the compound where she was being held.

The reasons for her abduction remain unknown, but multiple agencies, including but not limited to Interpol, the Central Intelligence Agency, National Security Agency, and Arrow Tactical are currently investigating the reason for her abduction and for the associated attempted abduction of her sister, and the murder of Felix Hernandez.

The signatures below are from Arrow Tactical team members who can verify the veracity of Dr. Watson's claims.

He reads it, and those blue irises become hard to see through his squinted eyelids.

"Do you need glasses? I can increase the font size."

"Sloane, you think this is what they're looking for?"

"What else could I provide?"

"I'm not sure, but I have to tell you, I don't like this at all. Maybe you're right. Maybe we jumped to the wrong conclusion about who is coming after you and why. But it strikes me as all kinds of FUBAR that you'd need to write a letter like this."

"What's FUBAR?"

"Fucked up beyond all recognition." He bites out the words and I cross my arms below my chest.

"What else am I supposed to do?"

"I'm not sure." He runs a hand through his hair. "But I can tell you that this doesn't sit right. Can you hold on to this letter? Come back with me. Let's meet with the guys in D.C. Let's see what light they can shed on everything that's happened."

"I have a chance to get my old job back. I can't risk… She's interviewing my replacement next week. I can't leave."

Frustration seeps through his pores and his frown. It's an expression I'm quite familiar with.

"I tell you what. I've got to go. They sent a plane here to get us. One of us needs to be on it. I'll meet with the men in D.C. We'll figure things out. But…just sit tight for the rest of the day. Can you do that for me? Arrow is setting up security for you. It sounds like they'll have you stay in the villa. It's more secure than your place."

"That's not–"

"Please Sloane? For me?"

"Okay."

"I'll call you when I land."

"Oh. We should schedule a call."

"What?"

"That's what I do with Sage. We schedule a call on Sunday. We could schedule to talk before or after that call."

"Are you serious right now?"

"Once I get back in the lab, it'll be manic. I have so much to catch up on." He's looking at me like he can't comprehend what I am saying. And that's fair. It's difficult for people who are used to clocking in and out of their jobs to understand dedication. "I'll speak to you on Sunday. That's only three days away."

"Wow."

He's wearing those hiking boots he likes so much, and they're still dusty.

"That's what you want?"

"I prefer scheduled calls. It's disorienting to get a phone call when I'm working. I know not everyone is like that. It's part of my differences."

I shouldn't have to defend myself.

"Is a Sunday phone call what you're seeing for this week, or is that what you're expecting from here on out?"

"I mean…" His tone sounds agitated. He doesn't like what I proposed. "We can add a few more calls in. The time difference will only be two hours."

It's awkward. I can't tell exactly why. But I have the same sensation I get when I break a rule, and I don't like this sensation. He needs to get to his plane, and I need to go see Dr. Kallio. I want her to see my draft of the letter and agree that she'll cancel interviewing my replacements. I'll let Max make changes to it, or anyone on the Arrow team really. It's a draft. We can make revisions to it.

"So, I guess this is it?" He stands at the door with his hands shoved in his pants pockets.

"You're not happy, are you?"

"I think I just thought something more happened between us..." He draws out the sentence, letting it hang there in the silence.

"You know, that's the thing about Sage's books. They end when the couple gets together, and you're supposed to imagine their lives being perfect. They don't show the day to day. And...this is my life." I don't know how else to explain it. What I am working on could change the world. It could give life to so many who might otherwise die. My work requires time. And focus. And really, he distracts me.

"What were your parents like?"

That's an odd question. One we don't really have time for. "Why?"

"I'm curious."

"They were exemplary parents."

"I get that. But what were they like as a couple?"

Memories of my parents surface. Mom at the hospital while Dad heated dinner in the oven. Mom driving through a drive-thru, only to be met at the hospital later with Dad after he'd had to work late. One of them would stay, one of them would drive Sam and me home. Shouting. Always behind closed doors. Tears. Over Sage. "They disagreed sometimes," I say, thoughtfully. "They saw a couple's therapist. But neither of them ever told us why. I always assumed it had to do with Sage being sick."

"They told you they were seeing a therapist but didn't tell you why?"

"They didn't tell us. But we spent a lot of time in the car, driving back and forth from the hospital. They never told us, but they didn't keep it a secret. We have ears. Why?"

"My parents loved each other. But they had a day-to-day reality too. Everyone does. But they also prioritized each other. I've always wanted a marriage like my parents."

"Marriage? You want to get married?"

"One day. I take it that's a negative for you?"

"Marriage is based on religious principles, and I'm not religious." It's a fantasy. I'm not sure why, but it surprises me that someone like Max would want the traditional construct of a marriage. He seems more open-minded.

"Well, then. I suppose it's better that we realized we want different things before we invested too much energy in scheduling phone calls."

I'm not sure what to say to that, so I focus on the unevenly tied laces of the out-of-place hiking boots he's wearing.

"I'll see you around."

A quivering sensation assaults my chest cavity. He's leaving to catch a plane. But this doesn't feel like a good goodbye. "Do you not want to talk this Sunday?"

"No, Sloane, I don't think I do." The room blurs, and it becomes hard to breathe. "Our paths are bound to cross, you know. Knox is like a brother to me."

"And he and Sage are going to have children." If something happens to her… She's all I've got. "I don't want her to go through a pregnancy. It's a risk."

"I remember." Again, he doesn't sound happy with me. But I'm only concerned for Sage. I just don't want her taking unnecessary risks.

I return to my laptop as the door clicks closed.

CHAPTER 27

Max

Like most terminals for private planes, this one is small, but given the Cayman Islands' location, it's on the luxe side. No one bats an eye at my gun bags. The corporate plane is here but needs to refuel before it turns around. Our departure time isn't slated for another forty-three minutes, and I'm camped out in a seat with a view of the tarmac.

My foul mood threatens to suffocate me. And it's my own damn fault. I should've seen it. Everyone described her as an odd bird. Different. Didn't Sage once tell me she was borderline obsessed with her work? Did Sage even use the word borderline, or is my memory playing wishful tricks?

The second woman I fall hard for, and she's the second one to decide I'm not worth it. But no, what am I saying? She offered to schedule a weekly call with me. *Holy fucking shit, I'm a joke.*

My phone vibrates in my back pocket, forcing me to shift in the hard plastic bucket seat. Damn thing goes through another series of vibrations. I'm not in the mood to read updates. I pull it out and lay it on top of the duffel at my feet. The thing continues to vibrate with five-second intervals of calm.

With a huff, and the reluctant realization something must've exploded, I bend and pick up the damn annoyance. Eight missed calls. Knox. Erik. Knox. Erik.

What're they doing? Playing tag team? I really do not feel like talking.

I click over to texts.

ERIK

Did you see the Interpol update? Sloane is a suspect.

ERIK

Photos on multiple websites. In Taiwan. Also Cambodia.

KNOX

Have you seen this shit? How's Sloane taking it?

ERIK

Bank statement details showing payments to her in Cayman accounts.

ERIK

Sloane Watson's name is suddenly popping
up everywhere on our searches. Rumors
circulating that she's bipolar.

KNOX

Can you call me? Sage can't reach Sloane.
She's worried. Something was wrong
earlier. Sloane wouldn't stop crying.

On our team server, I open the Interpol report. It's an updated version of what we originally read. Sloane Watson is a person of interest as an employee of Origins Laboratories. Only, the report has been amended to include photographs that have surfaced of her on location over the past two years. The photographs included in the file are grainy and appear to be taken with a long-distance lens. The photos themselves strike me as odd. An incoming call interrupts my review of the material. It's Knox. I answer through my earpiece. "Hey."

"How's Sloane?"

"I'm not with her. If you're asking how she's taking these revelations, when I saw her last, she was unaware." My voice strikes me as a helluva lot calmer than how I'm feeling.

"What do you mean? Where is she?"

"She's staying here. Said she ran into her boss and her old job is hers if she wants it. Which seemed weird as fuck to me, but now that I'm seeing all this—"

"She's not coming back with you to meet with the CIA and NSA? She thinks she can just blow them off?"

"Wasn't presented as a mandatory meeting. Although…I mean, has she broken US laws? She's working from the Caymans." *And she's not my problem.*

"Sage says it's all fabricated."

"Erik sent me a text saying they found Cayman Islands bank accounts. That doesn't exactly scream 'innocent.'" Knox has to expect a sister will claim innocence.

"Sage says the bipolar rumors are completely off."

"I haven't gotten that far in the report. But you've got to admit, everyone describes her as strange."

"Yes, but she's even-keeled, right?"

"She could be on medication. Look, I'm not saying the woman is evil. I know she's not. She's disciplined, and if she suffered from something like bipolar disorder, I'd expect she would stay on her meds. Who cares if that's the truth? But come on, she's obsessed with organs. I could see her rationalizing the illegal organ trade and being a part of it. Knowing what I know about Sloane, she'd justify it as helping others like her sister. But..." I scratch my jaw, thinking about the alleged bank accounts. "I saw that apartment of hers. If she's stashing money, she's doing so with a noble goal of opening a research facility or something like that."

"None of this adds," Knox says. "If she's involved in something like that, why come after her? Why come after Sage?"

"Maybe she pissed the wrong guy off. I don't know." My head hurts. I just want to get on the plane and put some distance between me and this case.

"Why couldn't our team find these bank accounts a month ago when we were searching high and low for any information on Sloane Watson? Now, suddenly, information is coming out of nowhere. The concerns about erratic behavior are dated from almost a year ago. If those posts had existed when we were doing our research, we would've found them."

A smear campaign?

I flick back over to the photos that struck me as odd. There's Taiwanese writing on a sign in the background, but it's blurred, and I don't know Taiwanese. But there's something else. The shadowy figures in the background all appear taller than Sloane.

"What are the chances a five-foot-ten woman is going to be shorter than all the other people at an Asian airport?" I enlarge the photo. One of the shadowy background figures is missing an arm. Another figure hovering near her on the sidewalk appears to have one foot. "This is an AI-generated image. How the hell did Interpol not pick up on that?"

"Click to the photos in Cambodia. They're real."

"Yeah, well, we know she was there. And we also know they didn't have a gun on her." The Cambodian photos could be legit.

"But then there are the bank accounts," Knox says under his breath. "And she chose to stay."

"I take it Sage isn't with you?"

"No. She had to go back to the school for parent-teacher meetings. I'm torn."

"About?"

"None of this has made sense. We've been assuming she had information someone didn't want exposed. But maybe this has always been about either trying to control her or force her hand at something. I can't think what would be in it for her to bring us into this, though. Unless it's a distraction of some sort."

"Sloane would never agree to someone going after her sister. She loves her sister more than anything…anyone in the world."

"You're positive about that?"

"No question. And, Knox, she rides a bike to work. A rusted beach cruiser. Her apartment's fine but nothing to write home about. No ocean view. For that matter, the view is of a parking lot. Money is not her motivator."

"Why did she choose to stay?"

"Her job."

"They offered it back to her?"

"If she could prove her story was accurate. Where all did you say posts are showing up about her?"

"Random blog posts. Industry, and when I say industry, I mean her industry, science-related groups. People she went to school with on Facebook. Some deeper commentary on LinkedIn, which is the only social media account she has."

"Would it be enough, do you think, to prevent her from being rehired?"

A beep sounds alerting me to an incoming call. It's Erik.

"I gotta go." I click and answer, "Erik."

"Did you look over everything?"

"Knox and I were just going over it."

"What're your thoughts on this?"

"Something's off." Sloane might be many things, but she's not conniving. "What do you think?"

"I think if any of this is correct, I've got to fire several on my team. But we hire good people, so that makes me suspicious."

"You know some of those photos are AI, right?"

"I didn't study them." There's clicking. "'K. Someone's checking them out. You'd think Interpol would do that, right?" He's gruff. Annoyed. Aren't we all? "Out of all of this, the bank accounts are the most damning piece of evidence. The rest is innuendo."

"Can they fake bank accounts?"

"Let me get back to you." The call ends.

CHAPTER 28

Sloane

The pit in my stomach aches. Something is wrong with me. Unbidden tears well up, and I have to inhale deeply to hold them at bay.

In North Carolina, it's later in the day. Sage won't be with her students. My finger hovers over her name. But what would I tell her? She'd ask questions, seeking to help me diagnose the issue. She'd ask me when the pain started.

And I'd tell her the symptoms intensified when the door clicked closed. When Max left.

"Sloane, sometimes you have to be willing to bend. Flexibility is a good thing, honey."

Mom said that to me. She repeated herself often.

The urge to vomit rises. I need fresh air. I just need to get to the lab and put all this behind me and re-focus. I need my routine. When I follow a routine, life is easier. I don't get so worked up when I know exactly what to expect.

I grab the old laptop with the draft letter that Max asked me to hold onto and my messenger bag, and I head out the door to the bike rack. One bike has a basket on the front, and I place the laptop in it. It looks lonely in the basket, but I need nothing else. If I bring my phone, I might call Sage, and I don't want to answer her questions. I need to get to work.

By the time I reach the Origins office, the wind has dried the tears I couldn't contain. The fresh air eradicated the nausea, but the crater-sized hole in my stomach weighs me down, and my chest aches with the pain of someone cracking open my breast-plate. I could ask Sage exactly what that feels like, but it's a metaphorical comparison. And if I hear my sister's voice, the tears will return.

The office doors are locked, but as I'm standing there looking through the tinted glass, a person wearing a lab coat exits the building. His sleek black hair looks familiar, and I must look familiar to him, because he holds the door open for me. His brown men's dress shoes are scuffed along the toes.

"Thank you," I say as I head inside.

No one is sitting behind reception. They only place someone there when investors are expected. My sandals click against the floor, and my reflection shines in the hallway glass. My messenger bag bangs against my thigh, and I lift the strap over my head so it hangs more snugly across my midsection.

I reach Dr. Kallio's lab. The door is ajar, and I peek inside. She sits at a counter, head bent, reading a report. I tap lightly on the door.

"Sloane. Hi. I didn't expect to see you here."

The length of her lab coat falls halfway down the stainless-steel legs of the stool. She removes her reading glasses and sets them on the counter.

"I brought the letter. The one you asked me to get for verification to prove my story."

"Did you?"

I open the flap on the messenger bag and lift my laptop. "It's on here. I don't have a printer." I could have emailed it, but I wasn't thinking straight...after Max. "It's a draft. The Arrow team is reviewing it and may make changes as well, but I thought you might have changes too. But you can see the draft version and, well, you won't need to interview anyone."

My chest cinches. It feels like I'm missing a lung or—no, I can breathe. It's more like my heart split open.

"Let's see it."

I take the laptop over to her and set it beside her glasses. The tip of her finger traces along the edge of the chrome. Her nails have been recently done. Instead of a color, this time she got the ends painted white and left the base a natural color. There's a name for that design, but I can't remember it. It looks pretty.

My nails are short and unpolished. My finger pad traces the edge of my thumbnail. It's a little rough from where I bit it.

"This computer isn't a work computer."

"No. It's one of my personal computers."

"Ah." The password box is displayed, and she turns the laptop to me for me to enter my password. Unlike Dr. Kallio, I don't have a written password list. I can remember my passwords. "Do you have access to the network from this computer?"

"No. It's an older computer."

"So, the only computer that you have access to the network is through your work computer?"

"Well, not without being on the VPN." I lean forward and open the file with the letter. "I can email it to you," I say, straightening my spine. "Dr. Kallio, has Origins ever considered opening a US office?"

"Not to my knowledge. Why?" She speaks to me absentmindedly as she reads my letter. It's a brief letter.

"I'm just wondering if maybe it's time for me to return to the States." It's been less than two years since I left, but things have changed.

"Are you asking because of Max Hawkins? The employee from Arrow Tactical that you've been spending time with?"

"Yes." I've never mentioned Max's last name to her, have I?

She closes the laptop lid and spins the stool to face me directly. "Sloane, you're a good kid. But you got in way over your head. We're not going to be able to re-hire you."

"What? Why?" Discomfort rises anew. My vision blurs. More tears are coming, and I can't stop them. If she doesn't want to re-hire me, I should leave.

"Where are you going?"

I pause, five steps from the door. "There's no reason to stay, is there?"

Proving my heart isn't literally split in two, it pounds hard enough to fray my nerves. Emotion wells in my throat, and it feels hard to swallow.

"No, there is. I need to talk to you."

She gets up and walks past me. She closes the door and locks it. Then she pulls the vinyl shade down over the glass pane in the door.

"What're you doing?" Instinctively, my hand falls into my messenger bag and the inside pocket. I blink rapidly, clearing the welling tears.

"I can't let you leave."

She pulls a phone out of her lab coat and taps on it.

"What do you mean?"

She presses her back to the door as if she's blocking me from leaving.

"I need to keep you here for your safety."

"What're you talking about?"

"You're delusional. You haven't been taking your medication regularly. We knew there were issues before you resigned with no notice, but we've had time to review your work, and it's clear you were suffering from psychotic episodes."

"No." I shake my head and step to the side. She's lying. But why? "Max was right, wasn't he?" My eyes burn at the mention of his name, but my adrenaline pumps hard through my veins and my eyes dry. "You are behind everything. But why?"

"Dammit." She checks her phone. Her lips press into a firm line, creating wrinkles all up and down. That's her angry expression. "I am not supposed to be the one who has to do this."

She charges past me to her desk, opens a drawer, and lifts a small pistol. Time slows.

My fingers wrap around the smooth edge of metal.

She points the pistol at me, and I take a step back. The end of the pistol wavers.

I take another step back.

"Stop. I can't let you leave. I need for you to stay here."

"Why?" Sam once told me that keeping someone talking is important. He also told me that distance is important. Not everyone who owns a gun has good aim. Most don't. That's what he said. I take another step back.

She locked the door, but it's not like I can't flip the lock.

She widens her stance and holds the gun with two hands. Someone taught her how to hold a gun and take aim.

"Why are you doing this?"

"I'm not the one calling the shots. You can't leave."

"Why did Anton Solonov tell everyone I couldn't be hurt?" If I'm going to keep her talking, I'm going to ask my questions.

"I don't know."

"Why didn't he just kill me?"

"That was apparently the plan, but someone interfered."

"Why? Why are you doing this?"

"I'm not behind this." She clucks her tongue. It's a sound I've never heard her make. "I don't agree with this. I wish I'd never discovered what is going on."

"What is going on?"

She points the gun straight at my chest. That's not an answer.

"You don't need to kill me." I inch back.

"If you don't stop where you are, I will have to pull this trigger whether I want to or not. Can you just stand there and wait?"

"You texted someone to come here, didn't you?"

"I didn't sign up for this." Her lips remain clenched and her eyes narrow. Her hands are steady. She's determined. It's the determination I need to be hyperaware of. All she has to do is squeeze her finger.

"What, exactly, is this? I don't get it."

"You really don't know, do you? That's exactly what I fucking told them, too." The words are bitter.

I inch back, and her arms straighten.

"One more inch, and I pull this trigger."

"If I'm going to die anyway, can you tell me what this is all about? I don't understand." *Keep them talking.* It's Sam's voice. His training. His coaching.

"I told them you didn't realize what you uncovered. But it was too big of a risk. You wanted to submit it for peer review. If they opened an investigation, it would have catastrophic implications."

"For organs?" The latest report I saw showed the organ transplant industry to be at two to three billion a year, tops. As far as medical industries go, it's relatively small.

"Use that brain of yours. Everyone thought you'd figured it out. But I was right. You only cared about the organs, right?"

Optimistic headlines flash before me. Headlines touting FDA approvals for drugs Lumina tested. Record breaking profit. Stock prices surging.

"The people in the compound. Lumina International is doing first round tests on them. And when they get sick, they sell their organs. That's why the incidence of cancer is so high on black market organs."

"For select products with tremendous promise, they'll do initial in vivo rounds in alternate locations before testing goes to India and China. It's a way to speed drugs to market."

Everything clicks. "Faster and cheaper than any competitor. And if someone gets sick, you harvest the organs. Which is a contributing factor to the transplant success rate stemming from the black market being so behind US rates. My report highlighted all the data and would've led regulators to Lumina's door. Eventually. Or...was there evidence in the data that would lead them to drugs already on the market?"

Her gaze flicks to the clock hanging on the wall.

I raise my hand. Wrapped around my fingers is a blade.

"Honey. Don't fight me on this." The literal meaning of honey is sweet, but her expression is mean.

"How many are involved?"

"Too many. I don't know them all. There's no way out of this." She actually sounds sad. "I don't have a choice."

I position my legs for stability and lift the blade.

"Didn't anyone ever tell you not to bring a knife to a gunfight?" Her lips curve into an almost smile, but nothing about this situation is smile-worthy.

"I throw knives to relax. I don't miss. Let me leave. If the people you work for are so powerful, they'll find me, right? Just let me go. Like you said, you weren't supposed to be the one to kill me. You are not a killer."

"There's too much at stake. I don't have a choice. I'm sorry."

Her trigger finger flexes.

A flick of my wrist. The blade spins through the air.

My hand is back in my bag, retrieving a second blade. Cool, smooth metal against my fingers.

The first blade strikes.

Directly into her throat.

The gun fires.

It's loud. So loud. I cover my ears.

The gun clatters to the floor.

My blade does too.

One hand clutches her throat.

Blood oozes between her fingers.

Her body remains erect. She wobbles. Her knees give. And she falls.

I told her I don't miss.

I lower my hands from my ears. It's quiet, but there's a distinct burning smell in the air. Reaching into my bag, I remove a third blade and step closer to her, blade ready.

"Tell me, who else is involved?"

Her mouth opens. Blood spills along the white tile near my sandals.

She reaches for me, and her bloody hand clutches my shirt.

"Just tell me. Is it everyone?"

Am I the only one who didn't know? That can't be possible.

Her eyes close. Her chest rises and falls. Blood spreads.

I need to get out of here. But first, I return the unused blades to my bag, and reclaim my blade from her throat and wipe it clean.

CHAPTER 29

Max

Erik's name flashes on my phone screen as I cross the tarmac.

"Erik." The one-word greeting is a tip-off to my mood. This whole mess is confusing as fuck.

"You boarded yet?"

"About to." A pilot in navy slacks and a white, button-down, short-sleeve shirt stands at the top of the stairs. He's holding a water bottle and watching an incoming jet.

"I've got a photo I'm going to text you. It's a frame from the security cameras."

I pause at the base of the stairs and use my hand to shield the sun from the screen. A photo shows Sloane exiting the front entrance of Origins Laboratories.

"She's going back to work there. Didn't I tell you?" I ascend the four steps to the entrance of the jet. Although, she agreed to wait. Matteo probably isn't in place yet. But, why would I expect her to heed potential risks?

"Look at that photo again. There's blood on her shirt. She arrived at 3:25. She exited at 3:52."

"She probably went to deliver a letter." The letter she said she'd sit on for a beat. "They haven't officially hired her back yet."

"Did you not hear me when I said there's blood on her shirt? That wasn't there when she arrived."

The pilot steps back, patiently holding out a hand for me to shake. I ignore him and focus on the still once again. Zoom in. Damn. It's definitely blood. It almost looks like she wiped blood off on herself.

What the hell?

I'm back down the steps at a run. I pop my earbuds in and switch the reception over. "Can you handle canceling the flight? I'm going to find her."

My bags are on a wheeled luggage trolley. I unzip the short duffel that holds my handguns, grab my Glock, load it, and tuck it into the back of my pants.

"Max. Hold up."

I scan the parking lot. I turned my rental car in, but there's a moped with the keys dangling. I'll return it.

"If the intel we're receiving is correct, she could've been a player all along."

"Erik." I've lost all patience with this guy. "You think she's behind someone targeting her sister?"

"Probably not. But she might've just exacted revenge on the person who was."

I sling a leg over the seat and flip the key. The engine putters. He's completely off the mark. "Has anyone come or gone since Sloane left?"

"No."

"Where is she?"

"We traced her phone, and it's at the villa. Is that an engine I hear?"

"Yep."

"Where are you going?"

"You say no one has come or gone from the lab since she left?"

"No one other than a security guard."

"Security patrols the grounds now?"

"Started two days after you two stole a laptop. Nothing suspicious about that."

"I'm going to head to the lab and see what I find."

"Why?"

"Well, you believe she killed someone, right?" The wind skims my face and rifles through my hair.

"Or maimed."

"Here's the thing. I don't buy for a second that Sloane is in on anything. Which means chances are, if she hurt anyone, it was in self-defense. She doesn't have her phone on her, so the best way for me to find her is to track her down. And that's going to where she was last seen."

Erik wisely does not argue.

"Where's Matteo?"

"I'll check." He ends the call.

It takes me fourteen minutes to reach the lab. There are no cars or bicycles in the parking lot, which means if the security guard is still on duty, it's probably the guy who lives nearby. I park the moped on the sidewalk at the side entrance.

The doors are locked, as it's a Saturday. I have nothing on me to pick the lock. My options are to shoot the lock or shatter the glass. I scan the ground for any kind of heavy rock or brick.

"Sir, can I help you?"

I spin to face the security guard. He's wearing pressed khaki shorts and an untucked short sleeve golf shirt with the logo that reads "Island Breeze Security."

"Ah, yes. Thank goodness you're here. Any chance you can let me inside?"

"You work here?"

And here goes. How to spin this?

He probably has a list of employees.

"I received a phone call from my girlfriend. She's hurt. She's inside. Didn't want to call an ambulance or anything."

"What do you mean, she's hurt?"

"She fell. You know, getting something out of one of those top cabinets in the lab. She's not supposed to be using the ladder when there's no one else around. Doesn't want to get in trouble. You know how it is."

"I was just inside. Didn't see anything. But I did hear something. Thought it might be an engine backfiring."

"She's in her lab. Down the back hall. It's ah… room 2A."

"Those doors are closed." He lifts his shirttail and tugs at a keychain that's hooked to his belt loop. "She shoulda called out to me. It's not like I care if she breaks rules. I'm just here to prevent theft."

He unlocks the door, and I push past him. "Thanks, man."

I tear down the hall. There are only two labs in this building that I've been in. Sloane's and Dr. Kallio's.

Smeared blood stains the white tile around the corner, and I sprint. The security guard's footsteps track behind me. He hasn't yet come across the blood, but he'll be there in seconds.

Tracks lead directly to Dr. Kallio's lab. If Sloane did this, she didn't bother to conceal the evidence.

I pull my gun and thrust the door open with all my might, going for the element of surprise. The door slams against the wall. No one faces me. If anyone's in here with a weapon, they're hiding.

The footsteps click down the hall at a fast pace.

A stream of blood flows to the door. Shoe prints. Two styles.

I track the prints.

Find two navy heels. Pants. Blouse.

The chest rises.

She's alive.

The source of blood is a knife wound in her neck.

"What the…"

"Call emergency services. She's alive."

"Shit! Holy fuck." The security guard is not a happy man.

I step forward and check for a pulse. It's faint. There's a lot of blood on this floor.

Her eyelids flutter. "You're going to be okay. We're going to get you help. Can you tell me who did this?"

Her lips move. I bend closer, both to hear her and to examine the wound. The blood flow has slowed, which isn't a good sign.

"Sloane."

The word is unmistakable. I sit back on my heels, taking stock.

It's a knife wound. Sloane killed the nurse with a knife.

I scan the room. And then I see it. A pistol. A Ruger Max-9. Three feet to the side of her.

Fuck. I was right. Self-defense.

CHAPTER 30

Sloane

The police will come for me. Maybe I should go to the police station and turn myself in. But where is it?

My phone is back at the villa. I'll go back, get it, and look up the location of the nearest police station. I'll explain everything. Someone has to believe me. I'll call Max. He'll believe me.

Behind me, a vehicle approaches. My bike is as close to the edge of the asphalt as possible, but the vehicle won't pass.

The front wheel dips off the edge of the asphalt onto the shoulder. The tire grips the packed sand, leaving deep treads behind. The sandy ground requires more effort to pedal. I wave, signaling to the vehicle to pass so I can get back on the road and traverse the smooth asphalt.

But the vehicle sidles beside me, matching my pace. The passenger window lowers.

"Sloane." My wheel wobbles. That voice. It can't be. "Are you okay? Get in the car."

"William? What're you doing here?" He should be in Switzerland.

"Thank god I found you. I know what's happened. Get in."

He can't possibly know what's happened. He's been away for nearly half a year. I push harder on the pedal.

"Sloane. Please. Where're you going?"

"You can't know what happened."

"I know everything. Let me protect you."

I slow, and the bike grinds to a halt. My foot hits the ground to keep the bike upright.

"What do you know?"

"That you're not safe. Are you bleeding? Are you hurt?"

"No."

"Here. Get in the car. Let me help you."

"Where did you come from?"

"Switzerland."

"And you just saw me riding on my bike?"

"No. I came for you. I found Dr. Kallio. Please. Get in."

I push forward on the pedal. I can't process what he's doing here. I don't want to process. All I see is Dr. Kallio.

"Sloane. Where're you going?"

"To my villa. I need my phone."

"Get in. I'll take you."

"I don't own this bike." I can't leave a rented bike on the side of the road.

"We'll put it in the trunk."

Sweat droplets drip from my temple. My thigh muscles burn, as do my shoulders. I slow the push of my feet, and the bike lurches. My feet hit the ground, and I straddle the bike frame once again.

The vehicle stops, and as William gets out of the car, a hotel transport van comes up behind and William waves it on, motioning for the van to pass.

I'm not sure my bike will fit in his trunk. He comes up to my side and places his hand on my shoulder. "Sloane." He pulls me into his arms and presses his lips to my hair. My muscles tense, and I pull back.

"I'm going to get sand in your trunk. If it even fits." The black leather on his pointed business shoes shines in the daylight.

His hands press down on my shoulders. "Are you hurt?"

"I already told you no."

"That's not your blood?"

"No."

"Good. Good. I've been so worried about you."

He opens the passenger door for me, and after I sit, he tugs the seatbelt across me, buckling me in. He presses his lips to my temple, then backs up and slams the door closed.

I jump at the harsh sound. My fingers are freezing.

The trunk pops open, and in the sideview mirror I see I was right. My bike doesn't really fit. The handlebars are a tight fit, and the back wheel hangs out the side.

"Why have you been worried about me?"

"You know I care about you, right?"

No, I don't. Or I guess I do. We worked well together.

"The bike doesn't even fit." There's no way it's not getting sand in his trunk.

"It'll do," William says as he puts the car in drive. "We don't have far to go."

"I'm not going back to my apartment," I tell him. "I need to get onto Church Street. Then it's just a little way."

"We'll do whatever you want."

"I need something at the villa." I bend my head back against the headrest. This isn't William's car. He had a convertible. This looks like an island rental. "What're you doing back?"

"Business."

"Ah." Business. That makes sense. "After we stop by the villa, can we go to the police station?"

"If that's what you want." He adjusts the rearview mirror. "I'm so relieved to see you."

He's dressed in dark tight-fitting jeans and a pressed button-down short-sleeve shirt. The shoes are work shoes, but he never wore jeans when he worked with us. He's not dressed for time on the beach either. There's a nervous air around him that reminds me of the way he was around me after we first had sex. If he thinks that's what we're going to do back at the villa, I need to set him straight. I'm no longer interested. "I met someone."

"Did you?"

"Yes."

"Is he back at the villa?"

"No, he's headed home."

"And you stayed behind?"

"Work." Out the window, the palm trees and cinderblock homes pass at a rapid clip.

His fingers tap the steering wheel. If he hears music, I do not. I roll down my window with a flick of my finger. The messenger bag sits on my lap, and I toy with the flap.

"And how is work going?"

"Awful," I tell him honestly. Dr. Kallio's words float back to me. It wasn't her choice. She was working for other people. People. And he said he knew what happened. He said he found her. "Did you know? Am I the only one who didn't know?"

"Know what?"

"Clinical trial companies are doing early-stage in vivo product testing on captive subjects. Humans." I rub my forehead, then my temple, where a dull pain throbs. "Lumina. Our primary investor. Maybe others." His gaze remains on the road. Both his hands are on the wheel in the ten and two position. "Did you know?"

"Take me through what you know." He ducks slightly and adjusts the rearview mirror again.

"Companies are doing illegal testing to speed products to

market." I narrow my eyes at him. "Lumina. Your employer. They get products to market faster than anyone else. They're the ones who are doing it."

"What evidence do you have?"

I place my right hand on the door handle and keep my left hand inside my messenger bag.

"Sloane?"

"The evidence is in a paper I was preparing for peer review. The paper explores the long-term viability of organ transplants done in black markets versus transplants done in the United States. What I uncovered, using statistical analysis, is that a high number of organs coming from specific markets had a significantly higher rate of cancer occurrence within three years post-surgery."

"That doesn't sound like evidence."

"It's not evidence, per se." I understand William searching for evidence. He's a man of science. But given all that's happened, I was clearly on to something. Something someone out there will kill over. Dr. Kallio was willing to kill for that person. Those people.

Is William one of those people?

"They're doing the research on unwilling subjects." I remember those people I tested. The fear in their eyes and the reluctant compliance.

"That would be problematic."

He flicks the turn signal as we approach the villa where Max and I have been staying.

Click. Click. Click.

I never gave him directions.

"How did you know where I'm staying?"

The gravel churns beneath the wheels as he slows the car to a stop and presses a button to turn the ignition off.

I unsnap the seat belt and open the door. I should've never

gotten in the car with him. Sam's words come to me as my feet touch the ground.

If someone tries to abduct you, never get in the car. Fight like hell.

Twice, now, I've gotten in the car. But I am not defenseless.

The beach is nearby. I can run.

William leans across the seat. His movement is slow, and his dark hair lends him the appearance of a shadow moving within the vehicle.

I can run into the house. Lock the door.

Inside the messenger bag, my fingers grope for steel.

William exits the car. The sunlight flickers against the grays mixed in with his dark strands. His elbow bends. The gun gleams.

He's holding a gun. My William. The man I regularly had sex with.

"So, you never left Origins? That was a lie?"

"Everything I told you was the truth. I was never supposed to be based here for long. My wife wouldn't move, so I agreed to come out and get things going, but the plan was always for me to transition back home."

"You're married?"

He gestures with the end of his gun, waving it between me and the house. "Let's go inside, shall we?"

"You never told me you were married."

"Technically, we were separated. You never seemed to care if I was married or not."

"I would have cared about that. I don't cheat."

"And neither did I. Sloane, I promise you, I care about you. If I didn't…" He closes his eyes and shakes his head while his lips move like he's having a conversation with himself.

"You're married." I trusted him.

"We worked things out when I returned home." He pinches the bridge of his nose. His eyes are closed like he's in pain. I'm the one who should be in pain. He never mentioned a wife to me.

He opens his eyes and uses the gun like it's a pointer in a presentation. "Get inside, Sloane."

There's no advantage to being indoors.

Keep him talking. Sam's voice comes to me.

"You once told me you don't like guns. Was that a lie?"

"No. I can't stand them."

Which means he probably hasn't practiced often. Most people who own guns have horrible aim.

I take a step back, closer to the path along the side of the villa. I can run along the beach. Dive into the water.

"Sloane, I did everything I could to save you." I take a step back. "There's no point in trying to run away. There's no escaping."

"What do you mean, you tried to save me?" Another step back.

"When they told me to handle the situation, I instructed them to keep you alive."

"Was I the situation?"

"Unfortunately. But I never agreed to kill anyone. We were bending some rules. That's all I agreed to."

"But this has been going on for years. It's…how long have you been working for them?"

"I didn't get involved until I moved. I swear. I took over for someone else. It was a good opportunity. That's all."

"You saw the report I was working on, didn't you? You saw my notations that I wanted to submit it for peer review."

"Sloane. You made notations of your plans to submit your findings to peer review on six different communal databases."

"And someone saw that?"

"I told them I could sell you on it. But they saw you as a risk. I should have just walked away. Let it happen. But I couldn't live with myself."

"You mean, if they killed me?"

"I'm not a killer. No one was ever supposed to get hurt. I volunteered to step up and take care of the situation, only so I could keep you safe. My plan had been to move you to Thailand. But I underestimated your connections. You never mentioned anyone other than your sister."

"They sent me to Cambodia."

"That was a temporary location. Didn't they mention that you'd be moved?"

He says this like that makes everything okay. "That place was disgusting."

"I wouldn't have let them keep you there indefinitely. It was… I had to sell the idea, and that worked."

"How did Sage fit into your idea?" Another step back.

"She's your only living relative. I thought she was the only one who would come looking for you. And I knew you loved her. If everything had gone according to plan, you would both have a good life together and you could continue doing your research."

"A good life?"

"Alive."

He's pointing a gun at me. The irony might go over his head, but I am aware.

"How do you know Anton Solonov?"

"Who?" He appears genuinely perplexed.

"The man you hired to drug me and put me on a boat."

"I never knew his name. I was given a number to call. I arranged it by phone and paid through… I just… If I did what they said, you wouldn't be alive. I offered up half of my payout as a bonus if they kept you alive." His words trail and the butt of the gun dips. "Sloane. You have to trust me. I am not a murderer. I didn't want you hurt."

"And you've worked for these people for how long? Since you moved?"

"Sloane. You work for them, too."

"No. I don't. I would never." He's wrong. My chest is too tight.

"Your work isn't close to coming to market. You haven't yet

endured the rigors of clinical testing. Lumina is one of the leaders in clinical testing. We help pharmaceutical companies around the world bring products to market. And there are rewards if we can beat everyone else."

"Am I the only one who didn't know what was going on?" Yes, I kept myself away from others, but it can't be everyone.

"Few know."

"Dr. Kallio?"

"She was recruited because one of the drugs she's overseeing will be going through the expedited process."

"These pharmaceutical companies, do they know what's going on? How Lumina is getting the products to market faster than others?" I take a step back.

"Where do you think you're going?" He takes a step forward. "Even if you get away from me, they'll send someone else. At this point, they know you've involved outside groups. They're not going to let this drop. You've already been discredited. They'll find you and make your death look like a suicide. Your best bet is to come with me. Let me hide you."

They'll send Solonov. Or someone else. That's what he means. "What if I agree to work for these people? I understand why you're sidestepping regulatory testing. I get it. And you're right. It's the fastest way to bring products to market."

"It's the best way forward." He reaches for me, and I step back.

I do not want him to touch me.

I step back. He steps forward.

"Now that you understand, would you be willing to join us? Work with us?"

"Yes." My lie is automatic.

"Well, let's go upstairs. Into the villa. Let's talk about it."

"Are you going to put the gun away?" He's still holding it.

He wavers, uncertain.

Run. It's Sam's voice. My heart feels like it's going to pound out of my chest.

"I risked my life to save you. And now you're playing me, aren't you?" Another step back. "You don't plan on working with us. You may think you're safer outside, but that's not the case. Yes, outside someone will hear the gun go off. But we're on a vacation island. Chances are anyone who hears will assume it's a car backfiring."

"Then just shoot me." One more step, and I'll be close enough to the corner of the villa I can take off running. It's a risk. But the farther away I am, the more likely he'll miss. I've never known William to practice target shooting. He can't be a good marksman.

But then again, I didn't know he was married.

The hum of a combustion engine steals William's attention.

And I'm off. Running.

My feet slip on the sandy path.

My gaze locks on the dunes.

Run.

Faster.

Run.

"Sloane!"

Max.

I spin, searching for him.

My chest heaves.

What's Max doing here?

Max's hands are up in the air in a defensive posture, but he's moving forward at a quick pace. And William's gun points at his chest.

"He'll shoot," I warn Max.

Slow down.

As if hearing my thoughts, Max slows his steps.

"Are you okay?" He directs his question to me. But Max is trained like Sam. And Sam would attack. That's what Sam would do. If he lunges for William, he'll be shot. William won't miss from so close to his target. At that distance, the bullet will kill him.

"I'm okay," I answer, edging around the corner of the villa, getting closer to Max. "Please be careful."

"Interesting request. Pretty sure you were supposed to stay put."

William's legs spread into a wide stance.

"William, please don't shoot him."

"This is your guy, huh?"

Max's hands are out at his side. He's not going to back down. Sam wouldn't.

"Put the gun down. Please."

"You know I can't do that."

He trains his gun on Max. All he has to do is squeeze his finger. He'll hit Max straight in the chest. In his heart.

William turns his head to me while his gun remains trained on Max.

With a flick of my wrist, the blade spins through the air.

Bullseye.

Literally.

William's body shifts. And then tumbles to the ground.

"Christ!" Max shouts.

My fingers wrap around another blade. It's automatic. Throw one. Grab the next. No time to spare in case of a miss. Sam trained me.

Max is before me, holding my shoulders. His hand goes to my cheek then lifts my chin. "Sloane, are you okay?"

His bright blue eyes question. His pupils are so tiny in the bright sunlight.

"He would've hurt you." My lips curl, and I instinctively inhale to hold back the tidal wave of peptide hormones. "I couldn't let him hurt you."

CHAPTER 31

Max

Using my body as a shield, I both protect Sloane from the man on the ground and from her seeing the destruction sown by her blade.

The silver blade sticks out from the eye socket where the tango took a direct hit to the left eye. The blade has to be inches inside the cranium.

His hand rises from the ground. He's conscious, and it looks like he might attempt to move the knife.

The handgun lies inches from his side.

I kick it away, choosing to ensure my fingerprints aren't on it.

The guy on the ground appears dazed. He's most likely in shock. Suffering from a brain injury. Hemorrhaging, perhaps.

I pull out my phone and dial emergency services.

The man on the ground's uninjured eyelid closes and his head lolls to the side.

"Who is he?" I ask as the phone rings.

"He would've shot you. I couldn't let him." Sloane's voice is shaky. She looks fucking petrified, but if she'd given me five more seconds, I would've taken the guy out.

I press my finger to his neck. His pulse is plenty strong. There's little blood stemming from the eye socket, which says to me he's most likely hemorrhaging internally. Judging from the placement of the handle, my guess is the blade extends four inches into his brain matter. It's fascinating he didn't die instantly.

"Where'd you learn to throw knives?"

"Sam. I don't like guns. He said I had to learn self-defense."

Throwing knives is one helluva self-defense. "In your apartment. That enormous block of wood. It wasn't art, was it? You use that to practice."

"Knife throwing relaxes me."

Off in the distance, sirens wail.

"Guns are loud. I don't like them."

Sloane's messenger back hangs in front of her body. One hand still lingers inside the flap.

"You got more knives in there?"

She lifts the flap. The inside is custom designed to hold flat blades. Below the blades are star-shaped knives. Christ. Absolutely savage.

Sloane's skin is flushed. Her eyes are glassy. Her index finger rubs back and forth over her thumbnail.

There's nothing I can do for the putz on the ground. But I can calm Sloane.

The sirens grow louder, cutting through the breeze. A passenger van zips by on the road, unaware of the tragedy on the drive.

"You sure you're okay?" I pull her to my side. Her arms are stiff, one hand still tucked inside the messenger bag.

"I'm not hurt."

I'm not so positive I agree with her. Years in the military have taught me there's a vast array of wounds, and the nonphysical can be as lethal as the physical.

"You always carry weapons with you?"

"Not always. But most of the time. Sage is the optimist. I'm the realist."

The sirens grow louder, and they'll be here any minute.

"You ready to answer questions? Medics will be here soon."

"I'll tell them everything. Do you think I'll go to jail for the rest of my life?"

"What? No. This was self-defense." She's so stiff in my arms. I rub my palm in a brisk motion up and down her arm, trying to bring her back to me, to the present. "Dr. Kallio was self-defense, too. I saw the gun."

"They both wanted to kill me."

"Do you know why?"

"Their boss told them to kill me. William was the one who wanted to keep me alive."

"Is that right?"

"They're using those people in the compounds to test all kinds of things. When they get a formulation that works, they begin ethical testing under legal scrutiny. My guess is there are drugs already on the market that were tested this way, and if this all came out, those drugs would have to be recalled. Both Dr. Kallio and William mentioned other people. Neither of them wanted to kill me." Her glazed eyes have me wondering if she's seeing anything.

I press the side of her head to my chest and wrap an arm around her, wishing I could remove her from all of this.

"Is Dr. Kallio dead?"

"Yeah." The ambulance will be here any second, but I'm not feeling particularly optimistic about the outlook for the man on the ground, either.

"I couldn't let William hurt you."

"Sometimes death saves life."

"Sam. He used to say that. You said it too."

The ambulance careens into the driveway, and the front doors open. A man in a uniform with jaw length dreadlocks steps forward, mouth open, aghast at what he's seeing.

"Aw, man. What the hellz happened here?" He bends to check the pulse. "Roger, get the gurney."

He glances up at us. "What happened?"

"Self-defense." I answer and gesture to the handgun.

"All right, man," he says, concern etched on his features as he no doubt evaluates the two of us.

He's joined by a man in a matching uniform, two tattoo sleeves, a silver hoop earring, and a shaved head.

The two men work in concert, and in less than sixty seconds, William is on a gurney and they're attaching an IV while wheeling him to the back of the ambulance.

The man with dreadlocks calls out to us as he's jumping into the driver's seat. "Wait here. The police will be here shortly to ask you questions."

"Yes, sir." I answer, but the ambulance is backing away before I finish.

We could leave and easily make it to the tarmac to get out of here before anyone connects our identities with the two knife attacks. But we're working with the law. Not against them.

The siren becomes more distant. I'm certain other sirens will come our way soon.

I text the team, letting them know what's happened and we'll be heading to the police station after they arrive on the scene. Erik texts that Matteo should be here in about an hour. I let him know we won't need him now. I'm not leaving Sloane's side.

Sloane's muscles are tight. Her body is like a board pressed against mine. "So, you're a knife thrower, huh? And you didn't think to share that with me when I asked about your hobbies?"

"I didn't want you to think I'm weird."

"Yeah, well, I kind of love your weird."

She sniffles and buries her face into my shirt. "Shh." I press my lips to the top of her head and hold her as tightly against me as I can. Emotion is good. She needs to feel it. Taking life is hard. You've got to do it a lot before it doesn't faze you, before that piece of humanity is wiped away.

"I can't believe I was a part of something like this. How could I have been so stupid?"

"Doesn't sound like you were a part of anything. You had the misfortune of discovering what's going on."

She sniffles. "I just keep seeing those faces. The people in the compound." She presses the side of her face hard against my chest. "They need to be rescued. You know that, right?"

The compound situation is a political shit show. But whoever is in charge made some serious missteps, because by going after the Watson sisters, they brought the sordid mess under scrutiny instead of brushing it under the rug as intended. "Interpol's following this. The crimes cross borders. This is their jurisdiction. They'll get involved."

"That meeting in D.C. I'll tell them whatever they need to know."

"I'll be there with you." My hope that the meeting will ultimately lead to US involvement in affairs in Asia isn't great. My guess is back in D.C. they just want intel.

"I don't need protection. You can go home." Her clipped words are bitter, but her body's saying something else. She's leaning into me, and damn if I don't love it.

"You may not need protection, but I'm still gonna be there. There's no one else like you, Sloane. You're going to have a hard time getting rid of me."

"You're the only person who says I'm different and makes it sound like it's a good thing."

"For someone who is so incredibly brilliant, you can be slow on the uptake."

"I know." She sniffles. "I should've figured out earlier what was going on. I should've refused to do anything they asked in Cambodia—"

"Sloane, I'm not talking about that."

I cup her chin and gently urge her to tilt those dark eyes upward. "I've fallen hard for you, Sloane Watson. You'd better believe I'm going to be by your side. Sure, Sam taught you well. But you're a better team player than anyone gives you credit for."

"Only with you."

"Exactly. And that's how it should be."

CHAPTER 32

Sloane

The Bodden Town Police station features spacious windows in a one-story building. They delivered us to this branch of the Royal Cayman Islands police service due to proximity and, as Officer Bogle explained, because of the serious nature of the incidents, the Criminal Investigation Department, or CID, must investigate them.

I expected handcuffs and multiple police officers shouting at me in an interrogation room, but I'm sitting in an open area with uniformed officers and regular people. Curious glances fall on me as they come and go. The distant voices in the solemn space sound hushed and blur into background noise.

In the open corridor, one detective asked me questions while another took notes. One officer pressed play on his phone to record the five-minute session where I explained what happened. The officer forced me to repeat myself.

"And you threw the knife? Both times? Just...threw it?"

"Yes, sir."

"You threw the knife?"

"That's what I said, sir."

"Right, then."

The detectives expressed far more fascination with knife throwing than whether I indeed acted in self-defense.

Thomas Edison famously said that until we stop harming all other living beings, we are still savages. I became a vegetarian because of his words. Attempted veganism, but vegan cheese is gross, and I'm so particular about food that a vegan diet simply would not work for me. Ironically, my eating habits don't matter at all. I am savage. There is no defense. Perhaps I don't deserve to go to jail under the current system of laws, but deep down, I do not regret my actions. Maybe I should have let Dr. Kallio kill me. But I would never let William hurt Max. I will kill again and again to keep Max safe. Sage used to be the only one, but now Max has joined her in the small circle of those I will kill to protect.

"Are we going to get that rain, do you think?" one officer asks another.

"Nah, Carly said last she saw, the radar shows it's blowing to the south of us. Might get some sprinkles, but nothing much."

Max strokes my back, the movement subtle and comforting. As promised, he hasn't left my side.

"I wish I had a book with me. Something to take my mind off what's going on around me."

"One of those romance books?"

He's teasing me.

"Nothing's wrong with a good love story."

I narrow my eyes at him, and he tips my chin up and presses his lips to mine.

Good sensations swarm in my chest. I rest my head against his shoulder and admit, "You're one of the few people I've ever told that I love romance books. Well, you and Sage."

"I'm honored. Maybe one day we can read one together." I pull back, wrinkling my nose. I'm not sure about that at all. He grins his sexy grin, and I know if he pushes, I'll read with him. Or maybe we can listen to an audiobook together.

His phone buzzes, and I absentmindedly read the text.

GINGER

I thought you'd be back by now. Is everything ok?

He thumbs back his response.

MAX

Y. Don't know when I'll return.

"Who is that?"

"My ex." His nails lightly scratch over my bra strap. "I told you about her."

"What does she mean?"

"You know she's staying at my place, right? She thought I'd be back."

"She's waiting on you?"

"I suppose."

The desire to pull away rises, so I do.

"Hey. She's nothing for you to worry about. She could be the last woman on Earth, and I wouldn't get back together with her."

"Does she know that?" The response comes out too quickly, and I cover my lips with my fingers. "Forget I said that. What needs to be said is that I don't like the idea of you going back to her. I don't have a right to not like it, but I don't like it."

"Duly noted." His hand returns to my back, and when I look over my shoulder, he's grinning.

"What?"

"I really like that you tell me what you're thinking. That's all."

And then he leans forward and brushes his lips across my cheek up to my ear. "You're the only one I want, Sloane."

A warmth infuses me, and it's from his words. The fact is easy to discern. And I'm about to let him know I feel the same way when the door to the outside swings open, and a man in a suit with a shaved head and a short salt and pepper beard approaches, extending his dark hand. I rise from the wooden chair and take his hand as he says, "I'm the Detective Superintendent. I'm given to understand you've come into some trouble on our fair island."

His hold on my hand is firm, his skin rough. His nails are cut short and filed evenly. The contrast of our skin color is striking, his deep ebony, mine pale and ghostly white.

He releases my hand and takes Max's. "And I understand you're with a company based in the United States? Maxwell Hawkins?"

"Yes, sir."

"There's a gentleman from Interpol waiting to speak with you. Well, he would like to speak with you both, but I'm hoping to get some time with Ms. Watson."

The Detective Superintendent's shoes are polished black leather with dusty creases. His suit hangs loose, and the lapels are creased unevenly in two locations, like maybe a heavy object weighed down on the suit coat and wrinkled it.

"Ms. Watson and I are together," Max says.

"Oh, in a professional or—"

"She's my girlfriend." It's the first time anyone has ever called me their girlfriend, and my face warms, quickly followed by a warmth blossoming in my chest cavity.

"Ah, I see. Well, unless you're married—"

"I'm not leaving her." Max's palm flattens on my lower back, and I fight the impulse to lean into his side.

"It's okay, Max. I'll be all right."

A tall, lithe man with black hair brushed back from a widow's peak enters the open room. His suit fits him perfectly, a sharp contrast to the detective's loose-fitting, wrinkled clothes. He's familiar. It takes me a second to place him. It's the man from the hospital.

"Charles, why don't we let them stay together?" The man possesses an air of superiority.

He steps directly to Max, hand extended. "Tristan Voignier. Interpol. A pleasure to see you again." His distinct European accent sets him apart from the others in the police station.

"Max visited Cayman Brac recently," Tristan says to the detective.

He did?

"Ah, yes. He was part of the team that trespassed at St. Luke's Hostel, was he?" the detective asks.

Tristan says only, "Not without reason."

I'm confused. Why did Max visit a hostel?

"So you say," responds the detective. He's smiling, as is the tall man, and I get the feeling I'm missing out on a joke.

"Charles, did you say you have a private room for us to meet in?"

"Oh, yes, my office. Right this way."

Max's fingers intertwine with mine, connecting us.

"Why did you trespass?"

Max smiles down at me. "It was when we were looking for you. It's nothing." He squeezes my hand, and I take it to mean he doesn't want to talk about it further.

Max guides me to a chair and drags another up beside it. Tristan Voignier closes the door behind us, shutting the four of us in a small room. This is the interrogation room I expected.

"First, may I say what a relief it is to find you alive and well, Ms. Watson."

I keep my gaze set on the floor, quite conscious that to comment on his statement might be perceived as defensive or inflammatory.

"Tristan, are you here because you have information?" Max's direct question strikes the confrontational tone I aim to avoid.

"Charles, would you mind if we have the room?" Tristan asks.

"For you? Not a problem. I'll visit the hospital and check on William Salo. Based on what you've told me, we'll set up security for him, should he stabilize."

I lose the will to fight leaning into Max. His arm curves around me, tucking me against him. "Do they think I'll go after him?"

My question is to Max, but I hear someone chuckle. Based on the throaty intonations, my guess is it's the Detective Superintendent laughing at me.

"No, they don't think you'll go after him," Max says to the room.

"Personally, I doubt he'll be much more than a vegetable should he survive, but it appears you've exposed some powerbrokers, Ms. Watson. Chances are good they won't want a liability sitting around in a hospital bed."

William was married, and I had sex with him. Many times. Oddly, no one has asked me about my relationship with William. If I were a detective working this case, I would ask those questions.

"Ms. Watson, can you please look at me while we have this discussion?" Tristan pulls out a chair and crosses a leg over his knee, exposing a pale, bony ankle and foot. His leather loafers bear a logo I've seen before but can't recall the brand name.

He's classically handsome, with an angular jaw and a straight nose. His lips don't smile, but his eyes do.

He yawns, and his hand graciously covers his mouth. "Please forgive me. I've been traveling."

"Because of me?"

"No, love." His fingers tap against his leg, and when I brave a glance, he's still smiling. "I was following Mr. Salo. Our sources of information are quite dependable, but they aren't so brilliant as to foresee today's turn of events."

"What can you tell us?" Max asks.

"I'm rather hoping you can tell me more than what you told the detectives."

"You listened to the tape?"

"Yes, I listened to the interview with the officer." He studies me. I feel the weight of his gaze, and my nerves spike. "You don't need to worry, Ms. Watson. Your character is not being questioned. What I'm most interested in, now that we understand the situation, is who the players are. Are there any names you can share?"

"No." Max's thumb crosses over the back of my hand like a windshield wiper, but I force my gaze to remain on Tristan, as he's the one asking the questions. "I didn't believe Dr. Kallio was involved until she made it known to me. Max tried to tell me, but...."

"And Mr. Salo?"

"It never would have occurred to me," I answer honestly. "He moved to Switzerland to work for Lumina International. I didn't think he was associated with us anymore."

"Did you get to know many of the executives from Lumina?"

"None. Yes, they are our lead investor, but I wasn't invited to any of the investor meetings. When investors visited, I would occasionally be introduced to them if they stopped by my lab, but that wasn't often, and I never paid close attention to the names or the faces. But Dr. Kallio and William made it clear there are others. I don't know if Lumina is the only company using the people in those compounds as test subjects or not. Neither of them said. But they both mentioned other people."

"Do you think it's likely this group will still come after Sloane?" Max asks the question of Mr. Voignier, and I stare at the scratched wooden chair leg waiting for the answer.

Mr. Voignier folds his hands, giving the question consideration.

"I don't expect they'd be keen to pursue her. Their failures in pursuing her have done quite enough damage. But once this mess is sorted, a wise course of action would be for Ms. Watson to return to the United States while this investigation continues." It's hard to swallow. "I have some connections. I'm willing to assist with your search for a research position if you'll do something for me."

"What?"

"This is confidential."

"I won't tell anyone." I glance up at Max, my boyfriend. "We won't tell anyone," I clarify.

"Quite right. As we investigate this matter, we need you to be a resource." I don't understand. "We simply ask that you be available to answer questions that might arise."

"Absolutely."

"We may need you to testify in an international court."

Max stiffens beside me. "I'll testify, if it helps. I don't have much information. I don't know any names. I'm awful with names, actually. And faces."

"I understand." Tristan's foot falls to the ground, and there's a finality to the movement, like he's done, and this is all that will be said.

"But I have questions. Are you going to rescue those people in Cambodia?"

"It's not a simple matter." He doesn't look happy. "One of the owners of those compounds is a wealthy, connected man and claims those people work there of their own free will and accord."

"That's not true."

"We're aware. Most of them are the equivalent of indentured servants. But we haven't gotten involved because there are situations like that all over the world, and it's a political quagmire. However, now that we know they're being used for illegal medical testing, it's a higher priority. But shuttering one compound won't end anything if we don't determine which company, or companies, are doing this, and who their customers are."

"William said it's a group within Lumina."

"Lumina International employs forty-six thousand people across the globe. It's a conglomerate of multiple entities."

"And you need evidence that ties to specific people?"

"Precisely."

"I don't have any names." I wish I did. While I wholeheartedly condone medical testing on humans, testing people against their will, or even under duress, is unequivocally unethical. "Typically, the first stages of human research are completed in India or China as both countries have less stringent legal standards. It's confusing to me why a testing firm would risk its reputation by doing initial testing elsewhere unless all they needed to do was test dosage. I could see a potential business reason to rush human testing to narrow the test parameters before taking it to the medical trial stage. Medical trials can last years. If there was a single parameter, like dosage, that you were uncertain about, you could shave off time. But, based on what I found, the testing was done years ago."

"And the drug would already be out in the market." He straightens his cufflink absentmindedly. "So, you don't think this testing is still ongoing?"

"No. Based on what I saw in Cambodia, I think it is. It would be done for products with significant potential financial gain and a reason to rush to market. That's what you'd need to look for."

"Competitive pressure."

"Exactly. But I don't know how Origins Labs was connected or why. We don't even do our own testing. We hire third parties to conduct the testing for ethical reasons. My best guess would be to look at who William worked with at Lumina headquarters in Switzerland."

He covers his lips with four fingers. His gold watch glints in the light. With a sigh, his hand leaves his lips and rests on the back of a chair. "So, knife throwing."

"Her brother taught her. He served with me," Max interjects.

"He passed away?" Tristan asks.

"Two years ago," I answer.

"I'm sorry for your loss."

It's an autopilot statement. Like 'have a nice day' or 'it's nice to meet you.'

"Ms. Watson?"

"Yes?"

"Can you take me through the report you wrote? We have some questions about the methods you used to extrapolate the data and the source files."

"We? Meaning Interpol?"

"Precisely."

"You're going to continue working on this case?"

"Most certainly. You have my word."

CHAPTER 33

Max

One Week Later

"All things under control there?"

I'm standing outside a conference room at the National Security Agency. Sloane is inside, in a meeting Jack Sullivan and Ryan Wolfgang arranged. If it weren't for their assurances I can trust these people, I would've insisted on remaining with her the entire time. But I trust Jack and Ryan.

In the room meeting with her are some I'm familiar with, such as Jack's daughter, Sophia Sullivan, a CIA officer, and Fisher, a former Arrow employee turned CIA operative, and the brother-in-law of Erik from Arrow's IT department, Logan, who coincidentally works for the NSA.

The question session evolved into a slide show of faces asking Sloane who she recognized from the Origins Laboratory, Lumina International, and Cambodia.

I stepped outside to take this call from Knox.

"It's good. Typical intel gathering. How're things there?"

"All good. We're moving into the rental this weekend."

"You still a happily engaged man?"

It was just a couple of days ago he asked and she said yes, but when we've touched base, we haven't been in a place to shoot the shit.

"I've never been more certain about anything in my life. This is right."

"I'm happy for you. I think she's good for you."

"How so?"

Sage is this tiny scrap with a giant heart. Whereas my Sloane is strong and lethal. She's tougher to get to know, but what's underneath is every bit as steadfast as Sage, and god help anyone who threatens someone she loves. And I'm one lucky SOB to fall into that category.

"What do you mean?" Knox asks again when I don't respond quickly enough for the new fiancé.

"I just think she's crazy in love with you and the two of you are going to be good together."

"Thanks. I agree. Things there are going okay? If Sage didn't have school, she'd be there right now."

"Tell her not to worry. They're just picking her brain."

"Room full of suits?"

"More or less. Some khakis and sports jackets thrown in for good measure, along with a couple of dresses and low heels."

"Does the scene have you jonesing to join the CIA, or NSA, or any other government acronym?"

"Not at all." I'm about done with uniforms of all varieties. Definitely done with all the formalities. "You know, Interpol's here too. Our contact, Tristan Voignier. In the room with her now."

"That's interesting."

"I concur. I'm glad Erik and the team proved all the shit posted was meant to shade her credibility. Otherwise, I'd be nervous they suspect her."

"Whoever tried to frame her was sloppy. The whole operation was sloppy. But it's all done, right? No one's thinking anyone's coming after Sage—"

"No, everyone here believes our girls are in the clear. These meetings have been about gaining intel to stop some of the lowlifes behind this sick operation."

"Our girls. Strange to hear you say that."

"Yeah, well." Truth is, I didn't see myself in another serious relationship for some time. But that time has come.

"A ring in your future?"

I try to imagine Sloane's reaction to a ring, but the conference room door opens. "Gotta run. Meeting's over."

I end the call, completely forgetting all about Knox as my gaze locks on Sloane. She's exhausted. A full day of interaction with strangers sucks the energy right out of her. I get that. What she needs is for me to get her back to our hotel, order room service, possibly a cheese pizza, and to let her decompress with a massage or her favorite form of exercise—sex.

"How'd it go?" I ask her.

"I don't think I helped." She's got bloodshot eyes, and her nails are worn down to the nubs. She must've started biting them after I left.

I wrap her in my arms. These few days have been tough for her. "Are you done?" I glance at the wood-paneled door behind her. "Do you have to go back in?"

"No." Her arms wrap around my waist, and her chin rests on my shoulder. "Tristan made some phone calls. I have an interview scheduled for tomorrow at a biotech firm in Delaware. They're doing the same cellular regeneration research I was doing."

"Really?"

"Will you come with me?"

"Of course."

"No, I mean, if I take the job. Will you…"

Her hesitation says she can't complete the sentence. But I can.

"Are you asking me to move with you?" She shrugs, and I follow her gaze to the floor. "If we can find a place together, I'll move."

"Well, you'd need to see the place. You might not like it. I don't know the area."

"If we don't like Wilmington, we can live in Philly or someplace nearby."

"You'd want to live with me?"

"You think we'd live in the same area and not spend the night together?"

Her dark eyes narrow and her head slowly moves back and forth. "What about your job?"

"I'll work it out."

"You know, they might not like me. I might not get the job."

"Hey." I lift her chin and stroke her cheek until she gives me those dark eyes for a precious second. "Work will work itself out. We've got other things to worry about."

"Like what?"

"Feeding you."

"You like feeding me."

She's right. I do. I can't wait to get in a kitchen and experiment. The fridge in the hotel room we're staying in was set too cold, and I inadvertently learned she loves frozen grapes.

She presses her lips to the side of my neck, and I close my eyes, reveling in contentment. Her teeth tug on my earlobe.

"There's one thing I want you to do for me, though."

"What's that?" I'm pretty sure I'll do anything she asks me.

"Stop the injections. It's an unnecessary risk, and they can harm your heart. I've only done a little research, but I don't like you taking unnecessary risks."

"Okay. Done."

"Really?"

"Yeah." I like that she cared enough to research what I'm taking. I like that she cares. After all, I care about her. "I wasn't doing any of the crazy stuff, anyway."

She narrows her eyes. "If you say so."

"I do."

"Good. Because I need you to stay healthy. I need you in my life." She says it like it's an admission, a weakness, but hearing those words does good things for my soul.

"Right back at you." She might not fully understand how true that statement is, but I have lots of time to show her.

EPILOGUE

Sloane
Three Years Later

"Sloane?"

Max appears in the doorway wearing an unbuttoned flannel shirt over a t-shirt that hugs his muscles in all the right places. He's not as muscular as he used to be, but he's still book-cover-worthy. He spends hours in the gym, which balances his newfound love of cooking. To ease some of his joint pain, he's transitioned from triathlons and crazy extreme races to rowing. As expected, he competes when possible, and often wins. When he can't get out on the water, he jumps on his rowing machine and competes virtually against folks all around the country. Some days he's up at four a.m. to get his workout routine in.

His mom once asked me if his competitive nature bothered me, and it was the strangest question. He never complains that I don't care for most food. Why would I complain about his habits? As long as he's healthy, there's no reason to complain.

That seems to be his take on me too. He's constantly leaving chopped-up cheese or mini pizzas on my desk. He sets out vitamins for me every morning, and he's perfected my all-time favorite morning smoothie.

He's not even a scientist, but he's become my favorite person.

For my part, I learned how to massage him, both with a handheld machine and my hands. I have cold compresses in the freezer and heating pads in the closet. He still goes regularly to a professional masseuse, but he says no one kneads his muscles like I do. We both get a lot out of his massage sessions.

His gaze falls to the present I'm attempting to wrap. The pale-yellow wrapping paper has little rubber duckies all across it. I had hoped the ducks would allow me to cut a straight line.

"Are you using a ruler?"

I'm wrapping presents for Sage and Knox's baby shower. Max told me I didn't need to buy everything on her gift registry, and I didn't. But I did make a habit of checking it periodically and purchased everything others did not purchase within the first week. I'm her sister, and I'm allowed to do that.

It's imperative she have everything she asks for, although I strongly disagree with her decision to wait to learn the gender. That makes absolutely no sense to me.

"I'm not good at wrapping presents." It's not something I typically worry about, but there will be a lot of people at the shower, and I don't want these gifts to look like a child wrapped them.

"You did a good job on those." He points to two presents I didn't wrap.

"The one without a bow is from Tristan and Lucia."

"Why'd they ship it here?"

"Because it's a surprise baby shower." I'm throwing the shower for Sage, and it's the first party I've ever thrown. Knox handled the guest list.

Tristan and Lucia plan on coming to the States after the baby is born. Max and I are going to meet them in Asheville and then travel with them for a long weekend in Napa. Sage and Knox won't be able to join us because they'll have a baby.

Sage's life is about to change. I still wish she wasn't doing this to herself, but I have accepted it and support her.

"Oh. I almost forgot. Another present arrived. It's already wrapped."

"What company is it from?"

"There's no return address. No shipping label." He leaves and returns with a box wrapped in shiny silver paper.

I frown at the box. "I have no idea what that is."

"You'll be surprised at the shower. As it stands, I'd say Sage is going to be thrilled with everything you're doing."

"These presents need bows. I was thinking I would add them when we get set up."

Sage believes she's coming to eat dinner at Edison's, a restaurant at The Grove Park, to celebrate the publication of my research study. When they enter, they'll walk into a room filled with balloons, presents, and friends. Knox and Jimmy invited almost the entire school. It was hard to get Edison's reserved, but it has a great view of the mountains, and it's a place Sage once told me she likes.

"When are your parents getting in?"

"In a few hours."

Max's parents are driving up from Florida and staying with us. I wish his parents could have met mine, because I think they would have liked each other.

I can't stop looking at the silver present. "Where's the box that came in?"

"Already broke it apart and put it in recycling."

"Max, there has to be something in there that will tell us who it's from."

"I promise you. There wasn't anything."

He grins his sexy grin. It's what he does when he needs me to chill out. And then he steps closer, and his pupils expand, which is what happens when his mind is on sex.

"If we're going to do that, then you have to wrap the rest of these presents."

"Getting tired?"

"I have five paper cuts."

"Hmm." He presses his lips to one particularly sore reddish cut. "Poor baby."

I lift his hand and press a kiss above his wedding band. We got married in Vegas over a year ago.

Marriage isn't something I ever wanted. It's not something I ever thought I'd agree to. But Max had a friend's bachelor party in Vegas. He convinced me to join him by telling me I'd love the hotel and I could spend time in the Canyon Ranch spa. I went mostly so I wouldn't be away from Max for too long. And we were walking by a chapel, not one with Elvis but another, normal-looking chapel without a line, and he asked me if I'd spend the rest of my life with him.

And I told him I hoped to. And he asked if I'd be willing to wear his ring.

And I told him only if he'll wear one, too.

And he said excellent.

He tried to guide me into the chapel, and I reminded him I'm an atheist. And he said he understood, but that it would mean the world to his parents if we took this step, and without him saying it, I understood. They mean the world to him.

An hour later, we were in the chapel. He told me we could do a big ceremony later if I wanted. But I don't want to. What we did was perfect, between us, and we have it on video, and his parents are happy. And so is Max. I want Max to be happy.

When Sage got married, she had a million images on Pinterest boards. Thankfully, I'm a spreadsheet queen, and in half a day we had her wedding planned and budgeted. On the day of her wedding, I kept thinking it was just like Mom and Dad would have wanted. We left spots for them in the family row, and lit candles for Mom, Dad, and Sam.

Marriage didn't make much sense to me, but I wanted it to be perfect for my little sister. And now that I have a husband of my own, I understand. I don't think I'll ever tire of seeing that platinum band on his ring finger because it means he's mine. He's my person.

His lips press against my throat, then find the spot right below my ear.

"Is everything ready in the guest room?"

"Yep."

I tug at his shirt as he backs me up to the wall.

Neither of us is working today. I never took vacation days before, but Max makes them worthwhile.

"Are you thinking up against the wall?"

I like it when he presses me against a wall and takes me. I like it on a table. The kitchen counter. The sofa. Shower. Anywhere with Max.

He doesn't answer, just gives me a lazy smile. And then he claims me. In the most savage way possible. And I love it.

THE END

Up next is Tristan's story, in Sinful Beauty.

When he lures the girl, it's just another day undercover until the unthinkable occurs...

She steals his heart and disappears.

Tristan

London, England

"Saint" peers into the conference room, checks the backside of the wooden door, glances over his shoulder, and enters, closing the door behind him.

An untraceable shell company reserved all the meeting rooms at St. Martin in the Fields. His caution is quite unnecessary, but I suppose it's habit.

Saint's gaze locks on a small white dome in the right quadrant of the ceiling.

"The camera has been deactivated," I assure him. "Our team currently controls the video stream on the property. Anyone monitoring will observe you entering the church, but they'll never see what you did inside."

"Hated the safe house, did you?"

Saint's question deserves the truth. "Required a bath after quitting the space."

Saint snorts and steps up to the refreshments a lovely woman named Patricia prepared an hour earlier. He passes over the wine and tea, opting for water.

"Do you know why this room is called the Peter Benenson room?"

Saint's an amenable chap, but he may not play along with my trivial question. I sit back, assessing his mood.

"He made a sizable donation to the church?"

"Reasonable guess. In 1961 Peter visited St. Martin's to reflect on two students imprisoned in Portugal for drinking a toast to freedom. From the pews of this historic sanctuary, Amnesty International was born."

Saint places the plate and glass on the table. He balls a hand into a fist and twists his neck, eliciting a cracking noise. "Two students. Does this story relate to two sisters?"

"Only in the loosest of senses." He picks up a scone, sets it on a small plate, and his nostrils flare. The American does not look pleased. "If you wish to meet elsewhere next time, we can. I recommend the countryside, far from London surveillance."

I'll meet anywhere, except the CIA's dodgy safe house. I stand out on that side of town. With London surveillance getting tighter by the day, and too many with access, precautions are warranted.

Saint pulls out a chair, flips it around, and sits on it backward, legs wide, facing me and not the table. His cowboy boots add to his American aura, a role he's been playing for so long I suspect it's become ingrained in his nature.

"The sisters are safe?" He looks me directly in the eye, reading me, weighing if he can trust me.

"Quite safe. I was with Sloane Watson in Washington D.C. two nights ago. She's unharmed and doing well. I helped her find a suitable research position stateside."

He shifts in his seat, moves one arm beneath his suit jacket, and lifts a handgun. He sets it on the table, barrel pointed to the frosted glass wall.

My gaze flicks between Saint and the handgun.

"I'm your friend, you know?" I'm not blowing shit up his arse. I've been his contact for years. Saint is deep undercover on a mission with the highest level of security, so high that I've only been partially briefed, and I'm in an elite group within Interpol with uppermost clearance.

"It was uncomfortable."

I narrow my eyes, deciphering his explanation for placing a gun on the table.

In my humble opinion, Saint's been too deep for too long. A man can lose himself when all his effort is spent pretending to be someone he's not. But he's not working for us, and it's not my call. I'm his liaison. His lifeline. He'd better damn well see me as a friend.

"Wasn't tickle fucking you. The gun really was uncomfortable." A trace of amusement plays across his face. It's not a smile, but the lips soften reflecting humor. It's good to see he's still capable of humor. "What else do you have?"

"Too little. We're tracking William Salo's colleagues and super-visors. If he wakes, he'll be a valuable intel source, but the doctors aren't optimistic. We've looked into the employee Sage Watson spoke with who claimed Sloane resigned. She's an executive assistant. Interestingly, she has family members in prison in Brazil, but we have yet to uncover a connection."

Saint's eyes narrow into slits, his head tilts, and his lips purse. "I've dug around on my end. The syndicate isn't behind it. But whoever is has Russian connections."

"We're looking for Russians?"

"All roads lead to Russia." He snorts at his dimwitted joke, scratches his jaw, and grows serious. "You're looking for a wealthy, connected individual or individuals with connections to a Russian cartel. My source says the contact is an older man, Swiss. I don't have a name for you. But it's someone within Lumina." An older

Swiss man matches the profile of a significant percentage of Lumina employees.

"Who's your source?"

"The information won't help you." He leans back and rests a forearm over the back of the chair, and one hand goes to his waist. "Why are you defensive?"

I hold up my hands, palms out, and cross an ankle over a knee, downplaying what he perceived as defensiveness. "Curious."

"You're looking for someone who has traveled to Moscow, possibly placed frequent calls to Moscow, but chances are he won't be sloppy enough to leave a communications trail. Might not even leave a travel trail. The contact with the cartel is the one who hired Zolonov."

Anton Zolonov has been on Interpol's Red Notice list for years. He abducted Sloane and contracted help to attempt an abduction of the other sister.

"If I get anything else, I'll let you know. But I've dug as deep as I can." I nod, comprehending all that remains unsaid. He can only dig so deep without risking blowing his cover.

"What do you have for me?"

He slides a burner mobile across the table. "In the notes app, you'll find a link to a file. Password LetThereBeLight, all one word. The file is a listing of bank accounts of four shell companies that will be contributing to candidates around the world. The bank accounts are from legal enterprises within the syndicate, but Kontinuum owns all four shell companies. The sole purpose is to influence elections and stoke unrest. If you find candidates with funding from these companies, then Kontinuum is backing them."

I slip the mobile into my inside breast pocket. "Anything else?"

"I'll be in Moscow for the next few weeks. I'll communicate through the normal channel for our next meet."

I pass a folder to him, which he promptly opens and flicks through. His face softens, and a thumb runs over one photograph.

The emotion playing across his typically nondescript expression speaks volumes.

"They're doing good." He says it more to himself than to me.

"It's my understanding the younger one got engaged."

"No shit. To who?"

"An American. Arrow employee. We've crossed paths a couple of times. Likable fellow." I recall him at the hospital in Kuala Lumpur. "Serious."

"Name?"

"Ah, Knox." I rack my brain, but the last name eludes me.

"No fucking shit." The grin on Saint's face is one I've never seen before. "The scoundrel. Would've never seen that coming." The guy looks genuinely pleased, relaxed, and, dare I say it, happy. It's a new look for him. "They're getting married?" I confirm with a nod. "Good for them. They'll take care of each other." He's thoughtful. "Can you do me a favor? Find out when they set a date. And can I get you to send an anonymous gift? Can you do that without creating any red flags?"

"Certainly."

He closes the folder and slowly slides it across the table, returning it to me. "Don't let this case fall through the cracks."

Saint threatened to blow his cover, and the entire op, if Sloane Watson wasn't extracted safely from Cambodia.

"You have my word." Of course, Saint doesn't know my true identity or my connection to Lumina. If he did, he would understand there's no way in hell I'll let this case grow cold. "And you plan to remain in place?"

"Quitting isn't an option." His eyes narrow, and he transforms from human to operative. "Interpol will crack down on the operation in Cambodia?"

"From a diplomatic standpoint—" Saint raises an eyebrow and his fingers closest to the handle of his pistol twitch. "Don't get punchy. I give you my word we'll catch the person who ordered hits on the Watson sisters."

"That's not good enough. Take them all out. Every single one. They're like ticks. Smash only a part and the full body grows back."

———

The story continues in Sinful Beauty, releasing September 12th, 2024.

NOTES

If you read *Stolen Beauty*, then you already read this…but in case you didn't, here it is again with an addition for Savage.

What's real? What's not?

The Cambodian compound is real. You can read about it more in the *New York Times* article "The Online Scam Industry Is Thriving. Cambodia Plays a Key Role."
https://nyti.ms/3I1B3j9
Obviously, I don't know what goes on inside those compounds. This is a work of fiction.

My father was denied twice for a heart transplant, once in Florida and once in North Carolina. The numbers on the wait lists for organs don't include those who don't qualify for the list. I suppose my experience watching my father go through the extensive testing required to see if he could qualify for a transplant has stayed with me. I've thought a lot about the people who need organs over the years. There's no easy solution, but I do hope that one day we have more options. And science is making headway.

It's not unrealistic to believe that one day we will grow functioning organs in a lab, and indeed we are moving down that path.

New Guidelines Suggest Lifting 14 Day Rule — https://nbcnews.to/49wgasJ

New tissue engineering process brings lab-grown organs one step closer — https://bit.ly/3SXWrw4

Lab Grown Mini Organs Help Model Disease and Test New Drugs — https://bit.ly/42O8S0H

Also, when researching Savage Beauty, I read "But Everyone Feels This Way" by Paige Gayle, and it got me thinking that her truth is true for everyone to some degree. A color blind person goes through life thinking everyone sees the world with the same color spectrum until a test shows them differently. A vision impaired person thinks they just suck at sports or are clumsy and everyone is else is gifted until the day they get glasses and realize everyone else can see the ball at a much greater distance. Our perception of the world, and how we deal with it—how we feel it—varies.

FROM THE AUTHOR...
AKA IZZY

If you enjoyed the story, I hope you'll take a moment to leave a review. Five-star reviews truly do sell books, bringing me closer to the day when I might be able to do this full time. So I'm deeply grateful for them.

In case you are curious...

Stolen Beauty is technically the fourth in the Arrow Series, but it's the first in what I'm calling the Beauty trilogy. Sinful Beauty is up next, and it's Tristan's story.

The Gilded Saint will follow Tristan's story, and yes, that one belongs to Sam. Saint will kick off the final trilogy within the Arrow Series, and I'm thinking of it as The Den of Thieves.

The first three books in the Arrow Series are what I'm calling the Wolf trilogy, and these books are, in order, *Better to See You, Sure of One*, and *Cloak of Red*.

The Arrow Tactical series is a spin-off from the Twisted Vines series. And the Twisted Vines series is a spin-off from the Haven Island series.

GRATITUDE

Savage Beauty might have undergone a severe edit if it wasn't for the encouragement of Kimberly Hunt telling me that she loved Sloane and that while not everyone will love her, some will absolutely identify with her. Mr. Jolie said the same, and then Lori, my editor, peppered her comments with "I so get this" and "I'm the same."

For this one, I needed the confidence boost, and I so much appreciate their encouragement. Sloane is "different," but we live in an era where we're more aware of differences than ever and I'd like to believe more accepting.

Karen Cimms stepped in and found things that had me thinking… how did we all miss that? I love working with her because she's so detail-oriented and good at catching my errors.

Last, but most definitely not least, I am so grateful to my ARC readers. There are so many books out there, and when a book first releases, those reviews can make all the difference. I'm so grateful that I have ARC readers who want to read my books and sign up to get them with each release.

And of course, to my readers: Thank you for reading!

ALSO BY ISABEL JOLIE

Arrow Tactical Security Series

Better to See You (Wolf and Alexandria)

Sure of One (Jack and Ava)

Cloak of Red (Sophia and Fisher)

Stolen Beauty (Knox and Sage)

Savage Beauty (Max and Sloane) - Releasing June 6th

Sinful Beauty (Tristan and Lucia) - Releasing September 12th

Gilded Saint (Sam and Willow) - Releasing December 5th

The Twisted Vines Series

Crushed (Erik and Vivi)

Breathe (Kairi and David)

Savor (Trevor and Stella)

Haven Island Series

Rogue Wave (Tate and Luna)

Adrift (Gabe and Poppy)

First Light (Logan and Cali)

The West Side Series

When the Stars Align (Jackson and Anna)

Trust Me (Sam Duke and Olivia)

Walk the Dog (Delilah and Mason)

Lost on the Way (Jason and Maggie)

Chasing Frost (Chase and Sadie)

Misplaced Mistletoe (Ashton aka Dr. Bobby and Nora)

Standalone Romances

How to Survive a Holiday Fling (Oliver Duke and Kate)

Always Sunny (Ian Duke and Sandra)

The Romantics (Harrison and Zuri)

ABOUT THE AUTHOR

Isabel Jolie, aka Izzy, lives on a lake, loves dogs of all stripes, and if she's not working, she can be found reading, often with a glass of wine. In prior lives, Izzy worked in marketing and advertising, in a variety of industries, such as financial services, entertainment, and technology. In this life, she loves daydreaming and writing contemporary romances with real, flawed characters with inner strength.

Sign-up for Izzy's newsletter to keep up-to-date on new releases, promotions and giveaways. (**Pro-tip** - She offers a free book on her home page…just scroll down after arriving at her site.)

Buy ebooks and signed paperbacks direct from Isabel at www.isabeljoliebooks.com

Want to say hi? Email her through her website or reply to her newsletter…she loves to hear from readers.